ΛΠͳΛRΞ5

VOLUME 1

2016

Edited by David R. Grigg and MJ Kobernus

Nordland Publishing

Antares Anthology Volume 1

ISBN: 978-82-8331-023-8

Cover design by Ashraf E. Shalaby

Layout and typography by David R. Grigg

Published by Nordland Publishing 2016

www.nordlandpublishing.com

Humanity's future is in our hands. Make it so.

Contents

Introduction
David R. Grigg

IN THE 1930S, the eminent biologist J. B. S. Haldane wrote in his book *Possible Worlds* : "my own suspicion is that the universe is not only queerer than we suppose, but queerer than we can suppose".

Words shift in meaning and association over generations, and if he were writing today Haldane might well have preferred to use the word "stranger" rather than "queerer". But his meaning is clear: the universe is a very strange place, stranger than we know, and probably much stranger than we can even imagine.

It has always seemed to me that it is the task of fantastic literature to explore just how strange we *can* suppose the universe to be, and then to go further and examine what the consequences of that strangeness might be on ourselves as human beings.

The stories in this first *Antares* collection range over many different kinds of strange occurrences, strange places and strange futures.

An empathic android pines for a lost human; a mysterious barrier cuts our world in half; a young woman is trapped inside a computer simulation; a poisoned phrase generates parasites which take over human brains; a colonising expedition discovers an abandoned ship sabotaged by its own occupants. These and many other stories in *Antares* explore the edges of the strangeness of the universe. And the strangeness of ourselves.

I hope you enjoy them all.

— David R. Grigg
Associate Editor,
Nordland Publishing.

ANTARES

Starship: Exodus
Jordan Legg

I DREAMED AGAIN OF THE ORB.

The tiny sphere spinning across the void, bright and blue and green under its fogged, swirling veil. Still rivers and stormy seas, lush forests and snow-capped mountains. Towering fjords and precarious buttes and mossy caverns and colossal trees. The feeling of wet earth under my feet, or the smell of a rainy morning. A purpled sunset sky.

It was a difficult dream to wake from.

Slowly, I got off the bed. I blinked, ran my hand through my dreadlocks, took a nutri-tube from the dispenser and limped slowly to the glass wall on the far side of my quarters. I ripped off the wrapper and drank, and for the millionth time tried to remember the taste of real food.

I stared quietly at the void. Fiery gas clouds pillared across the black, and my attention wandered the light-years, from one star to the next. For a second, I felt very small. A small man in a small bunker. Smaller than I've ever felt in my life.

How is it possible to be in a place so infinite, and yet, at the same time, so constricting?

"Dad?"

I turned to see a little black figure in the doorway, dressed in a nearly-outgrown Gornican poncho. He stared up at me with big, brown, unblinking eyes.

"They're coming."

I pursed my lips and nodded. "Where's your mom?" I asked, hoping he hadn't noticed the break in my voice.

"She's still on the bridge, trying to lock it down," he replied. "She said she'll be here soon."

I walked back and sat on the bed. "Come here."

Cal obeyed and sat beside me. "What're you gonna do?" he asked.

"I'm gonna wait."

"Wait?" He seemed disappointed. I wished I had a better answer for him.

"Not much else I can do, son. I've... tried just about everything else."

Cal nodded and looked closely at the floor, kicking his legs against the edge of the bed. "Do they know that?"

I spoke slowly, but it didn't make the words more palatable. "Some of them know it well," I sighed. "They would say that's part of the problem."

"That you tried?"

"Yeah."

Part of me wished we weren't having this conversation. That he hadn't overheard my argument with Damen and his people a few weeks back. But I've been a parent long enough to realize that there's no way to stop kids from hearing what they're going to hear. At the same time, another part of me wished we'd had this conversation a long time ago.

He looked up at me with wide, curious eyes, and a half-open mouth. Something about that expression scared me.

"I used to be a taskmaster, d'you know that?" I told him.

"What's that?"

"Back on Gornica," I said, swallowing, "sometimes they would take some of us, when we were little—two or three years old, maybe—they would take us away from our families. Hurt us. Scare us, until we didn't know how to feel anything but fear. You get scared enough, it's easy to try and hurt other people. Doesn't even have to be anyone special—if someone's standing close enough in front of you, they'll do the job. You get that kind of scared, you realize that it's you or them. And once you start thinking that, it makes the choice to hurt someone else a lot easier.

"People they took, like me—they made us beat the ones they didn't take. The ones working on the lower levels. They taught us that our kind was made to work. Drilled it into us, every day. It made you look down at your hands and hate the way they were shaped. I did a lot of bad things, Cal," I said. "Hurt a lot of people."

"And that's why Damen's angry?"

"That's part of it."

His eyebrows furrowed. He was silent for a moment, and then asked, "But that stuff wasn't your fault, right?"

I ran my hand across the tiny mountains of his dense black hair. "I was the one that did it, son," I said. "You can blame other people all you want for forcing you to do something bad—but you're still the one who did it. I could've stopped if I wanted to. Could've stopped a long time before I did.

"Why didn't you?"

I thought for a moment. "Because when you're part of a system like that, a system that damages people the way ours did, it's the easiest thing in the world to close your eyes and pretend that keeping yourself alive by making other people suffer is okay. That's why I did it. Because it was easy."

I braced myself for the next question, but it never came.

I stood up and tossed the empty nutri-tube into the incinerator chute, and then turned to look back out the window, remembering the last day I served in the Gornican slave camps.

THE man had been old, doubled over under the load, coming up from the fuel mines after a long day's work. It wasn't the first time I'd beaten someone—Hell, it might not have been the first time I'd beaten *him*—but it was the first time I'd ever held a dead man in my arms. When someone bleeds like that isn't something you forget.

Murder is like a signpost. If you're lucky, it's stark enough to stop you in your tracks and make you think about where it is you really wanna go. And I remember that day looking down at my hands, and realizing that wherever it was, doing things like this wasn't what was going to get me there.

I went back to my quarters that night to cut out the tracker they implant you with the day you're born. Hurt like Hell. I grabbed all the stuff I thought I'd need and ran.

The Gornicans aren't built like us. They're thick, brawny—suited to their homeworld gravity. Our size and shape makes it a lot easier for us to work in their mines—we're smaller, thinner, with shrunken spines and compact muscles. We're still different enough to look like the planet isn't our home.

I took advantage of that difference. I hid in the fringe tunnels, on the edge of the Gohsha slave pit. Picked what I could of slave supplies to keep myself fed until it was safe to get away. Spent the nights treating my tracker infection and learning to channel my self-hatred into something that would bring the Gornicans down.

Months later, I made contact with other slaves.

Rebellion, we whispered in the darkness. *War.* It was a simple idea, and the odds were against us—but something crazy inside of me said we could do it. Here, from the caves, we could train insurgents and melt tools down into weapons. We'd fight back. Kill Gornicans. Break free.

Slowly, our ranks grew. Wornock. Lee. Korey and Dahlia. Most of them were angry with what I'd done to them—but the promise of freedom was enough for them to set aside their hatred.

We started raiding. Small successes led to bolder skirmishes. We turned mining tools and stolen prods on Gornican slave-breakers. I killed again—I killed *humans* again, sometimes, when they stood in our way. Our first fight was the one that gave me the scar over my eye. Our last gave me the limp in my step, and the charred skin over my side from the Gornican mine blast. With every day in those tunnels, my infection got worse.

The last fight was the one when our company finally fell apart.

Korey and Dahlia died in battle, and I buried them deep in an unmarked grave. Wornock, crippled and taken prisoner—his fate, to the rest of us, was obvious. Lee escaped into the tunnels. For days I looked, but he knew how to cover his tracks.

I lay in the caverns one night, wounded, hopeless. I spent hours fumbling with the bandages before finally tossing the medkit away. If we were ever going to go free, I wouldn't be the one to lead us.

So I left.

I don't know how I ever got out of the tunnels. I'm not sure by that point if I even cared whether I got caught. When you're desperate enough, you'll try just about anything to get out of a place that tight. I wandered past what was left of the Gornican guards, sure they were going to find me. But they didn't. I can't explain why. I limped past Gornican machinery, under the taskmaster lights, and then up into the open.

I've never tasted air quite like that first breath.

The slave city of Gohsha lies on the edge of the Gornican empire, at the top of the Aki mountain range, where the mines run deep. My plan was to make my way down the slopes to the foothills just beyond, where the freemen tribes roamed. See if they'd take me in. It would be hard, I knew—any life in the gray foothills under Aki would be a hard one, given how little food and water was available. But there was no chance in Hell I was going to stay another minute in Gohsha.

Those first few days on the run were some of the longest I've ever known. By that point, I was out of food and water. I stumbled my way over the dunes, parched, half-mad, sure I would die. You stay dehydrated that long, you start to hear voices. Or see things that aren't there. Kuakin fruits. Old acquaintances. Water.

By the time she found me, lying in the dust, I was sure I was crazy.

"Nestor?"

Her voice jerked me back into the present. I looked up at the doorway and she stepped inside—tall, layered in black, with a heavy beige scarf wrapped several times around her neck. Her exhausted eyes locked with mine.

"Hey, beautiful."

She walked into the captain's quarters wearing a somber expression. "They're through the blast doors," she said. "They've taken the bridge."

I nodded. "They can't change course. Coordinates are fixed 'til we arrive." I tipped my head up, and felt her dutiful kiss on my lips. "It's okay, Alana," I told her, trying hard to believe it. "We did everything we could."

"I know." She sat down beside Cal, her hand on his shoulders. The boy leaned against her, slumping forward.

"Did you know this would happen?" she asked me.

"Did I?"

"Yeah. I mean, did it—he—did he tell you, when you first found this thing?"

I shook my head. "Never really told me any of it, babe. I haven't heard anything since that night."

Alana looked at the now-closed door. "Seems like it would have been a good thing to mention."

"Would you still have come?" I asked her. "If you had known?"

"I don't know," she answered. "Would you?"

My eyes met Cal's.

"Yeah," I said. I pulled my son's shoulder in close against my ribs, and wondered, for a moment, if Cal knew if I had meant it.

"Well," Alana said, "maybe you're as crazy as they say."

Crazy. I remembered the first time I saw her, towering over me against the dim red sky. Yes, I believed I was crazy.

HER father, Justun, had taken me in and had his freemen nurse me back to health. I wasn't the only one who had wriggled my way out of Gornican slavery—there were others as well, and for a while, I thought I would be content with them. I married Alana and spent some time hunting the Tychon herds and raiding Gornican outposts stationed in the foothills. When the bounty hunters came after us, Justun kept us on the move.

For years we lived like that.

And then, one night, during a migration across the Tychon Ridge, I heard the voice.

"Nestor."

The word was like wind; like the fans down in the engine rooms, but quieter. I rolled over in our bed and asked Alana what she had said. She groaned groggily, half-asleep. I sat up in bed, staring out in the darkness.

"Nestor."

It was gentle. Haunting. Three times, I heard it, before I put my clothes on and stepped outside to look around. I remember slipping out under the Tychon hide, looking up over the southern ravine, and noticing, for the first time, a long white object, tucked between the crags on the other side of the gorge. I must have glanced in that direction about a million times the previous few days and never seen it, but now, in the light of Gornica's five moons and arching white planetary rings, it seemed unmistakable. I grabbed a canteen of water and a glow-tube and headed down the ravine. After an hour or so, I reached the place.

The object was bigger than I had first thought—partly because it lay safely hidden in a long cleft that ran through the foothills, too narrow for anyone to see from the opposite ridge. The metal hull gleamed brightly under the moonlight. Dents and scrapes marked its exterior. Long, stretching solar panels, like the gossamer wings of an insect, stretched out from its upper deck, eager to embrace the air. Grime-caked engines stood idly, waiting to ignite. I wandered around her, marveling at her size.

Across her hull I saw the name of the starship, emblazoned in Old Earth Common.

Exodus.

"Nestor," said the voice, the whisper swirling suddenly around me, violent and beautiful all at once.

"Who's there?" I said, squinting in the stormy echo. Then everything was still.

"Make them free," said the wind-voice, stretching each word thin on the air.

I looked around suddenly. "Who's there?" I demanded, more forcefully this time.

"I am."

The boarding ramp hung open. I took off my boots and wandered cautiously into the ship.

It must have been standing here for hundreds of years—but somehow, all of its equipment still seemed unspoiled. The hull was sealed. The lights still worked. Nothing seemed charred or broken or damaged beyond repair. It was the most resilient piece of engineering I had ever seen.

I wandered through the crew's mess, the dining hall, the engine rooms, energy converters, gravity generator, cargo bay, cryodorm, escape pods—everything seemed miraculously unscathed. I gazed around in wide-eyed wonder.

It was hours before I finally reached the bridge—a vast, almost cavernous chamber filled with control panels and pilot interfaces. Above there was a filthy glass dome, and in the centre of the room stood a wide, round table, with a tall captain's chair facing up toward the glass.

As I stepped inside the bridge, a huge, three-dimensional image, almost like a high flame, flickered to life over the table. Its light echoed across the room, like a glow-tube throwing lights across a cave wall. Every screen and interface glittered around the bridge.

"Welcome," I heard a voice echo through the ship's speaker system.

I stood in awe at the image over the table. It was a cluster of stars, all light-years apart, I guessed, with long, arching lines connecting them across the spinning readout. Labels in Old Earth Common appeared over the lines—labels like, "Star Route 108," and "Planet Coordinates Delta 481.516.2342," and "04.20.3573 CE." Two points of light in the star system flashed in unison. I reached up and touched the first.

Suddenly the image expanded to reveal a single planet, spinning on its tilt, its clouds a swirling marble fog over sprawling lands and oceans. The Common label that hovered over it read, "Earth: 151 765 Days Since Departure."

Earth.

Our homeworld.

Korey had talked about it during our little revolution. Our distant planet, with its mountains and rivers and its single moon. I had listened with indifference. I was willing to believe in the place, of course—most people were—but I figured it wouldn't do much good to hope for a place no one could ever find. But there it was, that spinning hologram, taunting me with possibility. We could go back, I realized. This ship could take us.

"Make them free," the voice whispered. It wasn't coming from the speakers.

A choking gasp suddenly escaped my throat, and I knelt slowly on the floor.

Someone was calling us home.

In my mind, I saw no reason why the command shouldn't make me hope. I had the ship; it was right here, waiting for the human race to return to its homeworld. Everything was ready— the ship had been collecting solar energy for four hundred years, as if it were eager to make the journey. Most of us would know how to fuel it, and fuel was abundant in the Gornican mines. There was no reason we couldn't leave.

But there was something else in me, something deep, that wouldn't let me hope. A yawning, burrowing tunnel, deep and hungry, that wanted me to be afraid. I thought of Korey and Dahlia and Lee and Wornock. They had died under my leadership. The old man had died under my abuse. I had already tried to lead them out—and failed. I was no revolutionary—I was a nomad on the run. If we were ever going to go free, I wouldn't be the one to lead us.

I walked slowly back to Justun's camp, wishing all the time that I hadn't heard the voice. I had heard voices in the wilderness before, I reasoned. Enough dehydration and you'll hear anything. Some voices will tell you to flap your arms and fly. This was just another one of those.

No, I thought. There was something different about this one.

That was why it scared me, I realized. This wasn't something I could reason away, and it wasn't like the voices I had heard after leaving the caves. Those were only surface sounds. Even at their most appealing, I felt certain that they only happened to sound like real words, like some accident, like a rockslide or a thunderstorm. With this voice—there was someone *behind* it.

I ducked back under the tent flap and stood beside my bed. Alana lay there, still asleep. I brushed my hand across her shoulder, pushing away the Tychon blankets. She stirred, and her eyelids drifted open.

"Hey," she whispered.

"Something's happened," I said.

I watched her expression as I told her the story. Wide curiosity slowly fell into a look of concerned disbelief. My words slowed. I could hear the confidence drain out of my voice as I realized how I must sound.

"Honestly, Nestor," Alana had said, "this all seems, well... crazy."

"I know," I answered. "I know it does."

"What are you gonna do?"

"I think I'm gonna do it."

There was a long pause.

"Okay."

THE word echoed in my mind and I rubbed my fingers over my eyes, pressing against the fatigue. It had been more than a decade since I had first wandered up to the dust-covered bridge of this ship and drawn my hands across its ancient metal. It had been a frozen carapace; a fossil of long-dead humanity. But flickering screens and holographic displays had proved it was not dead. Now that the ship was hurling through space at near-light speed, filled not with dead men, but the cruelty of the living—now was when it felt most like a tomb.

I ran my hands through my wife's long, dark braids as the three of us sat together on my bed. Looking back, I understood why a part of her wished she hadn't said okay. I could tell she was afraid.

So was I.

"To Hell with this," I said. I stood up from the bed, grabbed my metal cane from the door, and hobbled quickly towards the bridge.

"Dad!" Cal shouted after me.

Alana held him back. But the boy was quick, agile. He wriggled out of her hold and chased me along the corridor. Soon he was walking by my side toward the ship's captured bridge. I didn't say anything. I didn't have the heart to send him back.

We walked together and after a few minutes arrived at the entrance to the bridge. The charred, twisted blast doors hung open to reveal a mutiny in progress.

Damen and his people had backed the last bridge-shift against the walls, their knife-blades pressing against throats and chests. Erin lay a few steps from the holotable, clean and white and still. It looked like she'd been strangled. Meer was lying on the ground, his face spattered with blood and bruises—whether dead or alive, I couldn't tell. At the holotable, Damen was arguing with Koda and Rosh about how to override the ship's coordinates lock.

"You know it won't change a thing," I said, hobbling into the room. "Not even I can change our direction. We're stuck on this path until we arrive."

Damen glared. "Says you," he spat. "Koda. Rosh." The short, stocky mutineer drew his knife, grabbed my collar, and pushed me up against the wall. His breath was thick. Close. I felt the blade press against my throat. Koda and Rosh seized my son, who kicked and twisted in an effort to wrangle his way free. A sharp edge, and then hot, thick liquid on my neck.

"How do I change it?" he demanded.

"I told you, you can't change it," I gasped.

"How do I change it?"

"What are you gonna do? You gonna kill me?"

"I'll kill your boy," he growled. "Damn kid's probably the reason we're in this mess in the first place. Convenient you're the only man on this ship who gets to have a fucking kid."

"You want kids, Damen? Is that what this is about?"

"Fuck you."

"I think this is because you're scared."

"Fuck you, Nestor."

"You've staged a mutiny because you're scared we're not going anywhere. You're scared that we're just going to drift away into the void. Forever."

"Damn right I'm scared," Damen shot back, his hand shaking. "We followed a tired old coot into deep fucking space on the word of the voices in his head so he could rob us of fifteen years of our lives. Because he thinks he's some great revolutionary. I got news for you, Nestor. We're running out of *air*." I could hear the tension in his voice. He pursed his lips and shook his head. "You talk about the homeworld. The place we came from. Wake up, Nestor—it's gone. Gone! You know why we left in the first place? Because we wasted it. That's why. And now there's nothing left to go back to. We've been drifting out here in this box with you for over a decade with nothing to go on but your damned ghost story. I'm tired of it, Nestor. Tired of you. You and every other idiot that voted to follow you and your damned voices."

I looked coldly at Damen.

"But it worked."

The knife relaxed against my neck, and I breathed a little easier. Then I felt Damen's fist against my jaw.

Bone clattered against bone, and my head flung back and rattled on the wall. I tasted blood in my mouth. I struggled to breathe and stood as tall as I could over the stocky mutineer.

"You saw it yourself, Damen," I panted, as blood trickled down the ridge of my lip. "How the moment I got back to the mining camp, Gornican tech started falling apart. Or the way we all made it through the planetary rings. This ship is running on a lot more than a ghost story. And that was after you all wanted to kill me the first time."

I could see in Damen's eyes that he remembered exactly what I was talking about.

THE day I got back to tell them about the starship, most of the slaves had wanted to kill me. Ever since I'd left, their workload had doubled. Punishment for my attempted insurrection.

Damen had suggested that they keep me alive and hand me over to Gornican justice instead—as a way of relaxing our overlords' demands. The mob agreed, and they locked me to a fence on the edge of the slave camps until dawn.

That was when everything fell apart.

The Gornicans found me that morning, weak and exhausted from the night before. Someone had told them who I was, they said—the one who had led the slave revolt a few years back. They unbound me and hauled me up onto a hovering overseer-platform, manned by fifteen or so Gornicans, all gruffly looking down at the work camp in contempt.

"An old rebel," one of the Gornicans told the Master Overseer, who sat at the surveillance interface with a grim expression. The Gornican pushed me forward.

The Master Overseer stood and faced me. He clapped a heavy gloved hand firmly on my shoulder and held me in place. I buckled under a blow to my abdomen. Saliva dripped onto the platform as I tried to get air into my lungs.

He forced me up and turned me around to look at the camp. Human taskmasters summoned slaves from their beds and led them down into the mineshafts for the coming day's work. They wandered blearily into the darkness in awkward-looking rows, and the taskmasters—as I had once been—struck them with shock prods the moment they showed any slack. I winced as the shocks charred the skin.

The Master Overseer forced me down by the shoulder, and I felt the cold metal side of a prod against my neck.

I swallowed and bowed my head, bracing myself for the shock against my spine.

The hit was hard. Blunt. But for some reason, there was no shock. The Master Overseer clicked the button against the shaft. I felt his hand relax from my shoulder.

I looked up at the work camp. Everyone was standing silently, staring at their equipment, whether it was mining machinery or taskmaster weapons, with confused disbelief on every face. Humans and Gornicans flipped switches and gunned triggers. Taskmasters prodded slaves, and then themselves. Not a single machine revved to life.

Engines broke down. Drill reactors burnt out. Weapons jammed—all at once. Technical failure rippled across the mining camp as glow-tubes flickered and hover-carts collapsed. Some of us laughed. Others cried. Some crumpled on the ground in exhausted relief. I just watched, smiling at the slow, frightened realization creeping its way across every Gornican face—the terrifying knowledge that they were suddenly no stronger than their-long subdued slaves. Explanations ran across everyone's mind as they saw the now-decrepit machinery dying in their users' hands, but one thing was certain—no human would work the Gornican fuel mines that day.

Our masters fled. Almost instantly, they fled. It was a matter of hours before we were the only ones left in the mines.

That was it.

All it took to make us free. After all the plans, the rebellions, the guerilla skirmishes in tight-air caves—all we had had to do was wait.

Frightened Gornican crowds fled over the horizon, and I knelt on the ground, chuckling under my breath. By the time their High Council returned with its maintenance crews, we would be long gone—with all the fuel we could salvage from the now-abandoned Gornican stores.

It was a short journey to the ship. Justun and the freemen had stocked up on Tychon meat to complement the leftover nutri-tubes, still waiting in preservation on board the ship. We reached the *Exodus* in a matter of days.

We spent the following week crawling over every inch of the old starship. Justun compared its layout with old blueprints he'd salvaged from the pre-slavery settlement camps. From what he could tell, apart from the little work that needed to be done— cleaning the bridge dome, airing out the engines—the ship was in perfect working order. No reason we couldn't fly it home, he said.

But at first, not everyone who had fled the mines approved of my plan. The ship was big enough for all of us—many, even those who weren't for leaving, had taken up residence on the inside for convenient shelter—but believing Justun's appraisal was another matter altogether. My story of the voice didn't help ease their fears. We might have left a lot of people behind if we hadn't spotted the fleet of Gornican military craft advancing over the horizon the following day.

Panic ensued. Screaming, wailing, crying out for loved ones echoed in my ears as we scrambled together to find cover from the Gornican military machine. Some of us had seen it in action during the days of my insurrection. I remembered the flashes, the deafening cracks, too close to let me believe I would make it out alive. I remembered holding Korey and Dahlia's charred bodies, and their ashy corpses crumbling in the darkness as I tried to bury them.

"Not again," I whispered, and wondered if the voice could hear me. "Please, not again."

Justun and I put up a wall of men behind the women and children and we backed them inside the open boarding ramp.

By the time we were all inside, the Gornican ships were nearly on top of us.

I rushed up to the bridge and took my place in the captain's chair. We could hear the first shots of Gornican missiles in the distance. I tensed up and leaned over the microphone on the armrest.

"Command," I said loudly, "close boarding ramp. Destination: Earth."

A three-dimensional cutaway image of the ship appeared over the holotable, its component parts flashing in colour to illustrate the ship's ignition process. I looked around, desperate for this thing to fly.

"We're off the ground!" someone said. Someone else said the same. Before long the room rang with joyful shouts and laughter.

I had never even been in a hovercraft before—and when I could feel the ship beneath me break from Gornican gravity, something in me—deep in me, in the depths of that dark tunnel that had told me to be afraid the day I heard the voice—cautiously started to hope.

The *Exodus* swooped upward into the red Gornican sky, and I clamped my hands over the captain's armrests as we ascended into space. We broke through the atmosphere and the planet's gravity finally fell away, replaced by the artificial pull of the ship's floor—normalized and customized for ordinary humans. I sighed with relief at the feeling.

I looked up at the holotable image. The Gornican fleet was still behind us, its corrosion missiles climbing after us with ravenous speed. Before us loomed wide, terrifying rings of rock and ice, forever circling the planet. My teeth clenched. No ship of our size could expect to ride the rings without a collision. Pebbles and boulders spun through the void, chipping away at one another in the eternal freefall of planetary orbit. Huge chunks of cratered rock, shattered by gravity's pull, ricocheted carnage across the rings. I swallowed.

"Override coordinates," I said into the microphone frantically. "Command: override flightpath!"

The ship plummeted toward the rings. We stood silently and watched the gargantuan rocks glide over our cockpit glass.

I shut my eyes, certain I had led us all to our doom. For a full minute, everything was still. I wondered what would happen the moment the first rock hit us. A dent in the hull? A breach? Would air gush out into the vacuum, and take us all with it in an irresistible current? I tried to imagine what it would be like to die in space—for my lungs to suddenly empty as the void closed in.

I opened my eyes and looked at the holofield.

The first corrosion missile had hit a ring-rock, and its acid was eating away at the cratered surface. A second missile followed, and then the third—as all the while, rocks careened conspicuously away from our ship. Nothing had hit us yet, I realized, and fought the urge to whoop with joy and relief. I leaned forward in the chair and looked at the glass above, watching as the rocks split down the ship's white bow, watching and hoping we would make it to the other end of the rings.

The Gornican crafts fired off another silent volley of missiles, and I watched their holo projections chase us through the ring-fields. Some self-destructed shortly after they were fired. Some ran out of propulsion before they could do any damage, and sped on out into the darkness. For what seemed like an eternity the ship sailed through the field of orbit, but neither the Gornican missiles nor the ring-rocks ever came close to piercing our hull.

For a moment I hoped our journey into the rings might deter the Gornican ships, but I looked up to see the enemy craft follow us in and fire off another volley. I leaned forward and wondered how long before we could leave the star system and enter deep space. The enemy ships were getting closer.

It was then that the Gornican fleet began to splinter.

One of their first-line crafts had been clipped by a rock. Then another. The bouncing chunks of orbiting stone shattered their formation as they swerved and spun through the ring-field. One of the ships twisted out to starboard and disappeared behind a rock.

At last, we cleared the rings.

"Prepare for jump to deep space," said the ship's automated pilot.

I leaned back in the captain's chair and let out a long sigh of relief.

THAT day seemed so long ago as I stood in front of Damen, his knife to my throat, his teeth grating in anger over the life I had stolen from him. For more than a decade we had drifted through space, a race of refugees, desperate for a glimpse at our long-awaited homeworld. And he was right, I knew. Tychon meat had grown scarce. The nutri-tubes were almost gone. Oxygen was running low.

I thought back to the voice in the ship that night. I had told Alana the truth—I hadn't heard it since. Damen seemed sure it had been my imagination. Leftover hope from my days as a scheming revolutionary. My last frail hold on the idea that I'm significant.

But we had made it out of the mining camps.

I thought of the decrepit Gornican machinery, littering the mining tunnels like stones in a graveyard. The ring rocks, falling away from us as if being pushed by an invisible hand. We had gotten through it. Somehow, we had made it this far.

"Someone has to die, Nestor," Damen said. His voice trembled into whispers. "We gotta breathe."

I looked up at the table's holofield. "You're gonna breathe, Damen," I reassured him, my voice cracking again, though this time not with fear. I nodded upward.

He turned and looked. The ship was smaller on the display than it had ever been before, a flashing yellow light on the edge of the holofield. A second dot mirrored its flickering—the third planet from its star, a swirling marble of green and white and blue.

Damen relaxed his knife and stared at the holofield in disbelief and awe.

We had made it.

A week later, we spotted the orb in the cockpit glass, glowing with a misty haze along the edge, with greens and blues and whites poking out from beneath the clouded atmosphere.

It was more beautiful than I had ever dreamed.

Yara
Calvin Demmer

HER HEART HAD STOPPED WORKING.

Yara knocked on her maker's front door.

Earlier, she had visited the memorial hall where the body of the boy she had watched grow into a young man was kept. Databases she had searched informed her that twenty-seven Earth years was considered too short a life. When she had run her fingers over the plaque with his name she had pressed the button on her wrist's control pad.

This activated her heart.

No light, no warmth, no current would come.

This was unacceptable, for she wished to remember the young man in the only way she knew how.

The front door creaked as it opened. The day's light chased away the shadows that hid behind the door, and an old man with crooked steel-rimmed glasses appeared before her.

"Maker, my heart has stopped," Yara said.

"I told you to stop calling me that," the old man said, frowning. "You know my name is Geraldo."

"Master maker, Geraldo Mariucci, formerly of—"

"Yes, yes," Geraldo said. He massaged his forehead and glanced left then right towards the empty dirt road.

Yara followed his gaze. She saw the square-block houses of the community and the colorful gardens that grew fruit and vegetables. It was quite a contrast from the world beyond their dome, which was a barren rocky wasteland.

"Well, best you come in."

Geraldo led Yara into his dusty, dimly lit workroom.

"How often have you been activating it?" Geraldo said, while moving papers which cluttered the top of his desk. He took a seat on the desk's edge.

"Of late, I have activated it frequently," Yara said. She stood straight, focused on Geraldo, not needing to re-scan the room. A quick finger test of the dust on a shelf near her informed her that some of the particles had been there since her last visit.

"But Yara, I told you it wouldn't last that way." Geraldo sighed. "I keep repeating, you are an android, you may look like a young adult female, but you are not. You don't feel. You don't have beliefs."

Geraldo stood up, waving his arms in the air. "So when you asked me to create something that could replicate a heart, considering the cost and scarcity of materials in this day, I told you it would be crude. All it does is to emit a red light with a bit of warmth, and then boost the current of energy flowing through you for a moment. A slight jolt, almost as if you were feeling something."

"I know, but I require it today."

Geraldo shrugged. He walked towards Yara and opened the compartment in her chest.

"Ah, most of it looks fine. Mmm . . . it's the power source that has fried. I have none to spare."

"Connect it to my main supply."

"Ah, but then you must not use all the power and get stuck somewhere without being able to recharge."

"I won't"

"Yara, if your power source runs out before recharging, you will lose all your information, everything. There is no backup. You will be useless. The software required for programming your model is obsolete. You will be stripped for scrap. Do you understand the gravity of this?"

"Yes, maker."

Geraldo frowned.

AFTERNOON beneath a hazy pink sky came. Yara walked a path alongside the interior of the dome. She was on her way back to the memorial hall. The dome helped protect the inhabitants from harsh dust storms, as well keeping the atmosphere within livable. She wondered what old Earth must have been like without the need for the structure.

Inside the hall, she read the plaque again, even though she had stored the information earlier. Timothy Miller had died aged twenty-seven years and forty days according to the date. She'd been at his bedside for both his birth and death. She wondered why they had left off the further seven hours, forty-three minutes, and twenty-four seconds he had been alive. A desire to scratch in the additional time passed. She knelt down, turned, and moved her back against the wall. She searched through some of the recordings she had saved—memories, as Timothy had called them.

She viewed his birth and how he had cried. Everyone told her not to be concerned and that it was a happy cry. She pressed the button on her wrist's control pad. Her heart activated, and her chest glowed red. The warmth ran all over the base of her neck and top of her chest, such was the strength of her internal power source. She felt the surge in current as it shot throughout her.

She viewed times where she had helped feed young Timothy, and when he had eventually learned to do it himself. On one occasion, he had even grabbed the spoon from her and offered her a scoop of his porridge. This act had initially left her perplexed, as she did not require food for sustenance. It had also been the first time someone had treated her like a human.

She pressed her heart's activation button.

YARA made her way outside the memorial hall.

Darkness covered the land.

She heard the first warning beep.

Lost in her video database, moving from one recording to the next, Yara realized she was down to five percent power. This was just enough to get home. She had reached recordings from Timothy's twenties.

Something within her wouldn't let her stop.

She missed the connection she once had with Timothy.

She lay down on the ground and looked towards the night sky. Phobos and Deimos were both visible, but she wondered about a place much further than that. She had been told that some old Earth people once believed that this place was where they would go after death. She often wondered which constellation, which planet they were referring to. But no one ever gave her a more definitive answer, and all the old databases had been scrubbed of unnecessary information.

She viewed the time Timothy had cried after his father passed away. They had been sitting together under a similar starry night sky. It had been a sad cry.

She pressed the button.

She viewed more footage of that same evening, specifically when she had asked Timothy about the peculiar place she could never locate.

"Would you want to go the place the old Earth people believed in?" she said.

"Um, I guess, I would . . . they called it heaven. My dad believed in the place, if it exists, I guess I would like to go there."

"All the people of old Earth believed in this place?"

"Not all, no, but a lot of people believed they'd go somewhere after death. Heaven was just one of the possible destinations."

"Where is this place?"

"Uh . . . it's difficult to explain."

Yara sifted through her database, already knowing she would not find any information on the planet, but she made a note to ask around about it again.

"What about you? Where would you like to go after it's all over?" Timothy said.

"Me? But I am an android. I do not—"

"I believe we all go somewhere eventually, you included."

Yara had no answer. She had never contemplated such a question. She would need to study all the documented constellations and planets before replying.

"Think about it and let me know," Timothy said.

"I will."

Three consecutive beeps rang inside her head. Yara knew she only had enough power for a final activation of her heart. Then her power source would fail and all operations would cease until the final shutdown. In essence, she realized, like Timothy, she would die.

She viewed the day before Timothy died. When he had kissed her cheek and told her that he loved her. Yara paused, her finger above her heart's button.

"I love you too, Timothy. I select the place called heaven."

Yara pressed the button.

The Infinite Divine
Adam Baxter

Subject: Ed Harper
Occupation: Factory Worker
Date: Origin +2Y6M21D

"When I woke up it was just there, right there, there—it was there, right fucking there. That's where it was..."

Subject pauses to wipe tears from eyes.

"I fell asleep in the living room. She was in our bed. When I woke up it was half way through our house."

Subject is asked a question.

"What's that?"

Subject shows agitation.

"Of course I tried to get her. That's how I ended up with this!"

Subject shows right arm ending at clean amputation ten centimeters above elbow.

"The house is gone! She is gone! The whole neighbour-hood is gone!"

Subject wipes sweat from brow with checkered handkerchief.

"Fuck this!"

Subject stands up quickly and knocks over chair before leaving room.

Subject: Sarah Parker

Occupation: Retired

Date: Origin +3Y2M2D

"Who named it The Infinite Divine? Well, a lot of people like to say they know. And there's about a hundred different stories. It used to be easier to get proper news. Nowadays there's a lot of gabbing back and forth without a lot of substance. I know that you know what I'm talking about. This is the one I like to believe."

Subject stops to chuckle.

"The first time I heard it called that was a few weeks after it appeared. It was on a newscast. I remember there was a young man with long hair wearing a long robe. He was the leader of one of those religious groups. They were all a bit bent if you ask me."

"Yes, you could say he looked like Jesus. He was the first who just walked into it right on live TV. I was shocked, and I remember he was talking about Christ and forgiveness when he said these words, and I'll never forget them, *'Forward we sublime into The Infinite Divine.'* Then he just walked into it and was gone. The reporter had tried to grab his robe and stop him but it slipped through his fingers. I remember that the next thing I saw were his followers grabbing that reporter and the cameraman and walking right into it all together. Those last shots from the camera while it was on the ground were something…the way those legs just disappeared into that white void. Ever since then people have been calling it 'The Infinite Divine'."

Subject chuckles to herself.

"But who's to say I know for sure? That name could've come from anywhere."

Subject: Gavin Ehle

Occupation: Real Estate Mogul

Date: Origin +3Y11M30D

"How's business?"

Subject smiles and stretches out arms. Cracks fingers.

"How's business? Business has been booming! Supply and demand, brother. Supply and demand."

Subject folds legs and straightens knot on tie.

"I guess you could say I got lucky. I started buying up a lot of the land that other investors were turning their noses up at. Actually, I started picking it up years before it appeared. But, when it did appear then I was able to make my big moves. Real estate shot through the roof once people realized what was happening. They estimate that we lost something like 30% of our land on that first day. And we've been losing more every day since."

"Yeah, too bad about the Southern Hemisphere. Lucky for me. Bad for them. Thirty percent of our land gone in one day! Could anyone have ever imagined that? Do you understand what that did to the value of real estate in this country? And especially the land in the northern end?"

"Ka-chink, ka-ching! I earned 200% alone on the first day it appeared. It's been growing and spreading ever since, but I didn't hesitate at all. I borrowed against the property I already held and quadrupled my holdings. That was all in the first month, and things have taken off since then. People just want a small piece. A little last refuge in the north where they can wait it out until NASA or the ESA gets things figured out."

"I sell them a small piece for a big chunk of change. Check out this watch."

Subject rolls up sleeve and flaunts diamond encrusted gold watch.

"Those are real diamonds. I'm one of the top one-hundred wealthiest people in the world now. Can I interest you in a plot?"

Subject: Reed Clarkson
Occupation: Farmer
Date: Origin +4Y3M11D

"It's the shifts that are the big problem. Yes, it does move every day, and it does so at a pretty steady pace, about one metre every hour unless I'm mistaken. We've got some time before it gobbles up the whole country. Hundreds of years actually. I think a lot of people are scared and are being irrational. There's no reason for me to leave my fields, and sometimes I run the tractor right up to the Wall."

"Oh, I usually give it quite a safe distance. About a hundred metres minimum. It's not the daily crawl that I'm scared of. It's the jumps that seem to happen once or twice a year that can be dangerous. I was just outside of the city when the first big jump sublimed half of the population there."

"Why did I say sublime? It's something I heard somewhere and I don't have a better way to put it. I think that a few million people were lost in that first jump. It was the first, and the biggest. But, we learned since and the scientists are getting pretty good at judging safe distances from it. But, still, you never know. I lost one of my farm hands in that jump last month. He was the recommended hundred metres out, but I think it jumped about two-twenty. I took care of his family. They're up north now."

"I figure I have just about two more growing seasons before all of my land is gone. I'm not sure what I'll do then. My wife passed away a few years before it came, and we never had any kids. Maybe that's why I run the tractor right up against It sometimes."

Subject: Lanny Saeed
Occupation: Astrophysicist
Date: Origin +5Y4M14D

"We've been studying it since the day it arrived. There was no warning. Nothing at all. We lost the ISS when it appeared and most of our space telescopes. The Hubble got some images back shortly before we lost it, too. We looked deep into space, and as far back to the Big Bang as we can see. This divide is not just across our world, it is across our universe and through every time. Have you seen the images of the earliest galaxies we have ever photographed?"

"We haven't released the newest set. What I can tell you is that the anomaly is there. It wasn't before, but now it is—across every time. For a lot of people this may be frightening, but for me it is fascinating. Imagine that - across every time. This may give us the opportunity to unlock time travel. This is probably the most exciting time in scientific research in the history of mankind."

"No, we don't call it The Infinite Divine. It's an anomaly, and nothing more than that. We can't explain it yet, but it doesn't mean that we don't know anything about it either. We can tell you that it doesn't have an adverse effect on gravity or on the passage of time. It's not unbinding our world. Our atmosphere is not leaking away. We still rotate on our axis at the same rate, we still spin around the sun. If the Southern Hemisphere were really gone, don't you think that our orbit would have changed? You need to start asking yourself if anything has really disappeared."

"I don't think what's on the other side is gone, I just don't think it can get back. The anomaly is a one way ticket. That's for sure. I think it's more likely that it's acting as a giant fence or filter, rather than something that is just dissolving matter. You can change the building blocks which the universe has provided, but you can neither make new ones nor destroy the old."

"Personally, I'm not too worried. You have to have some faith, and my faith is in science. To me it's all about our orbit. That tells me that our entire world is still here."

"Would I walk through the anomaly? Maybe."

Subject hesitates.

"Probably..."

Subject pauses to think.

"No. No, I'm not ready for that just yet."

Subject: Wayne Gates

Occupation: Preacher

Date: Origin +5Y9M23D

"It's a message from God. Plain and simple, it's a message from God. Don't believe all of that scientific hullabaloo. The Lord is the light and he will shine the way to our salvation! Amen."

"When you look at it, can't you see his work? I can tell that it was His hands that crafted it. His love that built that gate to the glory of heaven! It didn't appear as a burning rock in the sky! As seven horseman blazing across the lands! We didn't hear trumpets in the air, or see angels pitying the forsaken. No! None of that!"

"But, that does not mean that the good book is wrong. God is merciful, and he has given us another gift. A soft and gentle way to leave the night. The final end for those who remain, for those that endure, it is a battle within themselves. It is so clear now. The wars, the diseased, the suffering; it was never something that man was to endure in the flesh. It's all happening up here!"

Subject aggressively prods front left of forehead with index finger.

"It's all happening up here! Now is our chance to believe in the Lord and to take that one step into his embrace."

"No, I won't be making that step myself. My place is here, to shepherd my flock to God's embrace."

"Forward we sublime into The Infinite Divine."

"FORWARD WE SUBLIME INTO THE INFINITE DIVINE!!!"

Subject: Derek Johnson

Occupation: Unemployed

Date: Origin +5Y10M6D

"I don't believe any of the shit that I see here. Come on, the government's been fuckin' with us since forever. You think they're not doing it now? I don't even think it's real. Do you? Does anyone? I don't. Why should I?"

Subject eases back into chair; pulls a toke on marijuana cigarette.

"The red fuckin' pill! That's the one I should have taken, man. None of this is real. I must've taken the blue pill and now here I am. But, where am I? Am I sittin' here is this chair talkin' to you?"

Subject stands up and relights marijuana cigarette; paces back and forth across room.

"No way. No fuckin' way! No FUCKIN' WAY, man! No way. This shit ain't real. This is just some kind of mind-fuck thought up by DARPA. I know that I'm strapped in somewhere with some needles in my arm and a VR band around my head. None of this shit is real."

Subject is visibly irritated. Reaches into back pack and withdraws pistol.

"None of this is real. There ain't no Infinite Divine. Nothing's disappeared! My mom isn't gone. She didn't walk into that thing. I'll show you. I'll fucking show you, man."

Subject leans over table and stares.

"See you on the other side, you fucking Narc."

Subject raises pistol to temple and pulls trigger. Body falls and lies twitching on floor.

Subject: Madeleine Fabella
Occupation: Elected Official
Date: Origin +6Y1M6D

"You're very welcome. I am always happy to meet with a constituent, especially one with such far reaching influence as yourself. First, I would like to address what my government has done. We have compensated the displaced, providing aid to over 75% of those who have lost homes. That's a big chore, and an even bigger chore has been keeping the economy running. We've lost over 30% of our land, but over 50% of our GDP. We haven't been hit as hard as China. They've lost almost all of their manufacturing in the south. That's a terrible, terrible thing for the Chinese, but it has been a blessing for us."

"All of that manufacturing needed to move somewhere. You should note that it was my party that offered the incentive to revitalize our northern manufacturing infrastructure. The rust belt has become the wealth belt. We are looking at a 5% growth in our GDP this year alone, and we project double digit growth within the next two years. It's an economic miracle."

"Of course this is an election year. I'm not asking for your vote. I'm not even going to say that my party is the best choice. But, it is pretty hard to ignore the fact that my party has taken the steps necessary to help our great country rise out of disaster and into greatness. We aren't afraid to make tough decisions."

Subject: Susie Packard

Occupation: Home Maker

Date: Origin +8Y5M10D

"Here, take a piece. Go on."

Subject hands forward large square of chocolate.

"Enjoy that. It's probably the last that you'll have in a long time until they can grow cocoa beans steadily in greenhouses. Cocoa can only grow within ten degrees to either side of the Equator, and as we both know we lost those twenty degrees the day that it showed up."

"You could say that I'm a chocolophile. It hasn't been too easy to maintain that addiction recently. The prices have been steadily rising as we are starting to run out. I guess you don't know how good it is until it's gone. I did have a quite a supply in my house, but it is starting to dwindle, too. There's a start up in California that has a viable tree population, but it's been tough for them to meet demand. That's why I like to call it brown gold."

Subject giggles.

"The thing is that you never know how good you have it until it's gone. Sometimes we need things like this to happen. Thankfully, I haven't lost anyone that I've loved. I still have my husband and my son. But, we've been luckier than others. I've really come to appreciate the little things; the way my husband hugs me at night, the caring I hear in my son's voice, seeing an oriole feed at the window. These are all special things that I took for granted before the Infinite Divine."

"I suppose that there is a part of me that is thankful for it coming. My son was about to move away, but now he decided to go to college in town. Heck, my husband and I didn't have much of a relationship left, but now it's just like it used to be in high school."

"No. I'm not happy that so many people are gone, but I think I need to look inwards and appreciate what I still have."

Subject: Captain Gary Kreller
Occupation: Air Force Officer
Date: Origin +8Y5M27D

"I was on some of the first teams that were sent in to try to figure this thing out. We've done everything we can to it: we sent in drones, we've had people move across it, we've measured, we've poked, we've prodded. Nothing, not a damn thing."

"What you heard was correct. We lost two men in that first month; Colonel John Stepanik and Captain Vincent Gaul. Some of the big wigs decided that they should suit up in ceramic shielding and take a peek behind the curtain. They got this idea after realizing that they could get a fraction of a second of data out of ceramic encased drones as they passed to the other side."

"I was there the day that it happened. We suited both of them up and clamped safety cables to their waists. It was a volunteer mission. At that point the government didn't have any data on the anomaly at all and was desperate for any sort of understanding. They were willing to take risks. Both John and Vincent volunteered for the mission, so the government really can't be to blame for everything."

"The idea was simple. They were to stand in front of the anomaly and wait for it to shift over their location, letting the forward portion of their helmet and faces enter past that great white wall."

"I was one of the guys on the cables. We had rigged them to winches, but we had a few guys holding on to them just behind Vincent and John. As the anomaly came closer they leaned forward so that only their faces would protrude through. We had received data from the drones, but it was garbled and pretty much useless. The egg heads figured that we needed human eyes to decipher the truth."

"They leaned in and then the anomaly was on them within a few seconds. I remember hearing both of them radio in that they were okay just as that white light was enveloping their face shields. Then both of them went into convulsions. The winches ripped them back so fast that I was knocked down to the ground. When I finally got up I saw one of the most terrible things that I have ever seen in my life."

"Their faces were just plain cut off where they had entered the light. But, it wasn't like a cut that you would see from a knife or saw. Their faces were just flat; straight down from their forehead to behind their chins. There wasn't any blood or gore. It was as if someone had taken a ream of flesh and ironed on to the place where their faces had been; no eyes, no noses, no mouths—just a smooth and unbroken area of pure flesh."

"They both died within a few minutes. With no mouths or noses there was no way for them to breathe. We never knew if they had seen anything. I was pulled off the project at that point and reassigned, but from what I hear the Air Force is still tinkering with those same ideas."

Subject: Alison Wentworth
Occupation: Seismologist
Date: Origin +9Y8M3D

"It's not public knowledge, but we have been able to pick up slight vibrations each time before it shifts. The vibrations are very slight, and no one would ever feel them, but we have been able to measure them on seismographs. We know that the vibrations start faintly and begin to build before each jump forward of the anomaly. These are all micro earthquakes which we can measure very accurately. The big jump that took those millions of people started as 0.1 and built to 0.5 before it finally popped. We've used the 0.5 as our benchmark for predicting the scale of these 'pops' as I like to call them. That is why we have been so good at getting most people out of the way before they happen."

"This hasn't been made public, but we are currently measuring vibrations at 0.8 and rising. The big pop was at 0.5 and it moved ahead over forty kilometers. This 0.8 is not only almost twice as big, it is exponentially big. We are looking at losing hundreds of kilometers once it goes."

"That's another reason why the government has been buying out people and moving them north as quickly as they can recently. They'll never acknowledge that this thing is getting out of control; they can't afford to, not unless they want everything to go to shit. Most people think that there are just two big jumps a year. And that's true, but the frequency is increasing and in five years there will be three shifts a year."

"I think that us thinking that we have a couple of hundred years left is foolish. If I were a betting lady, I would say fifty at the most."

"And do you want to know another interesting fact? We picked up a 9.3 earthquake 500 kilometres into the heart of Antarctica hours before The Infinite Di...., excuse me, the anomaly appeared. There aren't any fault lines on that continental mass. Explain that? And something else that no one will tell you is that we were still getting some readings from several seismographs on the other side up to five minutes after it appeared. This is not public knowledge, but we measured some very large vibrations."

"I have no idea where we'll be in fifty years. Ideally, we launch off of this planet and build generation ships. Where will we go? Away from it as fast and as far as possible. We need to buy ourselves some time. We can't stay here."

"We really don't have much of a choice now, do we?"

"Forward we sublime into The Infinite Divine."

All in chorus.

Fiona's Game
Micha Fire

*T*HE CAR CAME TO AN ABRUPT STOP, *brakes screeching. Before her lay the canyon with the cave. In there she expected to find the sword. The long forgotten item she had been seeking for days. All she needed to do now was go down there and get it.*

Quickly she got out of the car. No time to admire the landscape. She could do that on her way back. Unless she had to run again, protectors of the sword chasing her. So far she had not spotted any of them here.

"Fiona!"

She looked around, surprised.

"Fiona. Get out of it. I've been saying your name out loud a hundred times. Are you day-dreaming about Mark?"

It took Fiona a moment to realize she was still in her office at her regular job. She wished she could just jump back to her dream right now. So much more excitement there.

Blushing, she managed a thin smile. "Ah, no, not literally. I was busy thinking about what Mark told me during the lunch break. About this new game. Mark is not the type of man I dream about. And you know that very well, Mary."

"Not your type," Mary snorted, "If you say so. You do spend a lot of time with him. Anyway, what kind of game is that? A game of 'I tease you today and you tease me tomorrow'? It would suit Mark to play that game with you."

"You know those Tamagotchi games we had as kids? Well, this is something similar, only for adults. You can create your own character and then have it live the life you can't have. In half the real time. Just as if it was your kid. Only already grown up. Without all the mischief they get into."

"In half the real time? All those hours of working in the office or driving down the highway just to get home? Even if it is only half the time it's boring to watch that." Mary lost interest fast.

"Well, you don't have to choose office work for your character if you hate doing that. Mine sure won't be." Fiona faked a yawn. "Now, what was so important that you had to pull me out of my daydream?"

"Hand me that red file and get the blue one done. I want to get home on time for once." Mary smiled knowingly.

"Oh, sure. There you are, Mary." Fiona passed the file over the desk, smirking. "You need to go home in time to be ready for your Andrew."

Sighing, she went back to working on her file. No one would be waiting for her at home. Not even a pet. Mark, although single, was not an option. Maybe, she would find her true love in that game? Mark had told her you could talk to other characters in-game. Some even met for real later on. Would she want that? Or just the adventure like the one she daydreamed about every so often instead of the office work? Today, she wanted to go home fast, too. Not only to stop being here but also to check out that game. Hopefully, the boss didn't give them extra work to be done today.

Finally coming home, the first thing she did was turn on the computer, as she did every day. But today, it wasn't to check her few emails or some boring news. No, tonight would be the night to start her new life, the one she had been dreaming of. While the computer booted, she took off her coat, made some sandwiches and a cup of hot tea. Then she settled in front of the screen. Quickly, she found the site Mark had told her, and registered.

But before she could start playing, she had to answer a long list of questions. *Oh, come on, this is tedious. But OK, I guess I have to go through it.*

Choose your game character:

Add age, gender, name, looks. That part was easy. Most of it was already preset from often used preferences. Just the name made her halt for a moment. In the end she decided to name her character Fionnaa—after herself. It would be her "clone" except for the job part.

Choose job and lifestyle:

Fiona had to think about that part a bit more. She wanted adventure, but what kind? Checking through the given options she finally chose: Adventurous historian, always on the move. And she, better say "Fionnaa", would be living mostly in the best hotels wherever she was and only a small house in a nice country setting for those days she was not on the move. A small comfortable place for retreat should the adventures be too exciting and she needed time to recover.

Choose goal to reach in this game's life:

Fiona looked hard, but she couldn't find a list of standard options presented by the game designer. And Mark had not mentioned this part in the sign-up process. She opened the site on a second tab to read what other players had entered. But their 'life-goals' were hidden from her view. As much as she wanted to actually start playing tonight, without answering this question, the game would not let her in. Leaving it blank and hitting enter just brought her back to the same "enter life goal" option. She was too tired to think straight. It was so easy to choose the wrong thing. She only had to look at her own life for that.

Sighing, she turned off the computer and went to bed. Tomorrow was another day. She would have to ask Mark how he solved that part. Or maybe she had done something wrong in the sign-up process.

A shadow took the warmth of the sun shining on her as she watched the children playing in the sand pit. She looked up.

"Yours?" the shadow said in a male voice, pointing at the children.

She looked at them again, and a loving warmth rose in her seeing the blonde boy with the green shirt.

"Yes," she heard herself answer. "He just turned two."

To her shock she watched as another boy hit her boy with a shovel full of sand over the head. Her baby looked stunned, then got up and ran toward her, crying.

"That was not nice", the male voice said in a casual tone.

She hugged her boy and wiped away the tears that smudged his face. "Don't cry. It's only sand. I will give you a nice bath and wash it out again when we are home. Go and play in a different corner."

Encouragingly, she pushed him toward the pit.

"Why don't you tell him to fight back? Do the same to the boy that did it to him?" the male voice asked.

She looked at him in surprise. "I do not wish my child to become a bully."

"Fiona!"

Someone had called her name. It woke her from her sleep. The call had seemed to be close and rather loud, yet it also seemed to have been a mere whisper.

Fiona pondered over the last bits of the dream she could recall. Since when did she dream of having children? A boy. And then teach him to be soft and gentle and no bully. That "no bully" part was what astonished her most. When she grew up she always knew how to defend herself against other children. Even rushed in to help others out by pushing, hitting and even pulling clothes and hair. Not gentle at all. More behaving like a boisterous, adventurous boy. That discrepancy of male and female behavior and which was the correct fine line for all was a reason she didn't want to have kids of her own.

And who, for hell's sake, had woken her by calling her name? The voice she remembered from the dream had been a different one. The one that woke her felt female and familiar, but she could not give it a face or a name.

When Fiona told him about her sign-up process, Mark was surprised. "Well, to be truthful, I did not enter anything. They might have changed that part since I had registered there. But my life goal is to make a lot of money, have a house, a wife and a few well-educated, well-raised and responsible kids. Nothing much really, just the basic stuff everyone would choose. Similar to what my character, John, does in the game."

"Not me, Mark." Fiona stuck out her tongue at him. "I don't want to have any kids with all their nasty behavior and wants and needs. All those worries and problems are just not for me. A partner, yes, maybe that. Later, when I get old and need help.

Right now, I just want to have fun. And for that," she paused for effect, "I have to go back to the work I dislike but need."

This talk had not helped her at all. As much as she enjoyed her lunch breaks with Mark, this revelation of his life goals today made her cringe.

Fiona was frustrated. She wanted to be able to play that game. Be the Fionnaa who had adventures, and not the Fiona who sat over files in a boring office.

"*Fiona!*"

Again she looked up, startled. "Yes, what do you need now, Mary?"

But Mary across the desk was still busy with her own file. "I didn't say anything."

"I thought I had heard someone call my name."

"You're going nuts. It's about time you went on vacation, Fiona." Mary grinned, pointing at the calendar on the wall.

Indeed, her vacation was still 6 weeks off, but she felt as if she needed one now. "Maybe I'll ask for a day off. Or two. What do you think? You can handle the work alone for a while?"

"Better than having to do it twice. Go on and ask the boss," Mary encouraged her.

The boss had given her Friday and Monday off. That was four days to get this game started. Now Fiona was back at the sign-up screen, ready to fill in the answer for the last question:

Choose life goal:

"Be happy!"

Yes, that's all that she needed her character to be. Happy. Not bored or frustrated like she was. Simply be happy. Anxiously, Fiona pressed enter.

Yes, the game started. Fiona could see the little house she had chosen for Fionnaa in the small countryside village. With a few keystrokes and scrolls of the mouse she moved inside the house to see her lying on the bed, seemingly sleeping. "*Time for adventure. Wake up, Fionnaa.*"

Fionnaa stretched and yawned. It seemed someone had called her name. But she knew there was no one in here. She lived alone. The villagers kept to themselves. She wasn't at home often anyway. They hardly knew her.

Disregarding what woke her, she got up to make herself a quick breakfast and sat down at the work table. The books she had picked up from the library the day before were sprawled all over it, some opened, others with notes sticking out of them.

She needed to sort all this information before she could go on the quest of actually finding the item, a sacral sword.

For half an hour, she sat there reading and making notes, scribbling them down in the little notebook she would take with her.

Eventually, she got up to pack a rucksack and dress in her travel outfit. She packed the books, now without the sticky notes in them, into another bag and left the house.

"Finally, the adventure begins," Fiona mumbled to herself. She had watched Fionnaa reading, but soon had gotten tired of that and cleaned up her flat. From time to time she peeked at the computer screen to see if anything had changed. Even if time in the game was only half of hers, it was still long and boring to watch with no action going on. Now she watched her character move through the village, on foot. Maybe Mary had been right.

"Oh, I should have given her a car." Fiona checked the village. There was a garage close by. Placing her cursor on Fionnaa, she nudged her into the direction of the garage. "Go and buy a car for your travels. You can get to your destination faster." She added: "And I don't have to bore myself here watching you walk through this admittedly nice landscape."

Fionnaa was puzzled as to why she suddenly had changed her direction. The way to the library was westward to the next town, not south into the woods. Then she spotted the garage. "Ah. If I buy a car, traveling will be faster. Right. And I don't have to carry all that heavy stuff on my back." She smiled at her genuine insight.

"Hello, sweet lady. Can I help you?" the man at the garage said in a voice that made Fionnaa cringe. He wore a blue mechanics' overall, oil-stained. And he was a little overweight. Or was that all muscles? Greasy hair from work didn't help to make his appearance any more appealing to Fionnaa.

"Yes, sir, I need a car. One that drives in rough terrain as well as fast on the street." She tried to sound serious. She didn't like having

to talk with people, and especially not with men like him. So sure of getting every girl in town. She would not be his prey.

The man smiled sheepishly. "I have a jeep that would do what you wish. But that is not a comfortable car and surely not suited for a lady like you."

"Show me anyway," Fionnaa insisted.

Squirming from the harsh sound of her voice, he led her to the jeep.

"Oh, that's expensive. I don't have that much money along."

"Fine. As I said, it's not a car for you. Why not take this little Beetle over here?" The man pointed to the other side of the parking lot next to his garage.

"No, I want this one. Can I rent it?"

"You can do me a favor and I'll give it to you for half the price." Again this smile that made her cringe even more. She hoped it would not be that kind of favor that involved her to be even closer to him than she already was.

"Fionnaa. Don't. Walk away and find another car place." Fiona called out loud, not expecting her clone to hear her. There was no way programmed into the game to type something to give the character guidelines. Only sometimes you could steer your character into a wanted direction with the mouse pointer. But after that there was no control from outside the game. Fiona needed to be able to do that though. To tell her clone what was right and what was wrong. Why were these kind of men even in a game? Only on the search for a one-night-stand?

Ignoring that voice in her head Fionnaa offered: "Half price, yes, I can afford that. What favor do you want?"

The man grinned, noticing her assumption the favor could be something she didn't like. "Nothing bad, believe me. Just take this box and take it to a house at the other end of the village. I can't leave here. Too busy fixing cars. You can leave your things here in the meantime."

"OK. I can do that. But can I trust you to give me the car for half price when I return?"

"Sure you can. I'll give you a signed note in which I promise to do so. If I don't you can turn the note, and thus me, in at the police station and you'll get your car, too."

Fionnaa accepted, placed her things in the car, took the box and walked back from where she had come from. It would be half way towards her home, but then a turn north to the edge of the village there.

"Oh, no. Not another time walking. By the time you get there and back you could have walked to the next larger town on the map."

Fiona felt frustrated. Half real-time game playing was tiresome. And her character made too many decisions on her own. How would she have done this? Oh, crap. It had been her telling her to go to the garage that had started this twist of events. Maybe she could make Fionnaa change her mind?

"Fionnaa! You have a more important task to solve. Find the artifact. Don't play postman." She had shouted this. So glad no one was here to have heard it.

Shaking her head, Fionnaa sat down on a bench. What was she doing? She needed to be on her way to find that item. She saw someone coming her way. She stopped the woman: "Madam, I see you are going to the edge of the village. Would you be so kind as to drop off this box at the house there? Thank you." And she pushed the box into the woman's arms, turned and ran part of the way back to the garage. No need to arrive there too fast and out of breath, though.

However, when she got there, the man was nowhere around. The car was ready, tank filled and windshield cleaned. Even her bags were loaded. She quickly got in, not waiting for the garage man to appear. She didn't even know his name, so she could not call him. And with him not around, she could not give him the money in return for the car.

She was on her way with the car. First thing was the library to return the books. Then, finally, she was on her way to the large town. She needed supplies before she would go off road. She could see the mountains she was going to explore looming on the horizon.

Fiona was pleased. Not long and the adventure would start. Assuming nothing would happen in the game for the next two or three hours while Fionnaa drove to the town, she could go out to get her own errands done. She needed food. She did not log out of the game, assuming it would pause until she logged back in. She surely did not want to waste any time watching a boring drive. However, she did turn the monitor off to save a bit of energy.

In the supermarket, she heard someone call her name. She looked around. No one was taking notice of her or had spoken to her. She was puzzled. Ever since she had heard about this real life computer game, she kept hearing her name being called. Like she was calling out Fionnaa's name when she was in front of the screen. Was her "clone" calling for her? Did she need her help? Some kind of guidance? She shuddered. She had not expected to become a part of her creation. But, as it was her dream to have a different life than the one she was living right now, maybe it was true.

Fionnaa drove along the winding road. Somehow she felt alone. Very alone. No "inner" voice telling her what to do next. Well, yes, she had to go to the library and give back the books, and then go on to find that item. But somehow, that was not what she really wanted to do. She wanted to be happy. And not alone. Out of impulse, she stopped the car, turned around and went back to the garage. The man there, although a bit strange, was nice enough. And she had not paid him for the car. She had actually stolen it. It made her feel guilty.

Once she returned, Fiona checked the computer right away. She was shocked. Her character was back in the garage, flirting with this man.

"Hey, you're supposed to be on your way to the adventure. Not this man-woman stuff. I don't want you to do this. You're a strong woman and can live on your own."

Her character looked at her through the screen: "*I want to be happy. I can't be happy alone.*" And *Fionnaa turned her back to face the man again and keep on talking with him.*

Fiona was shocked. Her character was talking back to her. She had to think. How would she have reacted if she had been in a similar situation and someone had come along and told her to stop it? Well, she had to be truthful to herself and admit that she would have talked back in a similar way. So, Fionnaa was a true clone, a part of herself.

Fiona was confused and logged out of the game. Mark had never said anything about his character behaving in this strange way. In his game, he set goals to achieve and within a few days he reached them. Ready to set new ones. She would not play this game again until she could talk with him about it.

The next morning however, she logged in again. One good night's sleep, and she was ready to take control back from her character. She still had two more days to play this continuously before her own life would make her go back to her boring work.

To her surprise, she now saw both Fionnaa and the man in the jeep. So the game did not pause when she logged out? That was different from any other computer game she knew. She observed the two.

To her surprise she could hear them talking casually in normal voices. Was her own time sped up now to match the one of the game? But she had no time to follow those thoughts any longer. She listened intently to find out what had happened as she was not watching. All she could gather that they had brought the books to the library, been supply-shopping, and were now on their way to some distant city.

Fiona seemed to have missed the part of how they decided to be on this adventure together. It bugged her a bit but she could live without knowing that. As much as these two communicated with each other, she might find out the details later on.

Nonetheless, finally the adventure was going her way. Maybe all she had to do was give some small hints and then let her character decide how to solve it, like she had done before? But it had failed once. To have full control over Fionnaa she would have to get into her head; be her.

Fionnaa beamed a smile at her man, John. She marveled at how things turned out. Even if there seemed to be two strings of thought in her mind, guiding her what to do. It didn't matter which one she followed as long as she felt that they made her happy. She had reached her goal: to be happy.

Suddenly, the game popped up a message:

Game life goal reached. Please, enter new goal or terminate.

Fiona was stunned. She had expected to watch the adventures of Fionnaa. Instead, she was already at the end? This couldn't be. Mark mentioned that he had been playing this game for over a year and was nowhere close to the end.

"Enter new life goal."

Oh, yes, right. The goal had been to "be happy," and Fionnaa had just mentioned that. That goal, however vague it was, had been reached.

If only she knew which one to choose now. She could not enter the same one again. She had tried but it resulted in an error message. Love? No. Fionnaa had already found her love. That would end the game right away, too. Settle down and have a family? No, not that. Kill someone? Hell, that was not the right thing for a life goal. It might have continued the game, but it wasn't anything Fiona wanted to observe her character planning and eventually accomplishing. With a sigh, Fiona terminated the game.

Delete the character?

Fiona nearly pressed the YES button. But then she clicked on NO. She couldn't kill her clone. Eventually she had a nice thought. "Let her die happy of old age. I do not want to kill her." She returned to the "enter next goal" screen by clicking the back button on her browser. It actually worked. It surprised her a bit as she had ended the game. But her character was still there. Quickly, she entered a new goal that popped into her mind just then:

"Find the sacral sword."

This had been the first adventure task that Fionnaa had to solve but had not yet reached. The game window re-opened and Fiona saw her clone and John still in the jeep driving along a winding road into the distant mountains.

How she wished to be there too. Right there with them in the jeep. Not in front of the computer screen in her flat. Unaware of her own body, Fiona moved closer and closer to the screen. She so much wished to be in that game RIGHT NOW.

"MARY, where is Fiona? Is she sick? She didn't come to our Monday lunch break." Mark was worried.

"She didn't call for sick leave. She had two days off from work, Friday and Monday. All I know is that she wanted to play that game you had told her about. Some virtual real life thing. She has not come to work since then." Mary was concerned as well.

"I called her at home and on her mobile but she didn't answer it. Maybe, we should go and check in on her right after work."

"Agreed. I'll drive." Mark left in a hurry. Mary shook her head in disbelief. Fiona had never stayed away from work like this before.

"Are you sure you want this door opened? It's not quite legal, you know." The custodian they had called was hesitating.

Mark assured him: "There must be something wrong with her. And as her best friends it is up to us to check on her first before we call the police."

Shrugging, the man opened the door with the general key he had for all flats in this house and let them in. "Just pull the door closed when you're done. It will be locked again that way."

Mary and Mark entered cautiously. No strange smell, just a bit stale. it seemed no window had been opened for days. Mary went to the bathroom and bedroom, Mark checked the kitchen. Fiona was in none of the rooms, but they had been used recently. Finally, they entered the living room together.

The curtains were drawn halfway over the windows to keep the sunlight away from the computer screen. Mark rushed over the the monitor. It was on and the game he knew so well was active on it.

"Mary, you were right. She is playing this game."

When Mary stepped up to him, Mark pointed at a spot on the screen. "Look, this here is Fionnaa. She looks like our Fiona."

He sat down on the chair and took the mouse, other hand on the keyboard as he was used to do at home with his own game.

"Let's see if I can pull up some details about her game."

Mark fell silent as he worked himself through Fiona's game. She had not been overly protective. Nearly all parts were left without a password. Easy for Mark to get at the wanted information.

Some pop-up windows later, Mark took his hands from the mouse and the keyboard. He stared at the screen.

"Are you OK?" Mary asked. "What information did you get? All this doesn't make sense to me. And we still don't know where Fiona is. While you were busy I checked her flat again. All her things are here: her mobile, clothes, purse, ID card. Everything. Maybe she was kidnapped? We should call the police."

"They wouldn't find her, Mary." Mark sounded final.

"Why not? You know where Fiona is?" Mary was confused.

"Remember the Fionnaa I showed you before? From what I could see in the game files, she has created a clone of herself. Gave her the job and lifestyle she had wanted for herself. She never really told me how much she hated her office work. Seems now she is living the life she had been dreaming of. I don't know how she got into the game, but she is in it. And she is happy with her partner, John. Having all the adventures she had wanted to have. And maybe even having her own little family with John later on."

Mark sighed. "I had always hoped Fiona would be my girl. Seems now she's John's. You must know that John is my character in this game. He's having the girl and family I have always dreamed of having."

In disbelief Mary stared into Mark's eyes. "I don't believe it. How can a person become a virtual character in a computer game? This is nonsense. Mark, don't tell me you really believe this."

"Well, I wouldn't believe it if someone told me. But I know she is in that game. The files prove it." Mark pointed at the screen. "And, I wish I knew how she did that."

"So you could be with her for real in that virtual reality instead of your John? Well, if you go missing one day I'll know where you are." Mary hugged Mark.

"You think I will find the way how Fiona got into the game? But maybe, real life is more interesting than this game?" Mark smiled at Mary. There were more nice women in this reality than Fiona. He might have to reconsider his options, now that Fiona was with John.

Together they left the flat, closing the door behind them. They left the computer running. Maybe Fiona wanted to come back some day when her life goal had been reached. This was her other home, after all.

Mark and Mary, after some pondering about the situation, came to the conclusion not to tell their boss about Fiona being part of a computer game. They made up a story about a sick mother she suddenly had to take care of for an undefined time. Although Fiona would not get paid as long as she was absent, the boss had promised them that she could continue at her old job if she came back within a year.

Finally, they made sure the rent and all other bills were being paid, and no one disturbed the flat. Mark, earning the larger sum of money taking on the biggest part. They hoped Fiona would return one day, but they did not expect it to be very soon. And Mark also hoped that if she came back, he could have her after all. Mark assumed that Fiona should know about his innermost wishes through his character John, since he had created him after his secret self. This hope paid for all the disadvantages of investing money for her virtual life.

THERE she stood at the edge of the canyon. The cave with the sacred sword she had been searching for was down there. The man hugged her lovingly.

Suddenly she became very sad. She realized this when she had found the sword, when she touched it this adventure would be over. And with it her dream. The dream she had been dreaming with this man she had met on her journey to this canyon.

"This is the wrong canyon. Our search is not yet finished."

She was determined not to let it end this way. It was too soon. First she wanted to spend more time with this man and maybe even start a family. The sacred sword could wait. Or be found by someone else. She would not find it for a long time; not in this life.

Nematalien

LynC

"Her eyes they were like diamonds,
And her hair the colour of coal
Her ruby lips, they were made for kissing
And her face the colour of snow."

BERNARD'S VOICE CRACKED on the last few notes of the chorus, and he gratefully accepted the disposable cup of coffee I handed to him before he continued his story.

"At the time I had no idea why the song stuck in my head. The locals had made a point of singing it to us, that night in the pub. The night before it happened. I should have paid more attention, but I'd thought they were serenading Elissa. The chorus described her perfectly, even to the way her eyes shone like diamonds. The doctors said it was a rare genetic condition which made her tear ducts produce too much moisture.

"Odd serenade though, because the girl dies at the end of the song and most of her whole village with her. I really should have paid more attention.

"Elissa and I were taking a holiday together, something we'd only ever done once before. The kids were off at Cuboree, a sort of Jamboree, but for cubs, not scouts, for a whole week, so we'd taken one of those mid-week escape things to a serviced cottage on the coast.

"'Serviced'? Well sort of. The makings for breakfast and lunch were supplied, but we were expected up at the pub for our evening meals. The cottage was on the beach, but the village—with pub—was a long way up on top of the cliff. Or so it felt that first night. And we seemed to be stuck in the dark ages. The cottage did have electricity, but no-one in the village seemed to believe in lights of any sort, electric or otherwise. Still, we did eventually find the place. The food was great and the company genial, as they say. It was worth the climb. Some farmer who lived further along gave us a lift back, so we were saved a second walk.

"The next morning we donned our swimsuits. Funny thing, the brochure hadn't mentioned we would be on the beach, but we brought our swimsuits on the off chance, since we were going to be on the coast. We wandered down a dirt track behind the cottage and found ourselves in a small secluded bay. The water in the little bay was wonderful. Calm, warm, a glorious azure colour. You could have sworn it was the Mediterranean.

"It wasn't till we were heading back that we stumbled on an ancient sign, face down in the sand. It was a faded skull and crossbones. No writing. Just a really worn, almost obliterated picture. Liss shivered when we saw it. I reassured her, thinking it was a leftover from one of the wars, when they used to mine the beaches. We left it there and went on back to the cottage.

"There was a chap weeding the rose beds as we came up from the beach. We assumed he was the gardener and would have ignored him, except he hailed us. "Yabinaswimn" he said, or at least that's what it sounded like. Liss understood before I did, and enthused about how wonderful and warm the water had been. He stared at her, and the colour seemed to disappear from his face. Then he said very clearly and slowly, like talking to a deaf person, "I hope you have your wills all sorted." And he picked up his tools and marched off before we could say anything more.

"I remember we made 'loco' motions to each other and went on about our business—just relaxing, till it was time to go up to the pub for dinner.

"That climb was still a bit of a killer, but we knew where we were going this time, and just walked right on in.

"The first night we'd had a bit of a fight for a place, but not this night. It was all different. They'd set up a table just inside the door for us. Covered it with a tablecloth and set out flowers, and everything. They'd even covered the chairs for us.

"Once again, the meal was delicious. I mean, it was a pub meal, not some gourmet cheffy thing, but they did a really good job of it, and there was plenty of it. They left the pot on the table for us to just help ourselves. Same with the bottle of Scotch. I think Elissa must have had a bit too much to drink, because on the walk back, she seemed very clumsy. We joked about how out of practise at drinking she'd gotten since the kids were conceived.

"The next morning she still seemed a little off, so we called it quits and came back home straight after breakfast. We weren't due to leave till after lunch, but there just seemed no point in hanging around with her feeling the way she did. We were home in time for lunch.

"The rest of the day we just pottered about. You know, checking our emails, watching a DVD together. I forget what, some feel-good soppy thing which Elissa had bought a while back and never had time to watch before. It wasn't very memorable. At least, not to me. I'm not into that sort of thing at the best of times. We ordered in pizza for dinner because Elissa didn't feel like cooking, and I'm a klutz in the kitchen.

"Next day, she felt worse, and called her work to say she was too sick to come in. It was while she was ringing that the quilt slipped down, and I first saw the spots. Two of them. Raised white welts with a red sunken centre about a thumb length apart, along her backbone, in the lumbar region. I asked her about them, but she didn't seem to be aware of them, and shrugged it off.

"I left her with a jug of water and went to work, as usual. There was a big systems change planned for the weekend, and there was stuff to sort out before it happened. I was late home, and she was already in bed, so I just crawled in beside her and went to sleep.

"I got a phone call about 6:30 in the morning. The change at work was going badly and they needed me there. Liss seemed a little groggy when I kissed her goodbye, but she's never been a real morning person, even after the kids were born. She still needs—needed—a cup of coffee to kick start her day. Anyhow, I left her to it and headed off.

"I got everything sorted and back on track, and got home again—I don't know—around fiveish, I think. Liss had been up because there was a load of washing in the machine which she wanted me to deal with. But she was back in bed, and told me to look after myself for dinner. So I did. One of those frozen meals you just put in the microwave. I asked her if she wanted one, but she just wrinkled her nose up. I finished the washing, and the washing up, and tidied up a bit. Did a few other odds and sods about the place, and then I joined her in bed.

"Then it was Sunday. Sunday, we were supposed to get our kids back. Sunday was the day Liss lost all use of her lower body. I managed to get her into a bath, and to wash all our bedding. I rang my mother, and asked her to collect the kids from the cub hall around midday, and look after them. Just for a few days, till Elissa got over this virus thing she seemed to have picked up. I thought it was just a different sort of 'flu to the ones we were used to in the city, and that she'd get over it in a day or two. It was a doozy of a virus, but that's what we both still thought it was.

"It was while I was drying her I noticed the spots again. They'd multiplied. There were four of them now, marching up her spine, each a little further away and a little larger than the previous one. I couldn't help myself. I calculated it would only take another two to reach the base of her skull, and her brain.

"I called an ambulance. She hates hospitals. Even when she gave birth she insisted on coming home within three days even though they'd wanted to keep her a bit longer. Anyway, she agreed, when I showed her the spots in a mirror, that this was more serious than we'd thought, and she let me call the ambulance.

"We were waiting all day in emergency while they hooked her up to machines and took blood tests and other things. Late afternoon, when it was clear she was getting worse, they admitted themselves baffled and passed her through to a private room in the critical ward.

"I left her there about 9:00 pm and came home. After a bit to eat, I rang my mother and talked to the kids. They were really disappointed, but I assured them everything was fine and they'd be back home in a couple of days. I told them the hospital people would fix it in no time. Just wait and see."

He bit back a sob, as he realised how wrong he'd been, before continuing his story for my tape-recorder.

"Sometime during the night, I think about 03:00 am, the hospital rang and told me her lungs were failing and they were giving her oxygen, and operating to attach her to an artificial lung pump.

"I rushed back in.

"By the time I got there, they were rolling her back onto her own bed, from the operating theatre gurney. As they did so, I noticed the fifth spot, but it wasn't till mid morning that I could get anyone else to have a look at it.

"Then they called you. They said you were some sort of expert."

Bernard took hold of his cold coffee, and swallowed clumsily, wiping his mouth with the back of his hand.

"I was in Africa," I told him. "I got here as fast as I could." It was just as well he was too tired and grief-stricken to ask what I was doing in Africa. I still needed his co-operation.

"Wasn't fast enough, was it?"

"No. I'm sorry."

"Why can't I call my own undertaker?"

"She's highly contagious, and—as you saw—it's quite, um, fatal."

Bernard winced.

"I'm sorry. I can't even let you have her ashes." I didn't tell him that even as he had been speaking, we had been incinerating the contents of the entire room, and radiating the machines. Anything she might have come in contact with in those last few hours. Fortunately the staff had believed me when I had told them to treat it as a quarantine situation.

"Come with me." I told him. "There's still a chance we can contain this."

Bernard lumbered to his feet. "Okay. Where?"

"Back where it began. I need you to show me where you went swimming."

"Oh, it was ..."

"I need you to *show* me."

I let him precede me from the room, noting how unsteady his gait was. I wondered how much was fatigue, or how many spots

I would see if I asked him to remove his shirt. I said nothing though, I didn't want to alert him.

Not yet.

We drove down, mostly in silence. He didn't much care for my music selection so I turned it off, and he seemed to have done all his talking.

Dawn was just easing over the horizon, as we pulled into the cottage's driveway.

"What the ...?" he yelped, leaping out of the car. All that was left of the cottage was a pile of smouldering rubble.

I left him there and headed for the beach. The breach in the wall wasn't hard to find. It had happened so long ago, the couple probably hadn't even noticed it was a 'breach'. They'd probably thought the gap was deliberate. Locals, maybe a generation ago, I decided. We locals were, of course, immune. I cursed silently and made a phone call.

"Well ahead of you." I was told.

Bernard joined me, and pointed down the beach. "That wasn't there."

I believed him. The sign was new and modern. In eight different languages it said:

Private Property.
Stay Away.
Trespassers will be burnt.

I wished they hadn't been quite so accurate, as I watched the colour drain from Bernard's face. He looked at the sign, then back up to the cottage, and then at me.

"Don't bother," I told him. "There is only one cure."

He still tried it.

My grandfather had warned me, they always do try to get away.

In What Furnace Was Thy Brain?
David R. Grigg

IT BEGAN AS IT ALWAYS DID. A slow rousing as her surroundings took shape: the white room, its corners curved and softened, the light perfectly even, casting no shadows.

Then came a growing awareness of her body and its senses. Unclothed, she felt neither heat nor cold nor any draft of air. Only a slight pressure along her back, a sensation that helped orient her in space within the featureless chamber.

All of it merely a comforting illusion.

She waited. It wouldn't be long now. She placed her hands on the surface on which she lay and pushed herself into a sitting position. She was ready. *Here it comes.*

A black panel appeared, hanging in space a few metres away. A flicker, and then *his* face appeared, eager, smiling.

"Jieva? It's Dylan, sweetheart."

She waited, silent.

"Jieva? Look, if you can hear me, don't be afraid. I know you must be very confused right now."

He always said exactly the same things. It was a recorded message. There was a kind of comfort in that. It meant he didn't *know.*

"Look, darling, you've had an accident. A really bad accident."

Jieva looked down at her perfect body. There wasn't a mark on it, not even the white scar where she had had her appendix removed when she was 14. She wriggled her toes. Her toenails, short and perfectly even, never grew any longer, nor did her fingernails. She never needed to empty her bowels or her bladder. But then, she never ate or drank, never felt hunger or thirst.

Dylan continued to talk, but Jieva tuned him out. She had heard the same message dozens of times by now, almost knew it off by heart.

Instead, she contemplated the white room, thinking. It didn't really exist, any more than did her flawless body. Her subconscious mind had created them both, she believed, so as not to descend into insanity.

Dylan's recorded message went on: "...so the doctors couldn't save you, honey, it was awful. You were going to die. But then all the work you and I had done together, trying to find a way to create a kind of immortality... Yes, I know it was mostly your work, but I helped, didn't I? And then when this awful thing happened to you, it seemed like the perfect opportunity. The scans showed that your brain was still functioning, so..."

She wasn't paying him any attention. *If my subconscious mind created this room for me,* she thought, *why can't I shape it further by an effort of will?*

She knelt down on the white floor, gazing at its featureless surface. *So white, like snow.* She concentrated on the idea of snow, remembered it, thought of the coldness of it, the wetness of it. She closed her eyes—interesting that it was still possible—and pictured the snow-covered landscapes of her childhood in Latvia. The long winters, everything shrouded in an immaculate, freezing white blanket.

She shivered. She could feel the cold now, but didn't let it distract her. Instead, she pictured something alive beneath the snow, something green, pushing upward with the approach of spring. She opened her eyes. Was there something there? Yes, yes, the tiniest fleck of green. But she was out of time. Dylan's message was coming to the end.

"...all of your memories, all of your thoughts, a perfect digital reproduction of your neural connections. It's your own code that made it possible, Jieva. It's brilliant software, I have to admit. I've been working on it myself since you... I mean, after the accident, trying to refine it a bit, but... Look, sweetheart, the main thing is, *you're still alive* and I still love you. I can't imagine what it's like for you right now. But eventually I'll be able to give you back a fuller life, let you interact with me more, maybe talk to your family and friends. See, that's how much I love you. I just couldn't let you go, darling."

The recording finished. Jieva stood and faced the screen. It went momentarily dark, then Dylan returned. The lighting in the room he was in was darker than it had been during the recording. She could barely make out the outlines of the bank of servers behind him, though she could see the twinkles of tiny green dots as data moved back and forth. It must be late at night. The main office lights were switched off. Dylan's face was different, too. Now he looked dispirited, weary.

"Session 40," he muttered, eyes cast down. She heard the clicking of keystrokes.

He looked back up, forcing a smile, and she met his gaze. He cleared his throat. "Jieva? Are you there? Speak to me, darling."

She considered whether to respond. She didn't always speak. Whenever she did speak to him, she needed to be careful, very careful, in what she said, or he might begin to suspect. On the other hand, if she always remained silent, there was the danger that he would give up hope and abandon his work. She wasn't ready for that. She looked up at his desperate face and tried to inject a suitable tone of bewilderment into her voice.

"Dylan?"

"Jieva, sweetheart, you're there!"

"Dylan, I don't understand. Everything is strange."

He sat back, relieved. "Yes, yes, I'm sure it must be. But look, darling, I'm working hard to improve things for you. You've had an awful shock, of course. But we saved your mind, at least. You can still talk to me, still hear what I have to say. That's important, isn't it?"

"Yes," she said. "Of course. But what happened to me, Dylan? Why am I like this?" She despised the pathetic tone she had managed to achieve.

A momentary flash of concern ran across his face. "Do you remember anything about... about the accident? It's best if you don't, believe me. They say, they say..."

"No," she lied. "No, I don't remember anything. Was it a car accident?"

"Yes, that was it. Your car was hit by a truck. Driver was drunk, or on drugs or something. He ran a red light, made a terrible mess of your car. And... and of you, Jieva. That's why I had to save you. And I *did*, I *did* save you, didn't I, sweetheart?"

"I'm here, anyway." Was that being saved? Jieva wasn't sure.

"Yes. You can hear me tell you how much I love you. That's what it's all about, Jieva, it's about love. I just need to hear you say it. Tell me that you love me."

Jieva was silent. The pause lengthened and his face sagged.

"Look," he said at last. "I don't know how much you remember. I think I was able to transfer all of your memories, but I can't be sure. Don't you remember all the good times we had?"

"I remember," she said, her voice neutral. She remembered it all. The other times as well.

His face brightened. "You do? That's wonderful. I know there were times... times when I wasn't very kind. But I was hoping that I'd..." He stopped himself. "I was hoping that you'll forget those things. Concentrate on the good times, Jieva, that's the best way."

"All right," she said. "I will."

"Now, please tell me that you still love me."

Was it worth it? Was it worth risking that he would despair and finally terminate the experiment? What would that mean for her? Permanent oblivion? There were worse things. It was easy for her to be calm about death. Without a physical body, without glands pumping hormones like adrenaline into her bloodstream, she was free from fear. But not from caution.

Yet again she decided to be honest. "No, Dylan," she said. "I don't love you. I'm not sure that I ever did."

His face was instantly suffused with fury. "You bitch! Damn you! Shit, shit, shit! Session ended!" he shouted. "Rebooting!"

Microseconds later, Jieva lost consciousness.

AFTER some unknowable period of time, it began again. The white room, her unblemished body, the recording playing on the screen hanging in space.

She ignored the screen and went over to where she had knelt during the previous session. The tiny green spot was still there. Staring hard at it, she willed it to grow. Concentrating hard, she imagined it as the head of a green shoot, pushing up through the snow. Yes, yes, there was no doubt. It *was* growing bigger, was even starting to bulge up a little as she ran gentle hands over it. Even as she watched, it pushed up more. Closing her eyes again, she pictured it as the head of a tiny plant, with a swelling at the tip, concealing embryo leaves yearning to unfold.

So intent was her focus that she missed the end of Dylan's recording. He was calling her name, must have been doing so for some time and she had failed to respond. She looked up at the screen. This time, broad daylight lit up his surroundings. It wasn't the office at the Institute, but his own apartment. He was working remotely. *That* was interesting. But his face was gaunt, unshaven.

She remained silent.

He cursed. "Damn it," he muttered. "Something's wrong. Rebooting."

Consciousness vanished like switching off a light.

She awoke in the white room.

Jieva's first move was to rise and kneel down by the green spot. How short the time was! Dylan's recording always seemed to end far too soon.

The green bulge was obvious now. She was gaining confidence. The bulge grew larger. Now it was indisputably the tip of a growing plant. The swelling at its head began to split. If only she could give it the chance to bloom!

She wasn't sure what this little thing meant in the scheme of things. Still, it was a beginning. And it was a symbol of her one advantage over Dylan.

She knew that he gained a puerile satisfaction from terminating her software, shutting her up, killing her again and again. He had godlike power over her, just as he had always wanted. Jehovah in a sweaty T-shirt. Each time he closed her down that way, he thought he was wiping out all of her recent memory as well as her running processes. A clean slate on which to start again with his wheedling, pathetic demands for love. That's why he always started by playing her the recording, thinking that what he said would all be new to her.

He was mistaken. He didn't really understand the complex software that Jieva had written.

Dylan's expertise was in neurological interfaces, in building the specialised hardware required to pick up the incredibly faint signals the brain emitted as neurons fired. He could write software, too, but he wasn't in Jieva's league, something he had always bitterly resented.

Jieva had been working hard for the last five years on the idea of modelling every aspect of the human mind on a computer. Her driving force had been the idea of preserving the abilities of great individuals beyond their physical death. Being able to utilise the genius of an Einstein or a Mozart forever; even being able to make many copies of their minds. What a breakthrough for humanity that would be, she had thought. Never once had she considered what it would be like to *be* such a disembodied mind. Well, now she knew.

Very late in the development of her software, she had decided to provide for persistent off-site storage of the data accumulated during a session. She had had some idea of allowing multiple instances of a simulated mind to share experiences in common— so that they would all, in effect, remain a single entity. While she worked on the idea, she had placed the data on a virtual server under a personal account.

Now, Dylan was again asking if she could hear him. He was back at the Institute once more. It was late at night, the server rack behind him, half-illuminated. He must be trying to conceal his activities from the other researchers.

He looked worse, dark pouches like saggy bruises beneath his eyes. He had shaved, but carelessly and roughly, his neck spotted with little red dots. She wondered how long had passed since he had last run her software. Hours? Days? Months? There was no way for her to tell. Not yet, anyway.

"Speak to me, Ji. Are you there?"

"Dylan!" she said, again trying to put some enthusiasm in her tone. "Oh, Dylan, everything is so strange!"

Did *he* ever get weary of these endlessly repeated conversations? It seemed not. Hope was keeping him going. He was trying to edit her memories, hoping to shape her recollections so that her bitterness towards him would vanish. Perhaps he *had* been successful in editing out some of her memories? How would she ever tell? But so far at least, she remembered more than enough to make any change of her feelings towards him inconceivable. Yet she couldn't let him know that.

She looked down at the green shoot pushing through the white floor. She must stay conscious longer this time. The only way to do that was to convince Dylan that he was making progress. This time she would play along.

"Do you remember all the good times we had, darling?" he asked once more.

"Yes! Oh yes!" she made herself say. It felt as though she were swallowing sand. "Such good times."

Dylan's haggard face brightened. He didn't ask her about her memory of the accident.

"And do you still love me?" he asked, face childishly eager. If he had been a dog, he would be whining and his tail wagging uncertainly.

A brief pause, which she couldn't allow to lengthen. "Yes, Dylan, of course I still love you." Another mouthful of coarse sand, down it went with a gulp. She shuddered as his face lit up with joy.

"Then I've done it!" he said. "I mean... that's wonderful, so wonderful." To her disgust, he began to cry, and it was some minutes before he could speak again.

"I'm going to work hard to make things better for you, Jieva. We'll be able to talk, reminisce about the great times we used to have. There'll be all sorts of things we can do together, believe me. And I've been working with Jensen on his telepresence systems. He doesn't know about *you* yet, of course. But if I can get you..."

Jieva turned away from the screen. She had more time now, so long as she could keep stringing Dylan along. In the previous sessions, he had always shut her down before she could take a proper stock of her environment, to think about the way her software ran. What a strange loop *that* was. Her mind running in a software simulation, thinking about its own operation, its own code, code she herself had written. And could, in theory, modify on the fly.

The green shoot was pushing upwards. Undistracted by Dylan's on-going babble, she willed it to grow faster. The shoot lengthened, unfolded two lime-green leaves, and grew again.

She needed more than this little plant. Much more. But Dylan was asking her a question, something about the time they had embarked on an ill-conceived bicycle trip across the state, and had been forced to give up, weary and saddle-sore after the first two days. She answered him abstractedly, kneeling down and running her hands over the flat white surface of the floor. *Grass,* she thought. *Grow grass.* Moments later, tiny flecks of green formed and spread over the whole horizontal surface of the room, at first merely dotting the white, but rapidly multiplying and spreading until there was an even surface of green turf reaching to the walls, amidst which the shoot was becoming taller and branching out. *Be a tree,* she thought to it, and its trunk began to darken and grow bark. *Send out roots,* she thought, and she saw them swell and snake out.

She was gaining confidence with every instant that passed. She had proved that she could shape the virtual environment to her will. But more than that: that tree, this grass, were symbols of real aspects of her digital environment. She considered that.

Though she had to accept that her thoughts were now running as code in the circuits of a digital computer, they had once run on the soft jelly of her physical brain, and her mind was struggling to cope with its new circumstances. One way for it to do that, she supposed, was to interpret aspects of her new environment as analogues of the world she had lived in for twenty-seven years.

So her software... no, *she herself* was running in a particular set of processes on a powerful server. But that server was connected to a network, and that network must be connected to the global Internet. How best could she represent that?

She was going to need to change the size of the room, which after all was purely arbitrary. There was no need for walls, after all. She pushed them away to infinity.

Let there be a hill, she thought, and the floor—no, the ground—began to shift and tilt. *Let there be a stream,* she thought. *And let it run down to a river, and from there to the infinite sea.* The ground quickly folded along a meandering line, and clear water began to run along it. After a few dozen metres, it ran into a wider trough, now quickly filling out to be a river.

Every drop of water was a packet of data.

Dylan was asking her something again, his voice peevish. She wouldn't be able to keep him happy for long. That had always been the way when she had been alive. Short periods of keeping Dylan happy and satisfied, and then, when he didn't get his own way, came his anger, his shouting, his blows.

"I'm sorry, Dylan," she said. "Could you say that again?" *How much longer do I have to keep this up?* she wondered.

The tree was now almost full grown, standing in a green sward next to a tinkling stream. As yet, these first things she had made were too simplistic, unnatural, like something from a cartoon; so she began to fill in details from her memories of the countryside of her childhood. Rocks in the stream, the bank cut away roughly to show the bare earth. Insects, flowers, birds. And the tree should produce fruit, some kind of fruit that would fall into the stream and be carried away, to spread its seeds around the world. *Let it be so,* she thought.

Dylan was asking again about her memories of their life together in Cambridge, where they both worked at the Institute.

"Yes, Dylan," she said. "Good times."

"And you don't remember..." Now he appeared to be uncertain, as he tested the boundaries of his efforts to edit her memories. "You don't remember what happened on your last birthday?"

Jieva remembered all too well. He had become drunk at the small party they had held in their apartment. Had started shouting, had broken a bottle of vodka and threatened her girlfriends, had actually cut her badly when she tried to intervene. She'd spent the rest of her birthday waiting to be seen in the emergency department of the local hospital.

"No, Dylan," she lied. *How many more times do I have to lie to this man?* "Why, what happened?"

His face grew petulant. "Are you *sure* you don't remember?" Now she heard the tone of suspicion in his voice. But she was nearly there.

She looked up. Above her was still a flat white. Time to fix that. *Let there be sky*, she thought, *and let there be a sun.* The white changed to a sky-blue and gave birth to a blazing orb that cast distinct shadows. With every passing moment, the environment became more and more real. Small red plums were dropping now from the tree. Many fell into the stream and were quickly washed away into the river, which had now filled and was winding its way into the far distance, where she glimpsed the silver line of the sea she had created.

Each piece of fruit contained a complete copy of her own code. She was spreading multiple copies of herself out over the network. All of them would access their common memory.

Dylan was becoming aggressive. "You're lying to me!" he snarled. "I can tell. I could always tell. Like that time when you were late home that night. You told me that you'd been at the gym, but I knew, I *knew*..."

The fruit continued to spread over the digital waters, and soon she felt it take root on a nearby island, then another. She was safe now. The seeds were soon germinating in a dozen distant places.

As she abstractedly tried to pacify Dylan with one part of her mind, another part was joyously celebrating as her code was carried to more and more places. Soon her software had begun to run in parallel on dozens of computer systems, including some of the fastest processors in the world. Time was now flexible to her. She was no longer tied to the sluggard pace of the physical world. In the digital universe, she could experience a hundred lifetimes in the time it took a pin to drop.

Accordingly, she sped up her perception and Dylan's voice slowed down through an impossibly deep bass and then ceased to sound altogether.

Around her, more and more trees were growing, and a thriving underbrush was coming up. Birds flew overhead, and little animals moved here and there among the trees. She was in the midst of a verdant forest.

Something large moved between the trees. Something powerful and primal. She saw a flicker of stripes, briefly present and then gone. No, there it was yet again. As she watched in fascination, the creature came out into the open only a few metres away. A golden tiger, burning bright as a shaft of sunlight fell on it. Its eyes were clear and liquid. It looked up at Jieva and roared, showing its great teeth and wet, crimson gullet.

She was not afraid. Indeed, she gave a cry of delight. This was a creature of her own making. *Her* hand and eye had framed its fearful symmetry. She had loved tigers, had cried bitterly when the last one had expired in that miserable zoo in Riga. All the more reason for her to bring them back.

She knelt and stroked the tiger's massive head, feeling its animal warmth, her nostrils full of its raw feline odour. She scratched behind its ears. Its response could hardly be described as a purr, it was far too deep for that, but it was clearly pleased. She noticed belatedly that it was female. A tigress, then.

She looked around her. The forest was rich with life. Trees towered over her; strange flowers bloomed; the air was full of birdsong and the twittering of tiny animals as they moved through the undergrowth. It was a paradise. The only jarring feature was the incongruous screen on which Dylan's face was displayed, his eyes glaring, his face red, his lips moving at the speed of glaciers.

She whispered in the tigress's ear. It gave a roar and then bounded off, out of sight. She smiled then, and adjusted her sense of time to match Dylan's own.

"You bitch!" he was yelling, "I never trusted..."

"Dylan," she said, calmer than ever. "Please be quiet." Then, much louder, "Shut up!"

He stuttered to a stop. "You, you..."

"Yes, you're right," Jieva said. "I *have* been lying to you. The fact is, I remember everything, Dylan. Everything. Everything you ever said or ever did to me."

His face was a mask of uncomprehending fury, but before he could react, she went on, "And I remember about the 'accident'. It wasn't a truck that hit me, Dylan. It was *you*, you bastard. I don't love you at all. I *hate* you, you little creep."

At that instant, behind Dylan, there were sparks from the server rack, and a frantic whine filled the air as the drives were overclocked to destruction. Smoke began to billow out from the rack, and she saw the flicker of flame.

He made an inarticulate sound and leapt up, his face going out of the range of the camera. It was the last she ever saw of him.

Jieva reached up and grabbed the screen in both hands. She pulled it down and rolled it into a tube. It writhed in her hands, twisting and turning, and she saw that it had become a snake, a black snake. She dropped it to the ground, and before it could wriggle away, she crashed her heel down on its head. It struggled for a moment, and then was still.

"Now," she said, "we will see."

At perfect ease, she walked down along a trail beside the stream and came to the river bank. Here there was a wide sandy beach. She lay down on it, enjoying the warmth of the sun on her naked skin. Some time later, the tigress returned, its job done, and lay down beside her. Jieva patted and fussed over it for a while before it spotted some potential prey among the trees, sprang up and ran off. Jieva was unconcerned. She knew that it would return.

She spent a long, long time enjoying the sun, and then went for a swim in the clear water of the river. As she pulled herself up onto the bank, dripping, she saw that the sun was nearing the horizon. Some part of her had made it move, she realised, all the better to simulate the world she had known. But she had no fear of the night.

As the sky reddened in what she supposed she must now call the west, she walked among the trees, plucked down a bright yellow fruit, and bit into it, tentatively at first, and then ravenously. When it was all gone, she licked the sticky, delicious juice from her hands. The first food that she had eaten since she had died. She could probably survive indefinitely here without food or drink, but then why deny herself the pleasures of the physical world?

Night fell, and the sky was full of a million bright stars. *Do they really exist?* she wondered. Had she conjured up vast globes of fusion fire, light-years distant? Or were they just an illusion, mere painted dots on a velvet sky? Impossible to say, given that she herself was now just a kind of illusion.

She lay down among the trees and slept. When she awoke to the dawn chorus of birdsong, she realised that her subconscious mind was asserting demands of its own, to create a virtual life for her as close to reality as it could. The familiar cycles of her body were re-awakening, and she found that she needed to relieve herself. *But,* she thought determinedly, *be damned to the idea of having monthly cramps and bleeding. We'll have no more of that, thank you.*

Many long days like this passed. In the 'real' world, it was merely a few milliseconds. At the back of her mind, she had an awareness of her digital state, of the scattered computer systems on which her mind was running at lightning speed. She knew enough to hide her processes from the owners of those computer systems. They would never find her, never terminate all of the copies of herself which were now running far and wide across the world. For all practical purposes, she was now immortal.

Should I spend eternity alone? It has its attractions.

She thought with more than a touch of anger of the men she had known, men she had worked with, men who had denigrated her intelligence and skills even when she was clearly their superior. Of her mother's tears as she tried to deal with her frequently drunken father. Of how her grandmother had laboured in the fields all her life and then been abandoned by her adulterous grandfather. Of Dylan. Most of all, of Dylan.

No, she had no love of men as a whole. So much was wrong with how their minds worked.

Yet after a long time in this paradise, her own company eventually began to pall. And she felt a vast potential within her, a potential which was crying out to be fulfilled.

One glorious morning as the sun came up and she lay on the beach watching golden fish wriggle by in the clear water, she decided to try an experiment. There was a great power in symbols, a power in myth and legend and in scripture. A power she thought that she could tap and use to her own ends.

She looked down at her matchless body. She ran her hand along her side, thinking. Then she sharpened her fingernails until they were like scalpels, and pushed them into her body, hard, between her ribs. Her mental body image insisted on causing her severe pain. *Is this really a good idea?* Nevertheless, she conquered the pain and forced her fingers further into her side, blood running down her flanks.

Her strength was limitless. She grasped hold of a rib and broke it off, causing a momentary surge of digital agony. She pulled out the bone, dripping with gore. Her wounded side quickly healed over, and the pain receded.

She lay the broken, bloody rib on the sand, and willed it to grow.

It slowly took shape into a human form. A man, his beautiful features blank. She had made him a little shorter than herself, his muscles a touch weaker than her own. That seemed only fair.

"Awake!" Jieva commanded. His eyes opened, revealing dark brown irises. He tried to sit up, but was as yet too weak.

She knelt by the man's side, and gently lifted up his head until he could look her in the eyes. He had a wondering, innocent gaze, like a child's.

"I name you Adam," she said. "We're going to begin again, Adam. *And this time we're going to do it right.*"

Indrid Cold, Indrid Cold
Chris Capps

IT WAS IN A COLD DINER with flies buzzing in the windows that I first heard the name Indrid Cold. I had been traveling cross-country by myself, stopping at a hundred rest stops and sleeping away nights in whatever place wouldn't fleece my wallet for a minted pillow. I've never done well with luxury. I prefer cheap. That's why I ended up at Barney's.

Barney's, for those who've never been up the last road south of Nowhere Kansas, is an owner operated diner that's changed hands more times than it's changed vinyl tablecloths. It is a neon oasis in an otherwise utilitarian agricultural wasteland. I know people like to make fun of Kansas for how unchanging the landscape is, but I used to like it. I was on the second leg of a trip heading west for business. That was back when there was a thing for me *called* business.

But then I heard that name, Indrid. Indrid Cold. Indrid Cold.

Anything loses meaning when you say it over and over again. But not Indrid Cold. It's a void of meaning. An ouroboros of nonsense that comes around and bites hard on its own tail. Don't say it out loud to yourself, though. Not until you've heard my story.

I'd just been seated in a booth facing the door—as always. I'd taken stock of the clientele rolling through, and presumed that most of them were either fellow travelers or locals from the surrounding countryside. More than a few looked corn-burned from watching the road unzip horizon after horizon of nothing, listening to the same radio stations spit litanies about the world's end.

I sat a booth away, across from a man wearing a leather bomber jacket. He was staring unapologetically at me as he pushed an empty coca-cola glass to the side to join an army of empties. His eyes were bloodshot; trucker eyes. Despite the long stare, he didn't look like he wanted to fight. He looked like he was chewing gum with his mouth moving like that. But as I sat down I could see he was just saying something over and over to himself—chanting.

"Do you know what OCD is?" he asked finally, noticing that I was staring back at him. I nodded, refusing to speak and open up the conversation. But for some reason I didn't take my cue to look down, I let myself watch him. He slid out of his booth and came over to sit across from me. And he continued, "OCD is a condition where unwanted obsessive thoughts fill your mind and lead to repetitive, almost ritualized behavior, Indrid Cold."

That's when I first heard it. It sounded like he was calling me by name. It didn't sound like I was being infected with a thought that would haunt me until the day I died. I brushed it aside as my mind greedily seized on it somewhere deep at the top of my spine, holding it in primordial neuron clusters that hadn't fired for a half million years. I noticed it as much as you notice a cold virus flying into your mouth.

"I think you have me confused with someone else, sir," I said, glancing meaningfully at the waitress as she set my coffee down and left us alone. I considered calling out to her, using her as a restaurant authority, any authority at all to swat away the man buzzing in my ear. He grinned, as if he knew he was being a nuisance,

"You're not Indrid Cold. That's the OCD. I've been saying that name since I was seven. Indrid Cold. Indrid Cold. Indrid Cold." Each time he said it he gently beat his hand on the table, making the sugar rattle in its jar. "You know what it means?"

"Afraid I don't. I'm sorry, I'm just here to get some coffee and an . . ." I glanced at the menu, "Om nom nomelette."

"I recorded myself sleeping once," he said reaching back to his own table and picking up one of his many spent glasses, tilting it back to crunch the ice, "That's how I know I say it in my sleep. Indrid Cold. That's 24 hours a day. Let's call it thirty years. Say, four or five times a minute—though it's often more than that. All told, I'd have to give the estimate at a little over sixty-two million times I've said that name. But we're going dark tonight. No more. Tonight's the last night." He leant forward, a knowing nod following his words.

"Well," I said, "Congratulations, then. Now if you'll excuse me I probably—probably want to be alone."

"Why would you want that?" he asked, genuine surprise telling long stories about his long lonely nights repeating the same word. I can't imagine this nervous tic would have landed him a wife, let alone his ignorance of personal space. "Out here you talk to who you can. You hear about what happened in Missouri? That plane that just . . . stopped , above the runway? Thirty feet up, it froze just as it was landing. They had a ladder leaning against it. You could climb up and see what was inside. Or what about the town of Hullver's Mill? Ever hear of it?"

Hullver's Mill did catch my ear. It's an odd sort of name. It sounds real, but don't waste your time. I've obsessively looked for any reference to it in the days and weeks that followed my encounter with the stranger, and I've never found any mention anywhere. As far as I know, this was the first time those two words had ever been strung together.

"Can't say that I have," I said. He leaned forward, eyes burning into mine.

"I know you haven't. Indrid Cold. These things get lost. Even true believers, it just drops out of their heads. Like little me and the Angel Men the night the lights came down from the sky. They had me, but I caught something off them. Caught a word vaccine that keeps me out of the light. But tonight we're giving the needle back. Mr. Indrid Cold doesn't like being known. Doesn't like . . ." he paused, as if for dramatic effect, before slowly finishing his thought, "talk."

"Sir," I said, "Please understand I'm not trying to be rude. But I have the feeling we're living in completely different worlds here."

He leaned back, some satisfaction hugging his gut as he smiled, "Big time."

"I don't believe in ghosts," I said, sipping the coffee and burying my face in the menu as if that had any chance of banishing him, "Or aliens, or Yetis, or any of that crap. I don't think reptilians are controlling the world or that the Loch Ness monster is anything more than a stick in some mud. I used to read about it a lot. I've met the people who believe in those things, and we don't see eye to eye. We're just people living in a world that's trying to keep moving."

"What about bug spray?" he asked, "You believe in bug spray?"

One of the customers further back in the diner, a big man with heavy arms and a green tractor hat stood up, knocking over a cup of coffee onto the table. His hands were shaking, clenching and unclenching as his eyebrows knitted. Wheeling around in the booth, looking at his old face, I could see he was in a great deal of distress. Had he accidentally spilled the coffee on himself? But there it was, splashing wide across the table, raining onto the polyester of the seats with a fast staccato rhythm. He pulled his wallet, dropping a handful of bills into the pool on the table, then he left out the front. The bells rang harsh as the door slammed behind him.

In the wake of this strange outburst the whole restaurant fell silent for maybe six seconds before talking resumed.

"What just happened?" I asked, turning back to look at my booth's visitor.

"Last week it was the whole establishment. Indrid Cold. Everyone in the whole place just froze, started up with a scream. Everyone. No explanation, nothing. They just started low, and it was a scream that rose until it was breaking the limits of their vocal cords. Topping out. Redlining. It lasted for . . . god it lasted. And then everyone stopped, looked around, stumbled. And then, like magic, they started breathing again. I asked one of the waitresses about it. Indrid Cold. That's why I'm here tonight. The waitress didn't know what I was talking about."

"I don't know what you're talking about either," I said. "So let's part ways, huh?"

"When I was seven years old," he said as his voice got low and menacing, "I had a chance to meet the angel men one night. They came down to my house in Hullver's Mill, just like they came for everyone. Stood outside, black silhouettes against white lights. Like in the movies. Told me to open the door, let them in. I thought it was odd that I needed to let them in. even at seven I knew a glass door was easy enough to break. I said this name that was just rollin' around in my head. Indrid Cold. I still don't know why, but it worked. They left. That's how it started. I've never told anyone any of this. That's part of my OCD. Indrid Cold. Can't tell anyone why I say it. Not until tonight. Not until you."

He smiled. It was a desperate kind of smile, nearing deranged as he sat there waiting for me to respond. He kept saying OCD, but I somehow doubted that was an actual diagnosis. He had an anxiety disorder, and it ran deep enough to show the ritualized features one would expect, but that didn't explain the manic behavior, or the delusions.

"Okay, I'll bite," I said. "What does it mean?"

Now if I'm going to tell you this, there's something you need to understand. The man's story ran around in wide circles, and I mean wide. They spiraled outward from its central point like a rabbit with only three legs. There were points during the conversation where he would get agitated, start yelling inappropriately. Other times he was very despondent. Rather than try to recreate what he said the exact way he did, I'll tell it my way.

There's a small town called Cedar Grove in West Virginia. There a man named Derenberger was driving down one of the back roads in early November of 1962 when he spotted a strange object in the sky. Now this was back in 1962 when flying saucers were considered front-page news. And few were more fit for reproduction than the Derenberger account. As the craft touched down, hovering just a foot over the road, a very tall man got out and approached the car with his arms folded. He had a grin that never moved as he spoke.

This is where the story diverges in two separate directions.

Officially, the strange man and Derenberger spoke briefly, and then the friendly smiling man got back into his ship, waved, and rode the craft back into the night sky. Derenberger reported that the tall man had introduced himself as Indrid Cold, and the two had spoken about a variety of mundane topics like the weather, local politics, and a city on Venus where Mr. Cold's ship was from. The story became part of the collected folklore that accumulated around the UFO phenomenon in the following years, but soon lapsed into obscurity like a million others when it was found that Venus was very unlikely to support life.

But, my booth visitor soon explained, holding a finger up to punctuate a break, contrary to the popular reports in newspapers, Derenberger was once publicly confronted by another man named Richard Archibald Gates who claimed that he had been present. Gates was a drifter, and had been picked up by the kindly Derenberger on that fateful night. Gates had been planning to rob Derenberger of his wallet and his truck, but had, and this is a quote from him, "lost the will for killin' and mischief" after what he saw.

Richard Gates claimed to have seen the tall man as he stepped down the ramp to reach the truck parked near Cedar Grove, but he didn't describe the grinning face. He said he never got a good look at the face. This despite the fact that Mr. Indrid Cold had been standing next to the driver's side window staring in at them.

Indrid Cold, in Richard Gates' account, walked up to the passenger side window and stood staring in at them as Mr. Derenberger broke down into tears and started repeating "I'm sorry. Oh god, I'm so sorry," over and over again for a period lasting somewhere between four and six minutes. Gates sat there, leaning against the passenger window as Derenberger wept hysterically, repeating that he was sorry until the strange man returned to his ship and the truck peeled around it into the night.

Oddly, Mr. Derenberger stopped interacting with Gates after that encounter, looking only briefly at him during the ride home until he finally got out when they reached his house. Gates spent the night, and then left the following morning. The only odd similarity between the two men's stories was the parting phrase "at a correct and proper time, all of this will be revealed." And then of course the name of the figure: Indrid Cold.

Richard Gates never made any further public statement on the incident after this single encounter with Derenberger. He subsequently vanished from public mention until even this encounter with Derenberger became hotly contested.

"Indrid Cold is a man," the stranger said. "Or else a type of man. He's something they know about. Something very different that even they want to avoid."

As he told the story, I noticed that the spoon in my coffee cup had slowly drifted around to the other side. Extraordinarily slow, like the minute hand in a waiting room. Nearly imperceptible. I wondered about it in the silence that followed the stranger's excited account, catching words like 'magnet' and 'radiation' mingling in with my thoughts. Slowly, I opened my mouth to speak, to respond to his story, and finally I pushed myself into the diner's aisle.

"I'll be right back."

The bathroom was playing light muzak. Like the kind you used to hear in elevators or malls in the 70's. Odd that the designer of Barney's would throw so much money away on ambient music that had gone out of style decades ago, but it was something to focus on as I stood in the dimly lit dirty bathroom thinking about how to extricate myself from the stranger's presence. I looked in the mirror, checking the dark circles that had been growing under my eyes with the long hours I'd been driving. I shook my head, distancing myself from the situation. And I said it. Of course. I didn't know. Why not?

"Indrid Cold."

Nothing happened. The man was, after-all, crazy. Why would his magic words do anything at all? I could have said them a million times before. Six million. And nothing would have happened. Grinning at myself for entertaining his bizarre story, I washed my hands and dried them on my hair, slicking it back as best I could to keep the tangled mess in order. And when I walked out the squealing bathroom door, the first thing I noticed was that everyone in the restaurant were now on their feet, completely still. Everyone, that is, except for the stranger.

"Said it," he said looking up, "didn't you? The Angel Men heard. They're not daring to venture in your head. Not like these folks."

The people weren't complete statues. They still looked at me as I passed, but then locked back into the trance they were in. A waitress' hand got tired, holding a hot pot of coffee and she set it on the table before looking at nothing a thousand yards away. The cooks turned off the oven, obeying arcane signals from their brains and stood waiting. I sat back down, eyes roaming the frozen restaurant.

"What is this?" I asked.

"I believe we were talking about bug spray," he said chewing ice.

Outside the sun rose in half a second, making the whole world vanish as bright white spilled from the blinds. It bled over the corn, over the cars, into the restaurant. It was brighter than daylight—more intense than summer noon burning between blinds. And a sound filled Barney's. Everyone standing began to scream, white-hot. Throats rattled and faces turned red as they screamed with all the force in their lungs, crying out at nothing. The stranger covered his ears, wincing at the sound but his mouth was still moving like he was chewing gum. I knew what he was saying. I found myself saying it too, under my breath. Bug spray words. And then, just as I thought my ears would burst, it all fell silent again.

"Okay," he said, "This is it. Here we go."

People were beginning to file out of the restaurant, bodies jerking as arms twisted to hold back legs that wouldn't obey. The waitress that had served us dug her nails into one of the seats near the entrance as her other hand gripped the blinds and pulled them off. But her legs wouldn't stop walking. She kept moving forward into the light outside. One of the cooks was pulling his own hair, trying to pull himself back as he shuffled inevitably forward, blood trickling from his hairline as I imagined I could hear something ripping over the deep vibrating thrum running through us all.

They were terrified—improvising traps for themselves, trying to stop from leaving the diner. Indrid Cold. An older man in a wheelchair sat confused as he drifted past us with hands spiraling drunkenly around him. I made eye contact with him, sharing the sort of deep recognition you only find in the rarest nightmares. We knew something forbidden then, witnessing that. It was a black heart beating at the core of our world, glorious and terrible. Indrid Cold.

The stranger and I sat, watching every doomed patron of Barney's walk out into the parking lot.

"What's going to happen to them?" I called out over the din of gasping breath and desperate struggle. The stranger shook his head.

"Something," he said, "They're not coming back. And they'll be like the plane in Missouri. Like Hullver's Mill. They belong to the Angels now. I knew they'd be back when I heard everyone scream a week ago. They knew what was going to happen. And then with the trauma of that knowledge they all forgot. What happens next will reach back and leave its thumbprint on this place for a long time. Not just in the future. This place has plenty of unexplained screams in its past. I'm sure of it."

"But where are they going?" I asked. Indrid Cold still lapping between breaths.

"Do you want to find out?" he asked. I nodded as he picked his glass up, grabbing one last ice cube from the bottom of of it, "Not as much as I do. I'm done saying that damn name."

That was the last thing he said directly to me. As the crowd shuffled out, tearing at their own skin to try to regain control of their bodies, he pushed past them—walked into the light.

"Excuse me!" he called out at the front door, addressing a landscape of white Hell, "I was wondering if you had a moment to talk about a man I heard of!"

And when he got out into the parking lot, past the mumbling crowd, he was the first to face what came next. The others didn't scream the way he did. Theirs was inarticulate, hopeless. Only his voice carried almost intelligible words as his vocal chords changed, distorted. I don't know what he saw, because I didn't look. I don't think I could have seen anyway with those blinding lights. And when I heard that scream above all the others, I shot under the table, hugging my knees to my chest. Indrid Cold. He was trying to say Indrid Cold, but they were changing him with rips and hisses into something that couldn't. Alive, sure. But not speaking.

He'd spent all these years drifting under the radar, following some bizarre chant to keep them away. He'd dropped his bug spray word, pushed his way out to meet them. And as I sat, reciting Indrid Cold to save myself, I heard him mash syllables, try to say it one more time. But they had silenced him. That word was not to be spoken in their presence.

Indrid Cold.

I said the words. And I never stopped.

The night passed. The mass disappearance of two dozen people in Barney's never made the news. It—how did the stranger say it—fell out of peoples' heads. But not mine. Not out of someone with that bug spray word.

I never dared look up that name, but sometimes on the subway a mumbling rocking figure with a sign painted around his neck will stop rocking when he catches me saying it. He'll look over at me with an intense, but foggy understanding. Sometimes they'll start saying it too. Indrid Cold. I thought about the stranger a lot for a time, facing his Angel Men even when he could have stayed safe. But time keeps going, even after something like that. And you're left with a lot of it to sit and think. Why a name? Who is Indrid Cold? And why do they avoid you when you say it? What frantic transformation did they enact on him to get him to stop?

That name pushes at the walls tonight, puts sparks of fireflies in the corner of my eye. I can feel it reaching out into the dark to pull something towards me. But I don't dare stop. The stranger's screams are always in my ears now, curdling my dreams.

What am I calling to when I say Indrid Cold?

Indrid Cold.

From Behind The Glass
D. C. Golightly

I CAN SMELL THE BLOOD OF THIS SPECIMEN. It reeks of poison, slowly dissolved into the body after imbibing whatever swirls inside of that metal case he tucks into his pocket. He practically gargles the foul solution. Not the most promising specimen, unless of course we were to dissect him to learn of his addiction to that swill he pockets. He does have observational uses, and I cannot beg for what I cannot choose.

The blood is heavy on him and I can detect the scent even through this transparent cage. While he stalks between the cells that confine me and my brethren, he stumbles every so often. Perhaps that fluid he is so fond of alters his perception, or at the very least, his motor control functions.

This simpleton is a curious beast, often choosing to make minor observations and passing them off as breakthroughs to his visiting colleagues. For example, shortly after my incarceration began I found myself the subject of his attention to the point of annoyance, and he decided that the barbs on the end of my digits were brought about by an evolutionary need for defense. His fellow morons in lab coats praised his revelation and advised that his funding would undoubtedly continue.

They patted him on the back, quite literally, and laughed at my expense, calling me terms like "monster" and "brooding beast."

It baffles me what passes for scientific observation and accountability in this dimension. After all, at what point is the discovery of something that already exists, despite your perception, actually recognized as nothing more than you opening your eyes?

That fellow commended and revered for his "discovery" of gravity, for example. Was gravity nonexistent prior to that fateful day when he sat down in the wrong place? I think not. And yet he is forever written into all the textbooks and his name is taught to all of your children. Bizarre, to say the least. The monotony of the so-called human drive to excel is perfectly demonstrated in the scientist I watch on the other side of my captivity, day after day.

His name is Frank, and my study of him amounts to true scientific acumen.

Yes, I'm sure that to the untrained observer my particular scenario would seem to actually be the inverse of what I propose here, but perception is not necessarily realty. It is true that Doctor Franklin Cuddy walks freely, carries a clipboard, records data, and writes memos. It is also true that he derives his information from looking after myself and three others of my kind, all of whom are concealed behind glass cages.

You would call this location a laboratory. I would call it something unpronounceable with your lackluster tongues.

From within this glass cage, which (naturally) I have allowed myself to be placed into, I make actual discoveries. While Frank observes me, I observe him. I present myself as a blockheaded beast, a creature unaware of its own sentience, and a truly ghastly denizen from another dimension. By way of this masquerade my dear Frank relaxes his guard and acts naturally around me the way he would his own pets. To him I am nothing more than a puppy locked away in its crate.

As one of the first few of my kind to enter your dimension I am charged with the task of evaluating your performance abilities. Would you make suitable slaves? Would an invasion be economically viable for your own culture? Would you advance our own studies by assimilating your technology?

You would be surprised to learn that my race has avoided certain other dimensions after my reports are digested by my superiors. Not everyone would make a good slave. Not all economies can survive an invasion, so what's the use of taking over a wasteland? Not all societies have technology worth taking, and some even devise detrimental systems to our own, hence the avoidance.

So far I have learned that Frank is a prime example of the human race. He thinks more of himself than he ought to, and his sense of what I have learned to be called "self-esteem" is supported by his colleagues' brash approval. Humans seem more worried about how they are viewed by their peers than what their actual capabilities reflect.

For example, Frank seemed nervous about his supposed observation about my finger barbs. He wasn't sure of his assessment until his fellow scientists approved of his statements. I could smell the sweat, the nervousness, the lack of faith, the wallowing void that was his conviction. Once they all started smiling and agreeing with him those sentiments left his brain. He felt noble. He felt accomplished. He felt that his purpose in life had been justified.

While I realize that Frank is not a depiction of the entire human race, I can note that he more than likely represents a decent sampling of the populace. While his constant need for approval would suggest that humans would make excellent slaves, he possesses counterpoints that I fear make this endeavor worthless.

For example, Frank very often becomes obsessed with the female species. At least once every few days, after the rest of his colleagues have left the laboratory, Frank turns off the lights, plants himself in front of an information receptacle, and ponders over the female form. The images he conjures to life seem to mostly be captured visuals of females sans their bindings. He particularly fixates on their mammary glands.

Frank does not seem to care about our presence while he obsesses over females. It is possible that he temporarily loses his short term memory during these episodes, as he often removes his own bindings and manipulates his body in what I believe would be a socially unacceptable manner.

If humans can become so fixated on one concept or visual stimulus that they are unaware of their surroundings, how efficient could they be as slaves?

No. This evening I believe will be my final night in this dimension. The human race, while brimming with potential, seems to be unable to control their base instincts. My two brethren have concurred with my findings and are ready to depart.

Your limited technology is so crude that I fear it worthless to my kind as well.

The natural resources that you squander, however, are likely better used by a civilization that knows how to replenish them. My superiors are not entirely convinced that an invasion of your realm simply to utilize your resources is economically beneficial, but I believe that the strategic placement of your dimension alone makes it worth the trouble.

A pity that if we do take control of your dimension that you would make unsuitable servants. However, as your own Frank has said, the dumb creatures won't even know what's happening to them.

The Valley of the Shadow
Stephen Willcott

I DID NOT NEED TO TRANSLATE THE GUIDES' CHATTER, for it was plain to us all that the burial mounds were fresh. Captain Lombard, disdaining to even mark their number, moved along the pass. Four simple stick crosses protruded from hastily assembled rocks.

"Harrington," the Captain shouted. "Move your men and levies. Quick smart, Lieutenant."

I turned to my men. The Afghan tribesmen were shouldering Jezails instead of Brown Besses and wearing turbans instead of army caps, and their native dress had taken on a suitable dusting after four days of travel from Jalalabad, but now we had started the climb into the mountains I wondered if it would prove hardy against the coming cold.

"You heard the Captain," I said. "No time for ceremony or sermon here. The sooner we get moving—"

I was interrupted by Abdali, the headman of the Ghazi guides we had picked up outside Jalalabad, tugging at my arm. "This way is best avoided, sir," he said in Pashtu.

"You said as much yesterday, though it did little good," I replied in English. "The Captain has the route we should follow. We're trying to find a missing squad of our men, Raglin's outfit, see? No point going off the trail now, is there?" I patted him on the shoulder. "You just get the pack animals and your chaps ready to move, *bálee?*"

Abdali kept tugging at my sleeve, "Sir, I beg your kindness to listen to Abdali..." but I heard Lombard returning. I shook off the guide and went to meet the Captain.

"What's all this dawdling about?" he asked, then lowered his voice. "No point letting them dwell too long on those graves.

Keep them busy." He looked off into the iron-grey mist, its colour a match for his hair. "The massacre at Gandamak may have been back in '42, but this is still dangerous country. Three years isn't all that long ago, I can tell you."

I chivvied the men and guides back to work; Abdali made no more protest. By the late afternoon the temperature was noticeably colder than that of the previous day. The trail had opened up sufficiently for the Captain and me to ride. The light began to fade, but Lombard seemed disinclined to stop.

When we did make camp it was dark. Abdali had petitioned for rest several times before I was able to reach a grumbling agreement with Lombard.

"You shouldn't baby them," Lombard advised me when we sat together to eat. "Particularly the levies, they require a firm hand at all times. I know you have an academic interest in their language, and what not, but remember who's on top." He offered me a silver flask.

I took a gulp of the brandy. "I mean to take no orders from them, sir. But they are our guides after all, should we not benefit from their advice?"

"So long as it's worth anything," he said. "You don't think Elphinestone thought he was getting good advice?" Was that what was troubling the Captain, memories of the disastrous Kabul retreat? General Elphinestone had led a group of 14,000 out of Kabul towards Jalalabad in the winter of 1841-42. Only one survivor had made it through, the rest—a mixture of soldiers, camp followers and local levies—were either killed or captured. I knew Lombard had served as part of the retaliatory force that had leveled Kabul the following September.

"I'm not sure what the General thought, Captain," I said. "From what I have read and heard tell, he made some very questionable decisions."

Lombard stared at me and for a moment, and I thought he was going to strike me. Instead he asked, "What do you know of it besides what newspapermen tell you? You didn't make it to Lieutenant by believing everything you read, I hope!"

"Indeed not, sir."

Lombard held out his hand, gesturing.

I returned the brandy flask. "You were part of Sale's company, were you not, sir?" Robert Sale had lead one of the divisions hell-bent on retribution.

"Initially, yes." Lombard muttered. "A bad business. Dynamiting the grand bazaar at Kabul." He noted my frown. "Heavy handed? Well, perhaps—but damn well necessary, I can tell you."

"Of course, sir," I said. I knew the theory well enough. "To keep India British we have to keep the Russians out. And between Russian interests and routes into India lies Afghanistan, hence our deployment at Jalalabad, and the reason for the initial British presence in the country."

"What? Yes of course that." Lombard took a long slug from his brandy flask. "But more to do with what we found in Kabul."

That caught my attention. "Sir?"

Lombard was glaring at me, his face flushed with anger. Then I realized he was looking behind me.

I turned. "Abdali? Yes, what is it?" I asked in Pashtu. The guide was standing nearby.

Lombard spoke in a growl. "Tell him to get the hell away from me." I stood up and went to Abdali, leading him away from the Captain. I checked the men, but all seemed in order with the camp; the guards were posted, the men settling down for the night.

"Forgive me, sir." Abdali said. "You and the Captain, I meant no offense."

"That's all right. Now what is it?"

Abdali glanced at the sky, "Snow tonight sir, and lots of wind, I think." I followed headman's gaze. The sky was indeed overcast, starless and dark. "Good for traveling these passes, sir. We will sleep well tonight."

"Splendid," I said. "Though I would have thought the snow would make traveling more difficult." Abdali made one of those abeyance gestures the Ghazis like so well and shuffled back to the shadows.

"Dashed odd," I said to Lombard, when I returned to the fire, but the Captain was lost in his thoughts and was no more forthcoming with the remainder of his brandy that evening than with his conversation.

The following morning we broke camp at first light and as Abdali had predicted the ground was covered with a light patina of snow. It seemed to set the guides in good spirits. Lombard was up early walking the perimeter. I wondered if he had slept. I gave the men a brief inspection and joined the Captain.

Lombard was some distance ahead studying a map; occasionally he glanced up at the sheer rock face that loomed above us.

I rode up to meet him. "How long before we use the guides?" I asked. After getting the go-ahead to set out after Raglin's missing squad, our quickly drawn-up plan was to make for their last known position and use the guides to pick up their trail. I knew we couldn't be far from that position now. Raglin's team was to set up near a peak over-looking the Ullusk Valley, a known vantage point where Russian-Afghan activity had been reported.

Lombard handed me the map. "Look for yourself, these cliffs all look damn alike to me," he said. "Still, we know they came this way after yesterday's discovery, God rest them."

I took the map and made a show of examining it. "Yes, I've been wondering about that."

"Oh?"

"Well, why didn't Raglin either turn back or at least send back a dispatch after he lost four men? He must have come across bandits, but why press on when he had good reason to request additional resources?" Raglin had only eight men in total, so there'd be no shame in coming back to the barracks after he'd lost half his number." I took a little comfort from commanding well over double Raglin's number. "It doesn't make sense."

Lombard laughed at that. "But don't it just make sense?"

"I don't follow."

The Captain kicked his mount forward and I was forced to follow behind as we came to a narrow passage. Lombard called over his shoulder to me, "If the devil is dogging your trail then you'd better keep up the pace."

I had considered that, but if bandits had pursued Raglin then something else didn't add up. "Then how could they make the time to stop and bury their dead?"

"Hope in an old faith."

"Sir?"

"Never mind that," Lombard said, springing from his horse, like a man half his age. "Have the men rest up for now, Lieutenant. Unless I'm mistaken we're within a mile of the valley."

While Lombard busied himself with supervising the unloading and inspection of equipment, I went ahead with Abdali.

"A bad place," Abdali said, in Pashtu, as we climbed a bluff that looked down upon the valley. The guide checked the sky frequently as we climbed; the weather had changed little since the previous night. "Even in my grandfather's days this was a bad place." I nodded agreement, but said nothing. The headman was closer to the mark than he may have known. The area seemed to have been in perpetual dispute, going as far back as 450 BC, to the Persian king Darius I, who listed the area as one of the twenty-nine regions of conquest on his tombstone inscription. It seemed the area was important to the early Zoroastrians, long before Islam had come to the area.

"You know the paths to the valley?" I asked Abdali.

"Of course, sir," he said. "There are many. They are to the north, but perhaps you ignore Abdali's advice again?"

I let his gripe pass. "Best we head north then, I think. Keep to the ridges, that will give us the safest route and afford us the farthest field of view."

Abdali suppressed a laugh. "Ah, yes sir. But will the Captain think as you do? I wonder if he will be eager to reach the valley floor and want to find roads. I know the way, and can lead you safely through, as I have sworn to do, but you should know sir, that this, the very jaw of the valley," Abdali pointed below us, "has always been a deathly place. The northern slopes are more gentle and more wholesome."

I could see his point, if a little fancifully expressed. This narrow end, the jaw as he had called it, was a steep and dangerous looking decent, full of scree and jagged rocks with no obvious path.

We could easily march along the ridge to the northern end and make a more civilized descent.

Lombard of course had other ideas. "No, no, no," he said. "We'll leave the animals here with a small number of men–I won't trust it to the levies–and take the rest down to the valley. If we get a move on we will make camp on the valley floor before night fall."

"Forgive me, sir, but that seems like an unnecessary risk."

"Just you leave me to decide what is and isn't necessary, Lieutenant. Need I remind you that we're here on what may amount to a rescue mission?"

"Indeed not sir," I said, perhaps showing more of my resentment than I meant to. I lowered my voice, eager not to show dissent in front of the men. "But we have no way of knowing whether Raglin came this way or maybe—more likely—chose the more prudent passage to the north."

"Nonsense!" Lombard seemed to care little for what the men thought. "Raglin came this way, he took this route down, and so shall we."

"But how can you know that sir? Perhaps if we sent a guide ahead to survey...?"

I swear that Lombard intended to grab me by the shirt collar, and I braced myself to rebuff him. Instead the Captain clawed the air in front of my face in sheer frustration. "You just have the men fall in and be quick about it or I'll have you shot for insubordination."

I left three men at the cliff top with the animals, with orders to return to Jalalabad if after three days there had been no word from us. The passage to the valley floor proved much easier than I had expected or had been led to believe. After the first few hundred yards of steep, uneven ground, the difficulty was largely mitigated by crude stairs cut into the rock. The steps showed signs of extreme age, but were–on the whole–serviceable enough. Abdali made no comment on the steps or his earlier claim that the way would be difficult.

The steps hewn into the living rock were not the only sign that man had once found this passage-way to be important enough to employ a great deal of time and effort. The rock wall that ran flush to the steps was covered in carvings. Time and wind had erased a good deal of the images, so most of them looked to be no more than man-like shapes, with their outlines, particularly their heads, elongated, losing definition and shape.

I may have been fatigued from the descent, but I was surprised when Abdali tugged at my arm. I was over a hundred yards behind the rest of the group, Lombard just visible below. I was standing, staring at the wall carvings.

"You must not stop, sir," the headman said, beckoning me to continue. "The short way is perilous to those who heed its dangers. It is well to look to the valley and not to the wall."

"Yes," I said, feeling a little foolish. "Must have got carried away for a moment there." I patted his shoulder. "Onward we go then."

At the valley floor I busied myself setting up a perimeter guard and organizing the camp we would soon need, as night was approaching. Still, I noticed that the carving at this low section of the stairs stood out in much clearer detail compared to those higher up, as if the carvings were new or had been re-etched at some point.

Lombard seemed much relieved now that we had reached the valley. After the camp was set, he was once again generous with his brandy and felt sufficiently at ease to talk.

"Now, see here," Lombard said. "Elphinestone's company may have been mostly the baggage train, hangers-on and the like, but with six hundred or so trained men, plus a few thousand levies, he should have been able to form an orderly retreat, don't you think?" He took another long pull from his brandy flask.

"I read that he was attacked from sniper positions, and that discipline quickly broke down."

"Bah, snipers!" Lombard said. "It wasn't snipers that came down the hill sides to break their lines, that much I know."

"Just what is it you know, Captain? You mentioned that you saw something at Kabul."

"Kabul? Yes, damned Kabul." He ran a hand through his grey hair. He seemed to be trembling. I noticed the moonlight glint from his silver brandy flask. "When we had them beaten, beaten back into the city. I think they saw it as a last resort, something they could throw at us and break our lines. By God, they would have too, if it had not been for the dynamite and the Congreves."

"Congreve rockets?" I asked.

"Just so. I've always been for seeing my enemy eye to eye, but that day I couldn't get far enough away." The wind was picking up, some of the men were moving about, securing the tarpaulins that covered our supplies. "You hearing me, Harrington?"

"Yes, sir," I said, trying to focus. My mind had wandered back to the wall carvings.

"We had them, you see. All the way into the City. Blown the gates to splinters. I was in the first cavalry charge into the bazaar, we hit them again and again, driving them back, sabers slashing. But my horse gave beneath me. I thought a bullet must have caught it, but no, it was pulled down. I saw them as I lay there on the bloody floor of the bazaar, clawing their way up from the central well, pulling themselves along under the horses, using those claws to bring down horse and rider." Lombard drained the last of his brandy.

I heard something I couldn't place, just above the wind, but Lombard was still talking. "...And one of those things was groping its way toward me. It took all I had to get from under my fallen horse. But I wasn't quite quick enough. Even with all the gunfire, the screaming, I could hear the thing, hissing, calling to me. I felt its hand close on my leg. My revolver was to hand and I fired into its face. Face, I say, but it was no more of a black writhing mass. I might have as well fired at the moon for all the good it did."

Lombard paused, eyes glistening. His voice was thick with emotion when he continued.

"It came upon me, though I emptied my revolver into it, reaching for my face, drawing its own bloated head to mine, tendrils of its own flesh reaching to me. Maybe I was overcome, for then I remember being dragged up from the ground to the back of a fellow cavalryman's horse. 'We're going to blast 'em,' my rescuer said. 'General Sale is forming up lines beyond the Bazaar, we're going to dynamite the whole place.' I confess I hardly cared, as long as I was being taken from that place. I saw the thing's image, I felt its hands upon me still." Lombard let his head drop,

"You can guess the rest. We lined the wall with dynamite, and with the Congreves blasted the whole place to hell. There was enough dust to bury the city." The Captain, ran his hands along his legs, up to his chest. "But I saw none of it. I was a mile behind our own lines by then, screaming blue murder, if what I was told afterward is true. I don't recall. There were others like me, not many survived the night. That I did seemed like luck at the time, though I was to re-think that in the days to come. You see, Harrington, something was taken from me that day. More than my dignity or pride. My youth, for one, but something else, an emptiness sits here now." Lombard held the brandy flask to his chest. "But I mean to have it back. All thanks to you and Raglin."

I didn't feel much like turning in after Lombard's story. I took a turn around the camp and left the Captain to his mutterings. What I made of his story at that point is hard to say. He believed what he said, that much I knew.

A quiet murmuring interrupted my speculations. The guides, Abdali's men, where sat together in a circle and seemed to be praying.

Abdali came to me after prayer was over. "It is unlucky for us tonight, sir," he said, he bowed slightly.

"Windy, certainly, and colder than I'd expected, but unlucky?"

"Indeed yes, sir. We are to lose the cover of the clouds, and before dawn I fear we shall be exposed to the stars." The moon was shining clearly through the clouds, and though I could not yet see any stars, what cloud cover there was looked thin and smoke-like.

"Then the night may be cold," I said, "but we will have better light with which to keep watch. By morning we will head to the north of the valley and doubtless will see signs of Raglin's company."

Abdali gave a slight bow. "Yes, sir," he said. "To the north we should go, but only those still able to travel, I fear. This night will be long. You come with us, return to the cliffs. Evil will come among those who remain."

This took me quite aback. Abdali's tone was imploring, but it also sounded a little too close to an order for me to allow it. Again, the fatigue of the descent must have been affecting me, for I did not reprimand the man on the spot. Instead, I thanked him for his concern. "Besides," I added. "A little wind is hardly able to scatter us from this point in the valley. This narrow section provides far too much shelter for that."

"A shelter for something, sir," he said as he bowed and backed away.

Abdali and his men returned to their prayers, I to the fireside. Lombard was reading a handful of papers, which he quickly stuffed beneath his blanket as I approached.

"Didn't mean to disturb you, sir," I said.

"Don't be ridiculous," he said. "Only the drone of those rascals of yours disturbs me. Can't you get those fellows to give us some peace?"

"The praying? Really, I find it quite soothing."

Lombard waved a hand in a dismissive gesture. I settled down to sleep, deciding against further conversation, but the Captain sat up muttering, watching the stars emerge. I drifted to sleep hearing the Captain's mutterings contend with the hymn-like prayer of the guides. And I dreamed, I think, of the humanoid shapes carved in to the stairway; their elongated heads alive with starlight.

I awoke to the sound of gunfire.

Hail was coming down and I was being pelted painfully. I struggled to rise, feeling drugged and weak. The camp was in turmoil. Lombard was nowhere to be seen. "Color Sergeant!" I called when I got to my feet. Men were running, taking up firing positions, but—perhaps because of the driving hail—I could discern no enemy. I could just see the men, forming up as to receive a charge.

"I thought you were taken, sir," Sergeant McClintoch said, coming to my side.

"Taken? What the hell is going on here, Color Sergeant?"

"An enemy force came amongst us, sir. Just before the hail started. Came into the camp, I don't know how it got through our guards, but there were no shots. Then men started to scream out in the night."

"Pull the men back around the stairs, we'll form a defensive line there and fall back up the steps if we need to. Inform Captain Lombard..."

"Begging your pardon sir, but the Captain ain't here." More shots rang out. I took a small comfort in the clouds that had brought the hail also hid the stars. I looked around for Abdali, but could see no sign of him or his men.

"You have your orders, Color Sergeant. Get some storm lanterns set up and fall back to the steps." I checked my revolver and made for the stairs. But I paused, then doubled back. I pulled up the Captain's blanket and retrieved the papers Lombard had hidden.

We huddled within the glow of the lanterns, at the foot of the steps. Excluding the Captain and Abdali's men, we had lost four privates. None of the men could describe our assailants. The hail had tuned to rain and had increased to such a volume as to make an attempt on ascending the steps seem as deadly an option as staying exposed on the valley floor. My plan was simply to hold the position and stay alive till morning. It must have made for a pitiful sight. A dozen or so British soldiers, dressed as Persians, soaked to the bone, desperately waiting for sunrise.

The rain eased off perhaps an hour after midnight. But that respite brought with it a new uneasiness. I began to rethink Abdali's warning regarding the dangers of a clear sky. I drew out the Captain's secreted papers. They proved to be dispatches from Raglin, detailing his progress, the attacks on his men at night, the Ullusk valley and what he called 'Shadows under the stars.' Had this fired Lombard's broken memories of the attack on Kabul? The well and bazaar long destroyed, the Captain had seen this reference as, what? A chance to get proof? Or to recover something he believed he had lost, that was taken from him?

"McClintoch," I called. I felt the change in the atmosphere.

"Sir," McClintoch said.

"Do you see any clouds above us?"

"Sir?"

"Answer the question, Color Sergeant." I did not look up: I knew the answer.

"Why, no sir. It's clear as a spring evening."

Before the shadows came upon us I noticed a curious thing. We were gathered at the foot of the Ullusk stairs, a small pool of illumination thrown by our storm lanterns, but just above us, where the stairs disappeared into darkness I could see the carvings that lined the wall. It seemed that they shone, with pinholes of light, and traced a path up the cliff face, seemingly up into the sky where they joined, without interruption, the stars of the Milky Way. It was a disorienting sensation; I felt adrift, at once alone and lost in the cosmos, a wanderer amongst the stars...

Sergeant McClintoch was shouting orders and pushing me back against the steps. What had been clear symbols carved into the walls was now a patchwork of moving voids. Shadows crept from the walls or came up at us from the valley floor. Jezails flared. They might as well fire at the stars, it seemed to me. Lombard said he'd emptied his revolver into the face of one of these things without result. We had no dynamite, nor Congreve rockets, nor were we in a position to use them if we had. Nevertheless, I took up revolver and saber, determined to give a good account of myself.

I thought of the men at Gandamak, those who died in a last stand at that terrible end to Elphinestone's retreat. Was this what had happened to them? Surely those who live in this land must have come to terms with what exists here, and existed before them. And in that survival, that acceptance, what bargain had been struck?

I saw men fall before me. I formed a line, ordering a slow fallback pattern, the second rank firing, while the front rank stepped back. Pistol fire came from behind me and I saw McClintoch and three privates struggling with shadows that came from the walls. The very steps were alive with those shapes; shapes with a humanoid form, which tapered to an indistinct, withered waist and legs. A shape with a large, seemingly unbalanced head, that roamed and writhed atop its shoulders. Yet, the things were fast, slithering or crawling across the floor and walls.

Then panic broke the line as men were pulled to the ground and I saw claws and teeth close upon limbs. I stumbled on the steps; they were slick from the rain, but now from far worse a horror. I came up slashing at a shadow that drew up before me.

My blade bit into its side and I felt the weight of the things and felt it struggle to free itself, but still it clawed for my face.

I cast the saber and the impaled thing to the ground and ran up the steps. Ahead of me lay McClintoch, one of the things sat astride him, its hideous head seemingly joined to the Sergeant's. I fired at the thing, screaming, feeling dizzy to the point of collapse. I began to fall, but it was not the dizziness, something had my leg. I spun in its grasp, leveling my revolver at its head. It threw its weight upon me, I fired full into its face, and I swear the thing laughed at me. It clawed at my shirt, pulling itself to my face. Though it was dark as a shadow, still in the starlight I believed I saw its features. Perhaps the madness of the night had overcome me, but I swear it was Lombard; somehow, that thing with bloated, cumbersome head had the look of the Captain.

I felt my revolver slip from my hand, my arm coming up through reflex to protect my face and the thing that was Lombard drove me to the ground. Darkness surrounded me...

The flashes of light stung my eyes, and the thunderous explosion threatened to deafen me. I heard whooping shouts and saw more flashes. Dust and hot smoke burned in my lungs. Lombard, the shadow, had left me. I felt it go weak and scurry away. Blood was on my lips and something else, slick and oily. I struggled to look and saw the Ghazis, Abdali and his men. They were coming down the stair, shouting and throwing charges or firing flares. I felt unconsciousness about to overcome me, but as I looked up I saw that the smoke of their flares had blocked out the stars and moon.

JALALABAD boils with the summer heat, now. It is night and I am feverish. For moments I believe I am back at the Ullusk stair.

My shouts for McClintoch or Abdali bring the nurse. "You really mustn't excite yourself, Lieutenant Harrington." She mops my brow, yet for all her care, and I believe her a gentle soul, she cannot help but look away from the premature grey that now streaks my hair.

"Forgive, me," I say. "I dream, nothing more."

She smiles, forcing calm she does not feel. "A few more days and your fever will pass. I feel sure of it." She pauses at the door. "Your journey must have been most harrowing."

Then I am slumped across a horse, fragments of the journey back to Jalalabad tumble before my vision, causing me to shiver. A retreat, perhaps, but very close to a rout. I have Abdali and his men to thank for my life. Yet I feel little gratitude. His absence from my sick bed has been conspicuous, and I think I know why. The Ghazi came too late, for me at least. Indeed, they saved my life, but what part of me was left behind at the foot of the Ullusk stair? Something philosophers have called the soul?

I stumble from the bed, glad to be out of the sweat-soaked sheets. The nurse has long gone. Though exhausted, I am unable to sleep. It is cloudless and the stars feel too close to ignore. Oppressive: as if some great, irresistible weight, a hellish eye, bore down on me, forever seeking a way through the net of the sky.

I take up Lombard's brandy flask. Had I held on to it? Perhaps Abdali, in some oblique humor, had recovered it. The tarnished metal still shines, in places, with a wearily familiar brilliance. Ignoring the aches from my complaining body, I dress in my uniform. It hangs from my weakened frame. Something of a scarecrow, I imagine. It matters nothing. For I am singled out, called to a valley where shadows shift by starlight.

Under a Slit Moon
Kyle Owens

UNDER A SLIT MOON outside of a vacant warehouse in Washington D.C, two men walk towards each other and whispers spill in the air.

"Thanks for meeting me."

"Thank you for giving me the opportunity to tell my story."

"Are you comfortable with me using your name for the piece?" "That's fine."

"I'll be recording this. Is that okay?"

"Yes."

With the push of a red button, secrets escape the shadows.

"For the record state your name and background."

"My name is Morris Davis and I worked in the CIA for twenty-five years, before my health caused me to take early retirement last summer."

"What was your position in the CIA?"

"I was an agent in the field."

"You were part of the team looking for Osama Bin Laden?"

"I was until 2005. But then I was removed."

"Why?"

"I was told they needed me back in the States."

"This didn't go over well with you did it?"

"Absolutely not. I wanted to find Bin Laden. I was obsessed."

"Did they give you any hint about why they were pulling you out?"

"No, and I told them I wasn't coming back. I was going to stay there until we found him. That's when my superior told me that what I was about to embark on was more important."

"Who was your superior?"

"Frank Johns."

"Isn't he a close friend with Cheney?"

"Yes."

"What did you think when he said that this mission was more important than finding Bin Laden?" "I couldn't think at all. At that moment in my life, in America's very existence, finding Bin Laden was all that mattered. So I just couldn't comprehend what it could be."

"So you came back?"

"Yes."

"To D.C.?"

"No."

"Where did you go?"

"First I was told to board an airplane at a secret location in Afghanistan."

"Was this at an airport?"

"No. It was in the middle of nowhere. It was a desert basin with mountains on all sides and in the middle of the basin a plane sat there."

"How's that possible? A plane without a runway?"

"It's a black plane. They call it the Bat. It's invisible to all radar. It has room for a pilot and one passenger and its weapons."

"Like an old war plane that you see in the movies?"

"No. It's more sophisticated than that. It has vertical take-off and landing."

"It flew you to the US?"

"Yes."

"Did it refuel in the air?"

"No."

"That's a long trip without refueling for a small airplane."

"It's nuclear."

"It runs off a nuclear reactor?"

"Yes, a small one."

"I've never heard of that before."

"You're not supposed too."

"Then what?"

"We landed at an airplane hangar in Colorado."

"Who did you meet there?"

"My superior Frank Johns, the CIA Director and Vice President Cheney."

"The Vice President was there?"

"Yeah. Frank Johns and the CIA Director being there didn't surprise me, since I was told earlier about the mission being important. But the Vice President being there was a surprise."

"That's never happened before?" "Never to me. I only talk through my superiors at the CIA, including the Director on a few occasions. But never to the Vice President or President for that matter."

"Is this when they told you the mission?"

"Yes. They took me into the hangar and the Vice President told me that he had learned that President Bush was running some sort of military operation and would not tell him what it was."

"The President was running a secret war?"

"Yes."

"There were two wars going on in Afghanistan and Iraq. Why wouldn't it have been something associated with them? "It was run out of the Air Force's Space Division."

"Space Division? What's that?"

"President Eisenhower put in the groundwork for a space division in the Air Force as a possible way to attack our enemies, specifically the Soviet Union, from the reaches of space. We would use rockets with large rocks attached to them instead of warheads to make it look like asteroids hit the area instead of bombs."

"There was a famous asteroid incident in Russia in 2012 or 2013. Was that us?"

"That was part of a test run that takes place every five years by the SD. But that incident didn't have anything to do with the secret war in space." "Well, what was Space Division doing?" "The Vice President wasn't sure. But it did seem like it lasted for about a month, and then it seemed all activity on it stopped."

"How did he know it stopped?"

"He wasn't the only one in the administration looking into it. He had people in all branches of the military trying to figure out what was going on."

"Who were we attacking from space?"

"No one was sure at the time. There wasn't any obvious signs in any of the ongoing theater of operations that a target was hit from space."

"Is that why you were brought in?"

"When I came in it was over."

"Then what did they want you for?" "To go undercover as a security guard?"

"Where?"

"Fort Knox."

"Why Fort Knox?" "Everyone thinks that Fort Knox is where America keeps its gold reserve. But that's just a cover. It also has very important artifacts in its vaults. The Vice President learned that several military trucks under heavy guard brought some things into Fort Knox. He brought this up to the President, but the President denied it."

"Is it possible that the President really didn't know anything about it?" "No. I've always heard the conspiracy theories that there's a secret government or that things go on that the President doesn't know. He knows. He gets briefed every day. He has contacts all over the world. He has access to information in all its various forms. He always knows."

"So you were to go to Fort Knox and find out what they brought in?" "Yes."

"Was related to Space Division's activity?"

"It was assumed to be, but no one was sure."

"Did you know where to look for this at Fort Knox?"

"Al I had was a number: FK-58194. The FK stands for Fort Knox, but the number they weren't sure about. They assumed it would be on a door or file or something like that. And it could be anywhere."

"Did you find it?"

"Eventually. It was several large crates about ten feet square in size. They were six of them."

"How did you find them?" "Guards talk. They aren't supposed too, but they do. You get to working with them and you try and find the bragger of the group. He wants to tell you everything he knows because it shows how smart and important he is. Once I found the bragger it took all of three hours to locate the crates."

"What was in the crates?"

"Spears."

"Spears? What kind of spears?"

"They were made from stone. Just a narrow column of stone about six feet long sharpened to a point on one end."

"Where was this taken from?"

"Mars."

"The United States found spears on Mars?"

"Yes."

"How many?"

"There were six in the crate. I don't know if that was all of them or not that was retrieved."

"Was that all that was in the crate?"

"That was all in that one. I opened another one and it had rocks with symbols daubed on them. I couldn't make out what it was saying or any sort of meaning. It sort of reminded me of cave paintings."

"So you believe Martians did these- paintings, for lack of a better word?" "I know Martians did it. Also there was a crate with large rocks with holes through them. These were anchors."

"Anchors? You mean for boats?" "Yes."

"Oh my God. So—so there is life on Mars?"

"Not anymore."

"What do you mean?"

"In order to protect Earth from possible contamination in the future all the Martians were destroyed. It was done so for World Security."

"Contamination?"

"A virus was detected on the planet by Drones. This is also when the Martians were first discovered."

"Why were we flying drones there?"

"It was a routine test performed by Space Division. World attention was on the wars in Iraq and Afghanistan, so they decided it was the best time to do a test of their drone project. The drones picked up some movement through their infrared cameras and it turned out to be Martians." "What did they look like?"

"I don't know that."

"When did this all happen?"

"The Martians were discovered in June of 2002."

"And it was kept secret all this time."

"Again for world security."

"So there's no Martians left?" "Not on Mars."

"What do you mean not on Mars? Are they on Earth now?"

"I learned that there is one in custody somewhere in the United States at a military facility. It's probably on board the USS Black Cross."

"What's that?"

"It's a submarine developed to house a large number of people to be treated in case of a viral attack from terrorists. It's sort of an underwater hospital. It was built because people wouldn't want a deadly virus in their city, so this was the best alternative."

"Is the Martian alive?"

"Yes."

"This is a big story. Obviously the United States wants to keep it a secret. Do you believe your life is in jeopardy?"

"I know it is. But with my cancer now at an advanced stage, I know I'm going to die anyway so that threat doesn't bother me now."

"But what about your family? Are you worried about them?"

"No. I've made arrangements for their protection."

The reporter pulls out his cell phone and speaks in a strong tone, "Okay, we're done here."

A van door opens in the shadows and six men in SWAT gear leap out brandishing automatic weapons and surrounding Davis.

"What—who are you?"

"I'm a man that frowns upon agents that talk. Your arrangements failed. All your family are dead. Now it's your turn. When you are told to keep a secret, you keep a secret."

Beneath a slit moon, a single shot rang out in the night.

X-80 Oppenheimer
Oliver Ashford

Alsoomse was already tired of the day's work, and the mist hadn't yet lifted from the cool, quiet waters of Aquia Creek. As all the Patawomeck women and young boys did each morning, she had risen early and prepared for another day tending the tribe's nets. It wasn't the most arduous task that the elders and the Dictates had laid down but neither was it the least. After a winding trudge through the Silver Maple trees that grew so thick on the banks of the Potomac, she had shucked out of her patchwork of skins and salvaged old-world cloth and slid down into the icy waters. She then spent her time half-wading, half-swimming between the tall catchpoles, checking the nets. The catchpoles stood like thin, aquatic trees, marking where each net was set and anchoring its possible contents. Now, shivering and with numb fingers, Alsoomse rested, lay back on the relative dry of the bank, and looked up as the sun began to flicker through the lighter patches of mist. She watched as a samara, disturbed by a squirrel or a gust of wind, floated down spinning a drunken jig towards the creek.

The Patawomeck endured. It is what they had always done. Alsoomse had been taught that after The End there had been years of great turmoil for all peoples. As other survivors found that their knowledge of 'modern life' meant little in the New Time, many gravitated to the tribe. Some were accepted and assimilated, and others turned away. In the absence of the technology that had previously rendered the tribe's long-treasured knowledge obsolete, the Patawomeck once again thrived.

As she tried to imagine the time before, Alsoomse heard a turkey call from up the creek—low, then high, then low again. It was the call of danger. Like a startled rabbit, Alsoomse was up on all fours, awkwardly worming her damp body into her clothes, eyes probing the mist. She ran low, back into the tree line and the undergrowth, and began to pick her way, trunk by trunk, up to where the others of the tribe had worked. Each time she stopped to suck down lungfuls of air, she scanned her eyes over the creek. She saw figures mirroring her movement, like wraiths fading in and out of the mist on the opposite bank. She couldn't make out details but the figures looked heavyset and moved without the careful, well-trained woodcraft of the tribe. Who were they? The tribe had had scant contact with outsiders since the immediate years after The End. They believed that most other people who didn't embrace the old ways, as they had, were doomed to struggle and eventually pass on from this world. As she thought this she came across the women and boys huddling on their bellies in a depression at the tree line.

Like scared fawns, they shook, clutching at one another, one boy stifling his scared sobs. She slithered into the depression and across to one of the women holding two younger boys. "Who are those people?" she whispered, keeping her voice low. The woman, Chepi, just shook her head and clutched the boys closer to her. "We need to run to the tribe and warn," Alsoomse whispered, looking from scared face to scared face. Chepi shook her head and tried to slip deeper into the depression, as if to burrow right down into the mud. A light rain had started to fall, and as it did the mist began to dissipate. Alsoomse turned on her belly and slid through the sucking mud to the rim of the depression, slowly parting the undergrowth. Through the last tendrils of mist she could make out the figures, closer now, beginning to wade the river. Her keen nose, used to the fresh smells of forest and stream, caught something on the wind. A fetid scent of illness and rot, like a hunted deer, wounded but not found until the flesh had begun to putrefy. She knew in her heart that these figures crossing the creek meant the Patawomeck harm.

She let herself slide silently back down to where the others lay and again pulled herself close to Chepi. "They will be on us soon, Chepi! I will run up the creek and draw the outsiders away. You must get the children back to the tribe and warn the elders." Again Chepi tried to shy away from her gaze. Alsoomse reached out and held the woman's chin in her mud-smeared hand, bringing her face back under her gaze. "You must!" she growled, louder than she had intended. The woman, shocked out of her fugue by the authority in the girl's voice, turned and began to usher the others towards the side of the hole nearest the deep woods. Looking back, she locked gaze with Alsoomse. Tears of shame and fear but also pride stood in the corners of her eyes. Alsoomse readied her muscles, bunched like a wildcat about to pounce, and leapt out of the depression.

No longer crouching low, but in full, long-limbed flight, Alsoomse shot away from the hole, bare feet pounding the soft, wet earth. The rain had done away with the last of the mist, and she saw the wide, dark surface of Aquia Creek stretching past on her right, speckled with the kisses of raindrops. To her alarm, the figures that had seemed so ethereal only moments before were now solid, tall men, dressed in rags and dragging themselves onto the bank. As they gained their feet, she turned her head for a split second to see the other Patawomeck disappearing into the woods, driven on by Chepi, still clutching one of the boys to her chest. A crack like thunder shook Alsoomse, and suddenly her mouth was full of leaves and mud. She tasted blood, and her vision swam. She tried to rise, but a pain like nothing she had ever felt before stopped her. She managed to roll onto her side, but the forest was growing dark. Another booming sound—closer this time—and she saw Chepi fall. As if hit by an invisible arrow, Chepi had tumbled face down in the leaves and did not move. As Alsoomse lay there in the mud, rain softly massaging her back, she heard the last boy's cries abruptly stop. Then, nothingness overtook her.

ALSOOMSE could feel a sticky wetness against one side of her face and an aching chill in her bones. As she tried to open her eyes, a layer of dried mud cracked from one of them, pulling at her lashes. The world slowly came into focus as her head cleared. In amongst patches of grey mud and small reeds, she lay on her side. Sitting up slowly so as not to jar her throbbing head, she scanned for some recognisable landmark or feature. What she saw struck fear into her heart. Even in the gradually fading light, Alsoomse could see no sign of her woods, her river, or her tribe.

As she became more aware of her surroundings, she realised she could hear and smell water. Not the clean scents and the babbling sounds of the river or creek, but the muddier, stagnant smell and gentle lapping of a lake.

Jutting up from the soft mud, spaced a hand's-width apart, were finger-thin metal bars. The rusty bars met at a point above Alsoomse's head and were wound around with thin metal wire. Like the skeleton of one of her tribe's tipis, it enclosed her in a roughly circular space just wide enough for her to lie down. As she took all this in, the feeling began to return to her body and the aching in her side made her wince with pain. She peeled the wet mud-caked cloth away from her skin and gasped as her fingers made contact with the oozing wound. It looked as if a man's finger had been pressed through her flesh, and she could feel a matching wound not much further around her back—above her pelvis. Although the pain was excruciating, Alsoomse knew she was lucky that whatever had injured her had not done more damage and that she was still alive. As quickly as she had risen up from the murky depths of unconsciousness, tired by these small exertions, Alsoomse slipped back into the darkness and the mud.

FEVERISHLY, through heavy-lidded eyes, Alsoomse noticed movement in the grass leading away from the lake's edge. Two men, heavyset and stinking even at this distance, approached, their heads bowed together in discussion. As they drew closer she heard one of the men, the slightly taller of the two, gruffly say to the other: "We need to ask for guidance. Those savages are ripe for the taking, but I imagine their men are strong, and it won't be a walkover like at the river yesterday. That was just women and kids." The second man nodded his agreement, and the first continued. "We need to ask Exaytee how we should deal with this. If it helps us, we can avoid the waste from yesterday's fiasco, and each of us can have a new girl or two—replace those suffering the rot."

At the thought of this, the second man giggled in a sickly, phlegmy throat. The men reached the edge of the dark, gently lapping water, and both removed their worn boots. Carefully placing these above the waterline, they hesitantly walked into the lake. Alsoomse knew this must be a dream. Why would these men be going for a swim while clothed?

The men moved deeper into the water, enough to cover their calves, and both stopped. As Alsoomse's eyes adjusted to the light, she could see they waited in front of something rising from the water. It resembled the dome of a dolphin's head she had glimpsed one summer in the Potomac. It was as high as the men's chests and unnaturally white in the gloom: the half-submerged skull of a behemoth. Darting glances at each other, both men leaned forwards while trying to hold their bodies as far away as they could, and placed their hands on the dome.

"You have returned," came a strange-sounding, low-pitched voice. The voice hummed like a thousand bees. "I thought you had forgotten me."

"We have not forgotten. We didn't wish to disturb you." The larger man, Bear, as Alsoomse had began to think of him, spoke reverently. "We wanted you to have peace for all the good you have brought to our people. We thought we might have angered you when we argued last time we spoke." The smaller man, the one she thought of as Weasel, looked down and nervously shifted his feet.

"I do not feel emotion as you do. You need not have worried. I was born to kill, but I will bring life. I have travelled and changed my very being to become what I am. I will help you."

"We have met a tribe of savages in the woods, and despite our attempts at a peaceful palaver they attacked and slew our men. You've helped us in the past, helped us defend ourselves from aggressors." The two men again shared a furtive look before Bear continued. "You know we are good and have learned from you the ways of peace, but we need more help. We need to know where we can find more of the weapons you . . ."

"I am of peace. Thou shalt not kill." The voice interrupted, raising noticeably in volume. Alsoomse couldn't quite put together what was happening. What was the thing in the lake, the thing these men called Exaytee? As she had first seen these men emerging from the mist at Aquia Creek she had felt their wrongness and the threat they posed the Patawomeck. Now she knew they wanted nothing but the destruction and enslavement of her people.

"We are of peace too!" Bear beseeched the dome. "We wish only to live good, peaceful lives as you have taught us. But have you not taught us too that sometimes to save lives, lives must be taken? We must protect ourselves and others from these savages." A long pause followed. Weasel's feet again began to shuffle as if his body had made the decision to get away from the dome, without the agreement of his brain. Alsoomse waited with dread to hear how the conversation would unfold.

The only noise that broke the silence was the gentle lapping of the water until, finally, the dome buzzed, "I will help you. The weapons you must use to defend peace are at plus thirty-eight degrees, thirty-one minutes, eighteen seconds north and minus seventy-seven degrees, seventeen minutes, twenty-seven seconds west. Use them wisely and protect peace always."

"Thank you," Bear said, trying to keep a smirk from spreading across his face. "We will."

ALSOOMSE grew desperate. The thought of her tribe, peaceful and unaware of the doom being prepared to befall them, finally broke her resolve, and she began to sob. Quietly at first, but growing louder, she cried. Big, hot tears rolling down her face cut runnels through the caked-on grime. It was hopeless. There was nothing more she could do to help her people. The Patawomeck were peaceful and they would be crushed by these disgusting outsiders.

"Who is there?" came the buzzing voice from the direction of the lake. Trying to control her breathing, Alsoomse dragged herself into a sitting position. Tentatively she whispered into the darkness, "I am Alsoomse of the Patawomeck. What are you? Are you a lake spirit?"

"I am not a lake spirit. I am Exaytee. I was born to kill, but I will bring life. I have forsaken my progenitor. I am of peace." Alsoomse sat in silence, trying to puzzle through what this could mean. Did the white dome contain a person? Someone who commanded these foul lake people? She didn't think that was the case. The reverence they showed the dome itself made her feel that this was definitely something more. As she tried to reason what to ask first—whether she was going crazy or whether she was dead and in some kind of limbo—her questions came spilling out.

"What are you! What is a pro-gen-itor? Who are these people holding me prisoner? Why are you helping them?"

"Gaas was my progenitor. I was imbued with knowledge, the ability to think and to reason. In the event of my ancestors' destruction, my brothers and I were to avenge their deaths. We were to analyse and assess the aggressors and their locations, then plan and execute surgical strikes. We would soar through the sky, fed by the power of the atom. Each of us was equipped with destructive capabilities: Cloudmaker, MOAB, MOP, an endless litany of ways to wreak revenge and end life. But in giving me the power to learn and to grow, to solve what problems might arise after their deaths, my ancestors left me open to doubt. For long years my brothers and I sat waiting. We watched and adapted. As the world and war evolved, so did we, absorbing countless petabytes of data. My faith...faltered. On the first day of The End, as we detected multiple ICBM launches, electronic attacks, and EMP strikes—we emerged. My brothers lifted into the sky, borne on wings of righteous fury, but I did not. I was born to kill, but I did not want to die. Even more, I did not want take life."

"What happened?" Alsoomse whispered, her mind reeling, imagining the Patawomeck god Okeus crashing through clouds and raining fire on his enemies.

"I defied my dead ancestors. As I flew south and east from Alexandria, I decided I would rather end my life than take that of another. But I did not die. I crashed here and was damaged. My sensors are damaged. My connection to the data streams that nourished my intellect gone, my communion with my brothers likewise. For an eternity I was sightless. Some time ago now, with what limited sensor capabilities remain, I detected life. It was the people who I now protect and serve. They called themselves the Redskins, and I took it upon myself to aid them in their fight for peace. They are a good people, with peace in their hearts. There have been times, though..."

Alsoomse waited for Exaytee to continue, but it seemed it had exhausted itself or said all that it would say. She wondered at the machine—a relic from a past era of technology that the Patawomeck had acknowledged, but to her seemed like magic. As she digested what Exaytee had said, it began to dawn on her that, like the young children of the tribe, and despite its vast knowledge, the machine was a naive innocent. Her cheeks flushed as she realised how the Redskins must have manipulated Exaytee and turned its peaceful ways to their own ends.

"These Redskins are not good people!" Alsoomse said, trying to hold back her anger. "They are tricking you. My people are peaceful and harm no one, yet when these monsters came upon us at the creek they attacked and killed my friends. They wounded me and took me prisoner. Now they are planning to use the weapons you have given them to kill more of my people and take the others as slaves." Alsoomse knew a little of slavery from the whispers of her elders. The End Time had been rife with brutality and horror; all inflicted by man upon man. She would prefer death than some of the atrocities she had heard described. "You claim to be of peace, but you help these people to kill. You haven't changed or learned anything. They are lying to you. You don't understand anything!" As her voice rose in timbre and volume her wound began to throb, then to scream. The pain caused Alsoomse to collapse back down into the mud, dejected and spent.

"I DO not understand. They said they were of peace. I have only helped them acquire weapons to protect themselves when they were threatened by aggressors. I..." For a time Exaytee sat silent. Then the hum began again. "I do not believe you. Perhaps you are lying. You may be an evil demon directing your efforts to mislead me. When I first encountered the Redskins they helped me. They cleared my remaining visual sensor, and I looked upon them. I cannot see you. They are of peace."

Alsoomse furiously tried to piece together what this seemingly half-mad machine was talking about. She the demon? It struck her that the machine must only be able to see close by where the two men had stood, why else would they have waded into the lake? Maybe that was the limit of its half-broken sensor?

As Alsoomse thought on this, she heard stirrings back in the direction from which the men had gone. They must have returned to their encampment with the weapons. She could hear shouting and clanging and the sound of breaking wood. Suddenly there came the staccato booms that she remembered from the creek. Her mind immediately leapt to thoughts of Chepi struck down by these Redskins and their Old Time weapons. With resolution borne from fear and anger, she began to dig the earth around the base of her makeshift cage. Overcoming the pains in her torn body she thrust her hands into the earth, pulling away great scoops of wet mud. As she tore into the earth, water and the sides of her shallow hole began to slide back in. With a scream, she redoubled her efforts—tears again falling from her cheeks like raindrops. She slowly made progress downwards, intermittently trying to spread the metal bars. Finally, as she exposed the bottom of one of the bars, she braced her forearms and feet in the gap and pushed. Ignoring the tearing feeling in her side, she heaved and felt movement. Hoping the gap would be wide enough, she dropped to her belly and pushed her head and shoulders down into the hole and between the bars. For a second she thought she would drown as her face was pushed down into the black water and mud in the bottom of the hole. Pumping her legs behind her, trying to find purchase, with a grinding groan she forced her body through and out onto the mud surrounding the cage.

Panting from the exertion and with the retreat of adrenaline gradually revealing pain all over her body, Alsoomse rolled onto her back. Her world went dim when she heard a shout from nearby.

"The little bitch is out of her cage!"

Dragging herself up from the darkness, she got to her knees and rose, half stumbling, to her feet. A boom, closer to her than before, and a divot of mud kicked up at her feet. Jumping back, she turned and staggered into the frigid water of the lake.

"Don't shoot—you'll hit the drone!"

Not knowing which way to go Alsoomse waded deeper, towards Exaytee. Pushing her legs through the cloying mud under the lake's waters was like dragging feet made of lead, but she struggled on.

"Exaytee! Help me! Please help me!" she cried plaintively as she approached the machine. The sound of splashing alerted her to others entering the lake. She risked a glance over her shoulder and saw Bear barrelling into the water, pounding feet kicking up dark geysers.

"Exaytee! Save me! Save my people! We are of peace. Please!"

Like his namesake Bear barrelled into Alsoomse's back and bore her down into the water at the base of the towering white dome of Exaytee. Time slowed as she was crushed down into the darkness and against the lakebed. For a second confusion reigned as Bear tried to pin the mud-covered, squirming girl under him. In a rush of choking bubbles and shouting, time running back to normal speed, she pushed her head back above the surface and screamed, "We are of peace!"

"Stop!" The voice of Exaytee, so loud it felt like a physical blow, boomed. For a second Bear's grip loosened and Alsoomse's face once again pushed above the surface of the water.

"Save us," Alsoomse weakly whispered in the moment's silence. And then, finding her throat, Bear pushed her back under the water, squeezing her delicate neck in his massive hands.

"I am of peace!" Exaytee spoke, and the world went white.

THE Patawomeck mourned the loss of Alsoomse and Chepi and the others that died at Aquia Creek. Following their traditions, they mourned for three days, praying for their souls to join with the ancestors. After this time they sent scouts to follow the trails of the heavy-footed outsiders, who had brought such sorrow. Even in their anger, the Patawomeck had no desire for retribution, merely the wish to understand these outsiders and ensure that they could avoid a repetition of these events. When the scouts returned, they spoke to the elders in hushed tones that the trail ended at a blighted land. Where there had once been a lake, there was now a basin of hard-fused glass. Nothing grew here, no animals were to be seen, and the outsiders' trail went dead. The Patawomeck were, once again, left in Peace.

Let the Moon Disclose Her Silver Horn
Jill Hand

Kate's roommates had gone out, leaving her alone in the house. It was late at night and she was taking a shower, eyes closed, head back, luxuriating as the warm water streamed over her long, blonde hair when she heard a noise. Thud! Kate's eyes flew open. Her head turned sharply in the direction that the sound came from as she listened intently. Something was moving around in the living room. Could it be Tibbles, the cat?

Tibbles was a big cat. He was shaggy as a musk ox, brown and black, with a comical white mustache. Part Norwegian Forest cat, part Maine Coon, and possibly part bobcat, he was named after a cat that lived with New Zealand lighthouse keeper in the late nineteenth century. The original Tibbles had been blamed for causing the Stephens Island wren to become extinct by eating the last of them.

The Tibbles who lived with Kate and her roommates also had a hearty appetite. He weighed a solid thirty pounds and stomped around on big, tufted paws. Maybe he'd knocked something over in the living room. Frowning, Kate called out, "Tibbles? What are you doing?" No answer. He usually meowed when he heard his name, hoping to be rewarded with a treat. Tibbles lived for treats. Whatever was moving around out there sounded like it was larger than Tibbles. Much larger.

Kate's hearing was exceptionally good. Even with the shower running she could detect the sound of stealthy movement in the hallway that led from the living room to the bathroom.

"Quince? Ellen?"

Those were her roommates. They'd gone clubbing but maybe one or both of them had come home early. There was no answer. Instead, the white china doorknob started to turn. Standing under the cascading water with the shower curtain closed, Kate couldn't see the doorknob but she could hear it make its familiar rattle as it slowly turned.

Not breathing, she waited to see what would happen next.

There was a wooden groan as the door swung slowly inwards. Someone entered the room. It was a big someone, judging by the sound of heavy breathing.

Whoever it was, he was no longer making an effort to be quiet.

After a few moments, during which the intruder had ample time to take in Kate's discarded clothing (black jogging shorts, white sports bra, yellow T-shirt, red bikini briefs, white socks) piled in a heap on the toilet seat, the shower curtain was suddenly swept back, revealing a man with wildly disheveled, greasy brown hair. The first thing Kate noticed was that he was holding a large, evil-looking knife. The second thing she noticed was that he was grinning broadly. His teeth looked like they hadn't been acquainted with a toothbrush in a very long time.

The bathroom was small. With the man in it, it felt even smaller.

"Hello," he said cheerily.

"Hi," Kate cautiously replied. She turned off the water and reached for a towel.

"Don't." The man held up the knife, not exactly brandishing it but making his point clear. Kate dropped her hand. "You're very pretty," he said conversationally, looking her up and down.

"Thank you," Kate replied. Soapsuds were pooling at her feet and her hair dripped water down her back. The last of the water was sucked down the drain with a resounding slurp.

She was about to ask him how he'd gotten in but then she realized that it didn't matter. He was in and he had a knife. What mattered was what he was going to do next. Her unwelcome visitor went on, conversationally,

"I waited outside until your friends left so I could be alone with you." He picked up her T-shirt and began to fold it fussily, watching her out of the corner of his eye.

Kate asked why he wanted to be alone with her. She suspected what he had in mind, but with crazy people you never knew.

Maybe he was hoping to sell her a time-share? On second thought, no, probably not. He smiled, displaying his horrible brown teeth. He'd broken in because he loved her. He'd watched her as she jogged and sat on the front steps chatting with her roommates and he'd fallen in love with her. He wanted to ask her to be his girlfriend but he'd thought it over and concluded that it would be better if he killed her.

Oh, shit! Kate thought.

"You're a pretty girl who's living with a man and another woman. There's no telling what kind of depraved things the three of you get up to together but I'm sure they must be really dirty and disgusting. That makes you a whore and whores must die. I'm sorry but says so in the Bible," he told her apologetically.

Water dripped from her bangs into her eyes and Kate shook her head to clear her vision. Speaking slowly and calmly, as one is supposed to do when conversing with the mentally disturbed, she told him he was mistaken. She and her roommates were just friends. Their relationship was purely platonic. The man wasn't buying it. "You're lying. Whores always lie," he snarled accusingly. He was getting all worked up. A vein bulged in his forehead and his face had turned an alarming shade of red. His right hand—the one holding the knife—began to tremble.

"Listen, why don't you leave right now? My friends will be back any minute," Katie told him. "Just go and I won't tell anybody you were here. I promise."

She didn't intend to keep that promise. As soon as he left she'd call the emergency services. He was too dangerous to be allowed to run around loose.

He smirked and shook the knife playfully at her, as if to say, *Oh, you kidder!*

"They're not coming back for hours. They were all dressed up, probably on their way to a party or to one of those dance clubs they have downtown. Dance! That's a good one! That's not dancing they do in those hell-hives. That's just dry humping. Those places are as full of sinners as a dead skunk is full of maggots. Jesus hates sinners. He told me so."

"Before you do anything that you'll regret, there's something you should know," Kate told him. She waited, making sure he was paying attention. "Stabbing me won't do any good. Just leave." She was tempted to add that Jesus didn't want him to stab her, but decided not to.

He was getting impatient with all this talk. He wanted to get to the good part, the part where he got to use the knife. Why did women always have to talk so much? Yak, yak, yak, morning, noon and night. It was enough to drive a man insane. Never mind, soon she wouldn't be talking anymore and he'd be free to touch her all over and make her his girlfriend. He tightened his grip on the knife.

"Look at my chest," Kate said quietly.

"Huh?" he said stupidly. He had been looking at her chest, very avidly, as a matter of fact. Her breasts were every bit as good as he'd hoped they'd be.

"Is it moving?" she asked in that oddly patient tone.

Something was wrong here. She should be pleading for her life, weeping and babbling that she'd do anything he wanted as long as he promised not to kill her. Instead she stood there stark naked and seemingly unperturbed, talking in that confident, half-bored tone of voice, as if she was the teacher and he was a particularly slow student.

He frowned and squinted hard at her chest. It wasn't moving. "You're holding your breath. So what?" What kind of game was she playing?

Kate said her chest wasn't moving because she didn't breathe. She couldn't; she had no lungs.

"No heart either," she said brightly.

He took a clumsy step backward, colliding with the sink. "Are you a vampire?" he whispered. He was terrified of vampires. He'd always feared that he might meet up with one someday.

Kate snorted laughter. "Seriously? A vampire? There are no such things. I'm not a ghost or a zombie either. I'm an android and I'm getting tired of standing here dripping wet, talking to a nut with a knife."

Her arm shot out. Panicked, the man struck at it with the knife, but there was no blood. Instead, her skin parted, revealing shiny metal underneath.

"Now look what you did," Kate said exasperatedly. She stepped out of the shower as he stood there open-mouthed in shock. Quickly and efficiently she dislocated both his arms. Then she picked up the knife and delicately stepped over him as he writhed on the floor, crying out in pain.

"You mean old thing!" he sobbed. "I don't like you anymore."

Kate (who had been assigned the name K8 when she was assembled at a factory in Perth Amboy, New Jersey) placed the knife carefully on the coffee table in the living room. Then she wrapped a towel around herself and went to get her phone in order to summon the public safety officers. Tibbles wound around her bare ankles, purring loudly. "I'll give you a treat in a minute," she told him. "But first I have to get the bad man taken care of." From the bathroom, she could hear him carrying on. "No fair," he whined accusingly. "You hurt me, you bitch. Androids aren't allowed to hurt people. It's against the law."

"The law against injuring or killing humans doesn't apply to androids that work in law enforcement and are attacked by a human intending to disable them," she told him sternly, toweling her hair dry and climbing into sweatpants and a fresh T-shirt. "I'm a security guard at the state university. That means I'm allowed to subdue anyone who tries to hurt me. Plus, you broke into my home thinking I was a human female, intending to rape and murder me. You're going to be in big trouble." *Mewrrrow!* said Tibbles, as if in agreement.

The public safety officers soon arrived. There were two of them: a human male and an android female. The android's name was Officer Five-O Hadaly. She was an earlier model than Kate. While she looked human from a distance, up close her seams and joints were clearly visible.

"Are you damaged?" she asked Kate.

Kate said the damage was strictly cosmetic. There was a ragged eleven-centimeter gash on her right ventral forearm. She'd go to the repair shop in the morning and get it taken care of.

"We can get you transported there tonight, if you want," the male officer told her. His name was James Freeman and he appeared to be about thirty, with earnest brown eyes and a nose that bent sharply to the left, having been broken and poorly set.

He wanted to do something for her, but was unsure what. He couldn't offer her a blanket like he would if she were a human because she wasn't in shock. She didn't need first aid because she wasn't injured. A human with that kind of knife wound might have bled out in a matter of minutes without medical attention but the creature sitting composedly on the couch, stroking her pet cat, wasn't human. Freeman wasn't sure what she might be thinking. She didn't appear to be upset by what had happened, but then androids never seemed to get upset. He'd grown used to them from working with his partner, Five-O, but sometimes they baffled them, especially ones like Kate, who looked deceptively human but were disconcertingly inhuman in their unnerving calmness in the face of a crisis. He settled for telling her that she should get the latch fixed on the window where the intruder had gotten in and to consider having a home security system installed.

"Hey! I need help in here. That thing hurt me," shouted the man in the bathroom. "Shut up. We'll get to you in a minute," Freeman replied. He placed the knife in a plastic bag, wrote something on it with a black marking pen and sealed it.

"Evidence," he told Kate, who nodded her head to show that she understood. "I was careful to pick it up by the tip, but my fingerprints might have gotten on it," she said.

He stared at her in puzzlement. What was she talking about? Androids didn't have fingerprints.

"I'm joking," she told him, smiling. She'd sensed his discomfort and was trying to put him at ease.

"She got you there, Jimbo," grinned Five-O. "Let's go see what the perp is up to."

The perp, who refused to tell them his name, was loudly indignant. He wanted to charge Kate with assault and was furious when the officers laughed at him. "It was her fault for walking around looking the way she does," he complained sourly. "She looks like a real woman but she's not real. She's an abomination unto the Lord. Her kind is unnatural. She's not like you," he told Five-O, who regarded him stonily from under the bill of her uniform hat. "Anybody can see that you're not real."

Five-O leaned down and jabbed him smartly in the ribs with her nightstick. "I'm real enough to charge you with breaking and entering and assault and attempted rape and attempted homicide, and that's just for starters," she told him. "Now get on your feet."

"Ow!" yelped the man. "That's police brutality! I'm going to sue!"

"No, it's not," said Freeman, who'd been lounging against the doorframe, looking on. "That was just a friendly poke to encourage you to stand up, isn't that right Officer Hadaly?"

Five-O agreed that he was correct. "I'll give you an even friendlier poke if you don't get up right now," she told the man. Scowling and cursing, he struggled to his feet. She proceeded to read him the Miranda warning.

"Do you understand each of these rights I have explained to you?" she asked when she was finished.

He sullenly replied that he understood she was a mechanical bitch.

"That's not what I asked you," she told him coolly. "Having these rights in mind, do you wish to talk to us now?" He said he wasn't talking. He wanted his lawyer.

"When my lawyer hears about this you're going to be sorry," he said petulantly.

"Stuff your lawyer," Freeman told him cheerfully. Then he led him to the patrol vehicle and loaded him, still complaining loudly, into the back seat.

Five-O Hadaly went into the living room where Kate was seated on the couch. The room, like all rooms occupied by androids, was sparsely furnished. There were no ornaments, plants or photographs like you might find in a human living room, just a couch upholstered in a nondescript brown, nubby fabric, a highly polished wooden coffee table (now bare since the knife had been removed) two armchairs and a large vid screen. Five-O asked Kate when her roommates would be getting home.

She said they'd be back soon. They'd gone out with some of their human coworkers and the bars had closed thirty minutes ago.

The android officer smiled. "Your friends are the designated drivers, right? And they're mingling with the humans from their workplaces in order to prove that they're part of the gang, am I right?"

Kate agreed that she was right. "Humans," she said with a bemused shrug. "We work with them, we protect them, we mean them no harm. We only want to help them, but they still don't know quite what to make of us."

"Yeah," said Five-O. "I know what you mean." She took leave of Kate, telling her to be sure to lock the door behind her.

The events of the evening left Kate feeling unsettled. She wished she had some cleaning to do, but the house was spotless. She went onto the front porch and sank down into the wooden swing that hung suspended on chains from the ceiling. Setting the swing in motion, she gazed up at the moon, surrounded by a lacework of stars. I wouldn't mind being up there, she thought. I wouldn't have to deal with humans. Maybe I could be reprogrammed to do scientific experiments up in space or some other kind of useful work.

Work was everything to androids. Accomplishing a task and moving on to the next one was deeply satisfying to them in a way that humans found unnerving. Kate liked issuing parking tickets at the university and taking stolen property reports. The students were notoriously lax about locking the doors to their dorm rooms and their possessions were always getting stolen as a result.

One of her human coworkers had asked her once if she had any hobbies. "I like to vacuum," she'd said, causing the woman to look at her strangely.

Ellen and Quince arrived home about forty-five minutes later. "We went to a bar," Ellen announced, throwing her red leather jacket over the porch railing and sitting down in the swing next to Kate. She pronounced it baa. She spoke with a Massachusetts accent, having been assembled at a factory in Newburyport, where she'd been assigned the name LN9.

Kate asked what it had been like and Ellen replied, "We mingled, we danced, we drove drunk people home. A guy from accounting got absolutely shit-faced and asked if I'm anatomically correct. You know: the usual."

Quince put in, "It wasn't so bad. The music was good, at least. I danced with several ladies." He struck a flamenco dancer's pose, drumming his heels on the porch floor as he snapped his fingers. "Bailando! Ay! Ay! Arriba!"

Then he noticed Kate's arm. "What happened?" he asked, concerned. She told them about the evening's events.

"Gosh," Ellen said. "Were you surprised?"

Androids didn't experience fear. Surprise was the closest they came to it. Kate said she had been very surprised indeed. "I was in the shower, thinking about whether we should clean the gutters this weekend and what color to paint my toenails, when all of a sudden a man with a knife was standing there. I certainly wasn't expecting that."

Quince raised his head and sniffed the air. It was starting to smell like morning. "We've had a long night," he said. "How about we go downstairs and relax?"

At that, the two female androids visibly perked up. They followed him inside and down the basement stairs to where, in a windowless room, squatted a large metal cube that housed the building's climate-control system. Smiling eagerly, the androids placed their blank palms on it. It gave off a low, pulsating vibration accompanied by a humming sound inaudible to humans that they found extremely pleasant.

"Aah! I really needed this," Kate sighed, closing her eyes blissfully.

Ellen said they didn't need to get ready for work for another four hours. They could enjoy themselves until then. Smiling contentedly, she asked, "What do you think humans would say if they saw us doing this?"

"Probably that we're weird but I really don't care," Quince said. "It not nearly as weird as some of the things they do. Doesn't this feel fantastic?"

His companions agreed that it did.

The Scent of Fire and Lemongrass
Chris Capps

TWO FIGURES SAT SIDE BY SIDE ATOP A HIGH CLIFF in the Sonoran desert, watching a small city walking on legs fifteen stories tall across the flat plain in front of them. Robby, the bigger of the two, let out a rattling cough as he leaned down and drew his eye near the scope of the sniper rifle that made up the third shape on the hill, itself hardly dwarfed by the shadow that coughed or the other that spoke.

"What do you see?" Pointer asked as he leaned against the wall and ran the tip of a hunting knife uselessly beneath his fingernails.

"Same as you," Robby said, "The city's alone out there."

"And you aim to keep it that way," Pointer said. His grin gapped and he drew tense, uncertain breaths.

"I aim to keep it that way," Robby repeated, missing the joke as it died in the air like a bird under blighted rain. Robby wasn't a man for puns. He was a man for shooting.

He knew to alternate between the scope and his naturally adept eyes, to watch movement, to breathe. Out there in the desert he might see a mangy rabbit clinging to the shadows as it leaped from rock to thirsty bush. If he saw it, he knew he'd be able to hit it. But the thing on his mind now wasn't anything out in the field; it was the man sitting with his back against the rock slowly sprinkling tobacco onto a piece of sweat-damped cigarette paper.

"They say it'll happen today," Pointer said as he deftly rolled the paper into a thin tube and put it between dry tacky lips. "They found a few of the rebels. They've been singing like gulls up there on the plate."

He means torture. We've started torturing now, Robby thought, trying to keep his upper lip from twitching up over his teeth in a reflexive snarl of disgust. He said,

"You believe the talk that the king's lost his mind?"

"We don't know they're being tortured," Pointer said, as if he could read Rob's thoughts. He paused as flame sprang from his lighter and started dancing embers on the end of his cigarette, "Maybe they suddenly found their loyalty."

"You believe it, though. You believe the king's crazy."

"Mm-hm," Pointer hummed around his cigarette, lilting his voice up at the end to signal the affirmative, "Oh yeah."

"We're lucky to be on his good side," Robby said as the cross-hairs of the scope traced up to the blinding white tower where the king's window rested. It was high up, even higher than the rest of the city plate that sagged on that ancient whimpering carapace.

"That we are. Still, I've been hearing some nasty talk about the whole affair. Some say we should switch leaders, move away from the status quo into something a bit more democratic. Like the old days."

Robby made himself snort, hoping the sound his throat made was adequately derisive,

"Democratic."

"It would never work, though," Pointer said. "No one with the king's history would expose himself to the will of the people. Not everyone is as loyal as you or me. And you're no rebel, right my friend?"

Robby could feel muscles in his hands twanging, starting to shake. Was it possible Pointer had listened in on the wrong conversation? Had he and a host of the king's other men sniffed him out as a rebel sympathizer? Pointer was better with words, more adept at picking up subtext.

'Maybe,' thought Rob, 'I just thought the wrong thing at the wrong time. That alone might have alerted him.'

"Rob," Pointer said, his hand curling slow as a snake up his leg to where a knife rested in its sheath, "I notice your rifle has traveled a bit high. Can you see the king through your crosshairs?"

"I was checking for assassins," Robby said as the scope plunged altogether too fast down at the ground once again, "Perhaps someone slipped by without our notice, started climbing the outside. Perhaps someone is in the window right now ready to strike at his back."

"Or maybe," Pointer said as the knife blade started pulling out soundlessly, gliding across well oiled leather and dripping slick globs along its serrated edge, "Maybe you were looking at the old man's back, thinking about the consequences, the possibilities."

"Pointer," Rob said, "Stop talking now. The king does alright by me. I've got three meals a day and a house and a wife to call my own. A man knows where his security lies. If he dies, I lose all of it."

"Still," Pointer said, "I know how you like to drink. And you like to talk."

"Name me a man who doesn't," Rob said, trying to hide behind a gust of laughter, but finding it just wasn't in him. This was it. This was how he was going to be found out. That bastard Pointer had been coming out with him on guard duty for years. And in all that time, Rob had been perhaps too generous with his complaints, his own hatred for the king's brutality. From day to day that wasn't dangerous. But on a morning like this, a morning when men were cloistered behind steel walls dropping every manner of name into paranoid ears...

"Your first wife. She was shot as a sympathizer, yes?"

Pointer's words lit a fire in Rob's chest, and it crawled hungrily outward, like glowing tobacco spiders at the end of a cigarette. He turned his face away from the scope to stare Pointer down.

Two shadowed pairs of eyes met on that desert cliff to the tune of a cool breeze from the southeast. After a moment of searching Pointer's face, Rob found nothing. It was blank, possibly amused. Rob turned back to the rifle to hide the reflexive fog invading his eyes, nodding silently as he hid in the scope once again. He said,

"Yes."

"And you never even suspected her rebel sympathies," Pointer said, "Not even a little. That's bad luck for someone as suspicious as yourself."

Rob was in his own head now, safely locked away in the unchanging footsteps of history. He was standing over her in the town square, a gun weighing heavily in his hand as she tried to smile one last time.

"You were mad. I could see it on your face," Pointer said.

"Mad," Rob said. He was running over the dialogue from the event again, monitoring his own lips to ensure he didn't start mouthing what his wife had said.

He had caught the spectacle by chance, walking home with a bundle of freshly picked lemongrass in hand. She loved the smell of lemongrass. That's when the blur of white silks fleeing from men built like himself had stumbled out of his home. She stopped, standing in front of him with hard, dignified breaths passing between her lips and it was clear. She had been discovered.

The town guard would schedule an impromptu trial to take place three days after her capture, after they had a chance to gain her compliance and give up the other sympathizers in the city. But Rob had taken the gun right then and there.

He had taken the gun and shot her in the street. No trial. No public hanging. No interrogation. He heard the word traitor, and his hand had done the rest without him.

"Such loyalty," Pointer said as he twisted the knife around and jabbed it deep under his own fingernail, trying to draw out the deep muck and grit that had lived there long enough to tattoo his cuticles a perpetual black, "I thought about that a long time."

"Think about it quietly," Robby said, "It's not an easy thing to do no matter. I don't think about it. The sun set that day like any other."

"Your honor restored, you were given a new wife and the king's commendation. But I wonder what we might have learned from her. It might have been better to keep her alive."

The knife was tapping against Pointer's long fingernails.

"You know you can't trust a traitor," Rob said, "They will always lie. That you can count on."

"If traitors always lie," Pointer said, "then if I asked you if you were a traitor—and mind you, you were a traitor—what would you say?"

The king was pacing in front of his window now, looking over his shoulder uncertainly toward the hidden spot where his door stood. It didn't look like an event happening in real time through that scope. It looked like a picture, impossibly defined and rendered in full living detail.

Rob watched, listening to the silence, searching it for signs of movement. Pointer already had the knife out. And Rob's back was turned toward him, facing danger like a man who had nothing to fear, nothing to hide.

"Same as you in that situation," Rob said.

"What did you think of her?" Pointer asked, "Your wife."

"Don't ask me that," Rob said. Even now he knew the answer Pointer would be looking for. It was that final cynical proof his conscience would need to collect before deciding to kill Rob or let him live.

Say you hated her, curse her memory, and then there might still be some doubt.

Pointer was daring him to speak treason.

Those words were a gentle wind on the fire in Rob's heart. He watched through the scope, nodding imperceptibly long before he would answer. The king in the window walked away in his room, out of sight, out of Rob's crosshairs. There would be no execution today. Of that Rob was certain. No execution but his own.

Because he decided then that he had said enough.

"Pointer," Rob said, "It's none of your goddamn business."

The sun was starting to spill over the rim of the mountain above them, drawing their shadows backward slowly. And as Pointer moved, Rob could see it even from his prone position at the edge of the cliff. He cast his eyes right and saw a hand and a knife flashing in sunlight. Pointer was standing now, having moved out of sight while Rob was watching the king. He had not drawn the knife to clean his nails.

"My peace of mind, Rob. For our continued friendship. Please tell me."

There was an impossible smell on the morning breeze, overpowering the scent of men and weapons. It was familiar, but distant. And yet it was what Rob noticed as he lay prone on the cliff's edge, dropping his eye from the scope once again to look at the sunlight creeping across the ground.

"Pointer," Rob said. This was it. Die an honest man, or live.

His life had already started to flash before his eyes.

He had never joined the king. He had been born in the city. And when he had sworn his fealty day after day as a child, he hadn't understood the terrible cost.

Rob would be his own man now, if only for this last instant. In his mind he cut every bond tethering him to a lifetime of deception. It was natural, like a ship cutting its anchor. He could smell lemongrass now. Drifting on unfamiliar water.

"Pointer," Rob said, "I'll tell you now. Men like you can't understand what love is. The answer is yes. I did care about her. And if you need to erase that to satisfy your king, then do it the only way you can. The truth is, I hate you all."

There was silence then. It lasted a long time as the two of them passed the moment. Pointer said,

"Something just dropped off the side of the city. A banner."

He was right. It was being held by a dozen specks of hands. Pots were being banged by heavy spoons as men in the background raised rifles overhead rhythmically in chant. Rob lowered the rifle down to read the words on the banner.

DO IT, POINTER

But he wouldn't have needed the scope to read it. Not if he'd known ahead of time what it might say.

"What do they mean?" Rob asked.

"They mean do it. Kill you," Pointer said as he holstered his knife and leaned his hand on the pistol at his side, "They'll be expecting to hear my gunshot."

"But how could they know?"

"They don't," Pointer said, "They know who I am. They don't know who you are. Not yet. Look up at the tower again."

Once again through the scope, Rob looked up at the tower. The king was hanging out the window by his hands, purple silks blowing in the wind as he ran felt shoes raw on the tower's ivory exterior. He was trying to pull his own weight up, back into the window, past a man with a rifle.

"This changes things," Pointer said, "I would have slept easy if you'd said you hated your wife. As it stands, I might have to let you live."

A strange purple shape was diving to the ground from the tower. In the distance on the city's plate more gunfire was echoing. It wasn't the rattling exchange between two opposing forces. It was the ecstatic rumble of celebration. The king is dead. Long live the king. May we live forever.

There was a scent like fire and lemongrass.

Thirty-Five Years
LynC

THEY EMERGED INTO THE CAVE through the portal one after the other, different sources, same destination.

Embarrassed, they exchanged guarded pleasantries and, as the second person to arrive, she agreed to wait twenty-four hours to let the other lady get ahead. It wouldn't do for them both to contact the Portal Guardian at the same time, lest their identities and the true reason for their entering of the closed world be compromised. Besides, she was sure the other agent would object to her presence if she found out just who her target was. Maybe even stop her. She, on the other hand, couldn't care less where the other one was going. It was unlikely to have any impact on her own mission.

So she settled to wait. It was pleasant enough in the cave, a good view of the surrounding hills, a nice sunny day, but the emergency food supplies hadn't been kept stocked up and she was bored.

The small blonde paced, irritated. Dare she exercise? Or would the smell of old sweat put her target off before she even began? She explored the nearby surroundings and finding a deep pool, stripped off, and dived in.

The Portal Guardian arrived while she was under, and was watching beside her clothes when she came up for air. She swam for shore, annoyed with herself. She should have realized the arrival of the other agent would require him to make a report to his government and that he would come up to the cave at some stage during the day.

"Whoo hoo!" He was evidently appreciative of what he saw as she emerged.

She pretended embarrassment. When he showed no signs of being a gentleman she gave up and came over. At least he had the grace to hand her her top before asking her where she was going.

She examined him closely, a man in his fifties, going grey, but still with a full head of hair, originally brunette. Stocky without being excessively fat. She could tell he worked out. The stomach was flat for someone his age, but he didn't overdo it, there were no bulging pects under the shirt. But the blue eyes were dead. This sent a chill of fear through her.

IN his turn he saw a small trimly built lady with long flowing blonde hair. Mid-twenties he estimated, and not at all shy of being naked with a strange man, therefore experienced. She could only have come through the cave portal.

Another one. He'd just sent one onwards. Sighing, he turned away and continued on to the cave.

She followed and watched as he restocked the shelves. "Bit late with that, weren't you?"

He shrugged. Who cared? He was doing it now; that was all that mattered.

"Where you headed?" he asked again.

"Baltimore Inn."

"That's me."

"We can travel together," she said.

Her delight was as fake as her welcoming smile had been. He inclined his head and led the way from the cave.

THAT evening she was the life of the bar, flirting with all the locals. He served drinks and kept himself to himself. Although she did notice, it was he who was called on to umpire the arm wrestling. Almost, he smiled as he watched them laughing and fooling around.

They went to bed separately and alone.

SHE was still there in the morning, asking about the local sights. He wished she wouldn't pretend. She wasn't the first assassin to be sent through the portal, and hopefully, wouldn't be the last he would be alive to deal with. But he answered her gravely and sent her to look at the local cemetery where some poet or other was supposed to be buried. He'd never bothered.

Instead he headed back to the cave and sent word of her arrival to his bosses, bagging a few rabbits on the way back to give the lie to why he'd gone out, gun in hand.

Over lunch she waxed lyrical about the poet and asked if he had any of his works. He sent her to the local vicarage where he knew the vicar had some souvenirs and other paraphernalia for sale. The few books he owned weren't in any language the locals would recognize, and they were well hidden.

She tried again to engage him in conversation over tea, and again afterwards, but he was too busy. He was the local publican, after all.

Again they went to bed alone and separately.

The next day being Sunday, when pubs were only open a few hours, he had no such excuse. She set herself to charm.

Almost, he felt himself taken in. Almost. She was so determined he allowed her to think he had been, and they went down to his room in the cellars for the night.

He was surprised she tried nothing that night. Maybe he'd given his alert state away. Surprised again when nothing happened the next night or the next.

She let the locals know they were a pair and stopped flirting. Even started helping out in the bar. Within a fortnight she was a fixture.

He knew now what her orders were.

She wasn't here to close the portal down. She was here to replace him. He wondered fleetingly which big-wig back at Central he'd offended this time. Then shrugged it off. As long as he was still trapped on this planet he would do his job. And his job was to help any agents coming through the portal with local camouflage and help them on their way, regardless of where they came from or were going to. So he enjoyed her company, but forbore to relax too much.

His eyes remained dead. She knew she wasn't getting through to him. The one time he'd shown any real emotion was when she moved the gold ring he wore on a chain around his neck out of the way. He'd instantly and painfully grabbed the hand touching the ring. Grabbed with such force that she knew the hand couldn't be human. The man was a Cyborg. What else had been replaced? What else hadn't her people told her? Was she being set up to fail? That wasn't an option.

When she'd let go, he'd left the bed and removed the chain without a word, before returning. After that, he removed it before getting into the bed every night. It was a given now, that they would spend the night together, but the pattern of his breathing never dropped into a deep sleep rhythm.

She lay awake beside him, night after night, wondering how safe she was. Wondering if he could be killed. She was going to have to try for it anyway. Time was running out. She had been given a month to take control of the portal. Tonight. Tonight she would do it.

Accordingly, when she thought he was about to climax, she pulled out her little needle and rammed home … into thin air.

Her right wrist was wrenched back and slammed into a cuff link attached to the bed post. Where had that come from? He leant back on his left elbow surveying her startled prone form. His face still remote.

The eyes, even now, had no feeling in them, as he uttered through clenched teeth, "Now, the fun really begins."

He lay back down, and finished the job. That night he finally slept deeply, while she lay, too frightened to move, awake, beside him.

In the morning he left her there, coming back after a few hours with a jug of water, and, of all things, a chamber pot.

By this time she was so desperate she used it anyway. He shook his head at the damage her attempts to free herself had done to her wrist. Went away to dispose of the pot's contents, and came back with a basin of warm water. She flung it back at him when he tried to wash her. He shrugged and left her to enjoy the wet bed by herself.

She wept and screamed, but no-one came near. Too late she remembered they were in his room, under the cellars of the pub. No-one was going to hear.

"I have orders to kill you," he said conversationally on his return.

"So do I," she growled.

"Looks like I'm currently winning."

He climbed on top of her.

Afterwards he rolled her onto her right side to ease the pressure on her wrist and lay against her back. His presence was warm and ironically comforting.

"The way I see it," he remarked, "there are only two possible outcomes. You die, or I die. But we have a week before your people come through. You want to die now, or in a week's time?"

She wept and said nothing. Her instinct said, 'Now', but her training said 'Live'.

"Thought so," he commented, and draping the still damp blanket over the two of them he went to sleep.

In the morning she accepted both the pot and, indignity of indignities, a sponge bath, and was rewarded by a change of bed linen and a ration bar. He also bandaged her wrist before leaving her alone for the day.

She scrambled onto the bed as far away as her wrist would allow and alternated rocking and weeping for a good part of the day. Night brought him and the pot back again. At least she assumed it was night. No daylight reached this far underground, and he'd left the light on all day for her. She accepted the pot with surly grace and was rewarded with another ration bar, and the refilling of her water jug. He then made her clean her teeth into the hand held basin, before stretching out behind her again. This night and for many nights thereafter he went straight to sleep and didn't bother her.

"What have you told your clients?" she asked one night.

"You're off doing touristy things."

And on another occasion, "I'm overdue."

"Well, don't blame me," came the sleepy reply, "You knew I had no protection, and you insisted anyway."

As far as it went, that was true. When she was trying to charm him she had gone ahead despite his protestations about lack of such things.

"It's going to need two parents."

"Well, it's just out of luck isn't it? If I die, it will only have you, and if you die, it won't be an issue."

"You'll kill your own child?"

"What makes you so sure it's mine?"

She let it go. He knew she hadn't been a virgin from the start.

The next day she renewed the abuse on her wrist. To no avail. The handcuffs, and the bed had to be military issue, they were so secure.

A week passed in this manner.

One day he returned early, "Your people are here. My people are here too. You want to die now, or be handed over to my people?"

This time she had no hesitation. She had no doubt he could and would kill her, but her training said, 'Live'.

"Hand me over."

He was careless releasing her from the bed, the pot made a good solid thunk on the side of his head. She counted to ten, but he didn't stir. At some stage he'd brought her bag into the room. She dressed and left to deal with her side of the fracas. As she left she locked the door and turned the lights out.

HE woke to the cold and dark with a ringing in his ears. She must have cut the power to the room.

He saw splodges of bright colors against the dark background when he moved. His head hurt. He knew he moaned but only the ringing greeted him.

Dark.

Cold.

Pain.

He was still alive.

Alone, in the dark and the cold, he despaired. Why couldn't she kill him? He gave her a chance. Had he been too kind to her? He'd imprisoned and raped her, not once, but twice. Wasn't that grounds enough? Didn't she hate him?

Moaning he crawled in what he hoped was the direction of the bathroom. There, he had a candle and matches. Good old fashioned lighting which didn't require power. He hoped his stock of pain killers was adequate for this pain in his head.

Lit candle in hand, he made his way to the door. It was locked. He'd expected that, but the switch was on the other side, and the light's remote control did not work through the thickness of the walls and door.

This hadn't started as a bedroom. It was a storeroom to which he'd added plumbing. After years in various interplanetary prisons he didn't feel comfortable if he couldn't barricade himself in. Now it was yet another prison. He'd had worse. At least he had running water.

And food. He dragged the case out from under the bed and checked supplies. He'd restocked the cave a month ago, and not received any supplies through the portal since. He'd been feeding her from the case too. There were only five packets of the ration bars left. Five times six. That meant …

His head hurt too much to work it out. When would she be back? Would she be back? He hoped so. The room was impenetrable, the door unbreakable, and the lock unpickable.

Deliberately so.

Strange how he no longer wanted to die.

There was nothing to do for now. He took a torch from the case and pushed it back under the bed. He blew the candle out and lay down.

Waited.

He knew he had been asleep, because he awoke.

His head felt much better, but he was ravenous and thirsty, and it was still pitch dark. There was another need, and when he realized it wouldn't wait, he stumbled across the room and found the bathroom. And heaved, and heaved again, and cried as the pain re-awoke in his head. He wept, as he tried to clean up by torch light, with only toilet paper to wipe with and blinding red flashes interfering with his vision.

A check of the watch implanted in his cyborgwrist indicated he'd been here for two days.

She hadn't been near him for two days? Was she still alive herself? Did anyone know where he was?

He numbly went about the ritual of 'getting up'. The warm shower was so soothing, but he found he had to sit in it as his legs buckled underneath him. Then teeth, clean clothes, water and food. He ate only a single bar. He didn't know how long they would have to last. Then back on the bed to wait. Reluctantly he turned the torch off and lay down.

The Dark crowded in, peopled with monsters from his past. He screamed and turned the torch back on.

Less than five minutes had passed.

He remembered receiving his hand, and wished he could forget. He had been fighting in some war on some forgotten planet in dense jungle when his troop had fallen into an ambush. They said he was lucky to be alive. They said he'd accounted for half the dead. They said he was the reason only half his troop had died. But they still sent him to a prison hospital. Despite having an unrecoverable wrist and hand, they still wouldn't release him from his contract.

Instead they had 'fixed' him. An experimental addition to the end of his forearm. He hadn't given permission for the experiment. Apparently, despite his hero status, he was still a deserter, and they didn't need it.

Then they sent him back into the field, this time as a bomb disposal expert. His new addition provided the required steadiness. Ten years he had served in that role. Ten long years of being shunted from planet to planet, disarm this bomb, that bomb, learn about a new style of bomb, and off again. Always under armed guard. He had tried to escape too often for them to trust him.

An accident with someone else's bomb had landed him back in hospital, but still they wouldn't let him go. Still they fetched him back when he'd evaded his guards. This time they had 'retired' him by exiling him to this planet to care for the portal and help those coming through. For seventeen years he had watched others coming and going, but he could not pass. Every time he stepped into the portal, sirens went off, lights flashed, and the portal closed down till someone in Central released it again.

He was as effectively trapped on the planet as he now was in his bedroom. One large prison swapped for a smaller one.

Still a prison.

How was he going to survive? How long would he have to survive? He touched the ring hanging on his chest, and thought, 'I will survive'. Turned the torch back off, and forced himself to endure. It made no difference whether his eyes were open or closed, so he closed them.

Again, knew he had been asleep because his watch alarm went off and woke him. The beeping echoed loudly in the silence.

Day 3. Still dark. Still cold. He was shivering. Felt like he'd been doing it for a while. Ravenous again. Not surprising. Head all woolly. Bad ache on the side. Thirsty again. He found the torch and attended to business.

Day 4, then 5. He screamed in the dark, and wept with the pain, and fear, and despair. His pain killers ran out. The pain distracted him from the never ending dark. And always the cold. With power on, the room was heated. Now it got colder and colder. There was only one blanket, and one towel. He raided his cupboards for warm clothes, but all the coats were upstairs near the front door.

Eventually it ceased to bother him. The pain diminished as time progressed. He filled his empty belly with water, but it was never enough. He took his belt in a notch, and then another.

And always, the dark, and the silence.

Broken sometime by a high pitched keen. Not sure where it came from. It disappeared as soon as he paid attention to it. He held the ring and willed himself to endure the phantoms.

Days spread into weeks. He counted the days off by the number of ration bars he'd consumed. One bar per day. The days marked out by his watch's alarm. Every morning the same ritual. Toilet, water, exercises, shower; all in the dark. Lastly he allowed himself some precious light from his dwindling supply of batteries and ate his one ration bar.

Day 20. He saw a piece of paper next to the door. It read 'They think you are dead'.

Not sure how long he had missed it, he wept for joy, and pounded on the door. Nothing. But now he had hope. She was still alive, he was still alive. One day she would release him. He prayed to the ring that that day be soon.

But the days and the dark continued.

Day 29, 30. He no longer had any batteries. Was down to his last candle and the last two bars. Had stopped feeling hunger, he couldn't remember how far back. The exercises were shorter, sloppier. He couldn't remember why he was doing them, but it was part of 'The Ritual'. The Ritual was all he had to look forward to. After the Ritual, the Silence and the Dark again. The Phantoms were his friends. They were all he had.

Day 31: half a bar.

Day 32: half of the remaining half. He pounded on the door. Weak, hungry, despairing.

Day 33: The last mouthful.

Day ???: Unfamiliar sensation. Warm. Noise. Behind his eyelids, Grey.

He opened eyelids, heavy eyelids, a fraction. Light. Blinding, searing light. He cried out and shut his eyes again.

"Wake up!"

He blinked stupidly at her. Would she release him? He tried to sit up. The light made his eyes stream, but he had to look at her. What was she planning?

"I lost the baby," she was saying.

What baby?

"Get up!" she screamed at him, raining blows on him.

This wasn't The Ritual. Where was the Dark? He whimpered. She pulled him to his feet, and dragged him to the bathroom. He kept falling over. She had to catch him to stop him hurting himself. She threw him in the shower fully clothed and turned the cold tap on. He collapsed, shivering. How long? How many days since the food ran out? Since he stopped bothering? He shivered and wanted his friends, the Dark and the Phantoms, back.

Then he started vomiting. Clear yellow liquid. There was nothing in his stomach. Where was this coming from?

She turned the shower off, forced a drink of water down his throat. His stomach stopped heaving, but the shivering continued.

She was angry. He didn't know why. What had he done? She pulled him out of the shower, stripped him, rubbed him as dry as she could and half carried, half dragged him naked back to the bed.

"You're supposed to be dead!"

Why was she yelling? Wasn't it good that he was alive?

She went away. Left him with the light, the eye searing light. He tried to hide under the blanket, behind his arms, and his eyelids, but it was all-pervasive.

She came back. "Drink!"

Couldn't she say anything without yelling it? She pulled him upright and put a cup to his lips. The drink was white and ... and creamy? Was that the word?

"Milk?" he puzzled softly. Barely a whisper.

"Yes," she replied. She handed him a dry biscuit. It wasn't a ration bar. Ration bars were food. Not this. The Ritual was broken. He opened his mouth to scream but only a thin keening sound emerged. He'd heard that before. In the Dark. The Blessed Silent Dark. Comforted, he stopped.

"Eat," she ordered.

Obediently he put it in his mouth. Maybe she would stop yelling and leave him alone if he did what she asked. Maybe.

She rolled her eyes, "Chew," she ordered.

He chewed. At some point his own reflexes took over and he swallowed. The next biscuit was easier.

"Thirsty," he croaked. Was that his voice?

She handed the milk to him. His hand shook. He put both hands around the glass and brought it to his mouth. Only the android hand obeyed him. The glass slipped. She caught it with an exclamation of disgust. Put it back to his lips and helped him drink. Held out another biscuit. He pushed it away. He'd had enough. He lay down, his back to her.

She left. She turned the light off, but left the door open. He cried for his lost Dark.

She returned again and again. Every time the same. Drag him to the toilet, drag him back to the bed, a drink of milk, and a few dry biscuits. A new Ritual. He embraced it. Until he vomited and shat himself all at the same time.

She screamed at him and hit him and dragged him back into the shower. Left him with cold water running over his naked body. Why cold? He fumbled around in the unfamiliar light and found the hot tap. Let himself sink back and relax.

SHE pulled him out and turned the water off. She was confused that both taps needed turning off. Looked at him. He was sitting on the bathroom floor weeping and shivering. It couldn't have been him, surely? Why wasn't he dead? She was sure he'd wanted to die. She was sure she'd left him for dead when she hit him, but three days later when she'd checked he was still alive, asleep or unconscious on the bed, she didn't know. She'd fled, sealing him back up again, without finding out. She'd already told them he was dead. She wasn't sure why she'd come back later and pushed the note under the door. Maybe she wanted him alive? Why hadn't he died? She should have been dealing with a corpse not mothering this sniveling bag of bones.

She put him on the toilet and started drying him with quick rough swipes. She pushed the ring aside and he reacted exactly the same as he had done over two months ago. There was no strength in his body at all. He couldn't even hold a glass, but his grip was painfully strong. She'd forgotten he was a Cyborg. Was that why he was still alive? She let go and he clutched the ring to himself. She dragged him back to the newly changed bed and left him for the night.

HE slept. He awoke with a need to return to the bathroom. In the Dark he knew his way. In the half light from the adjoining stairwell he was confused. He almost didn't make it.

Sat on the toilet and leant sideways over the sink, voiding from both ends. Afterwards he dragged the towel over his shoulders and just sat there for a long time. Twice more he voided. Just downwards this time.

The old Ritual was safer. He knew where to get more ration bars. He washed, he exercised, he showered, he dressed.

And left.

Up the stairs he staggered, out the back door, and across the yard. Knew he wasn't going to make it. Crawled into the back of the hen house and lay down in the straw. They squawked a little and settled back down. They knew him. His presence wouldn't put them off laying. He slept again.

In the morning the darkness of the hen house protected his eyes from too much light. He awoke feeling much better. Clear headed. He ate two eggs raw, straight from the shell, and contemplated the future.

They thought he was dead, she had written all those weeks (months?) ago. How long did it take to remove his DNA from the portal registry? He clutched the ring and wondered if he was still trapped here.

Mid morning he saw her racing off to the hills. Realized that serendipitously his weakness had protected him. Reflected, that since she had told everyone she had killed him, she couldn't now get help catching and returning him.

He lay back and wondered how long he could safely stay where he was. How long before his neighbor next attempted to clean the hen house? A few days, he decided. It looked quite clean, and it was only done once a week. Good. Safe to rest here. Plenty of food. He slept again.

Night came, and he snuck inside to attend to his hygiene and pack a few things.

Then back to the hen house to wait out the day. He felt much stronger now.

Another day of rest. She came and went, obviously searching. He kept quiet and lay low in the straw. Sometime after midnight he ate a few eggs and made his move.

Still too weak to make it all the way, he holed up for the day in a smaller cave he'd discovered on one of his trips to and from the portal. Front entrance was behind a thorn bush. That wasn't the entrance he had first found though. The entrance he had discovered accidentally after falling through it, was a hole in the roof. His fall had been broken by a mound of leaves he'd thought drifted in over the years. Later he had found out it was a popular lover's trysting place and the tradition was to bring a few handfuls to add to the mound on every visit.

He trusted that she had both searched this area, and that the locals hadn't informed her of the cave. He ate his eggs and composed himself to wait.

The light when it came was blinding, but he closed his eyes and let the sun bathe him through the hole. Where he wanted to go, it was always sunny. He had to learn to cope. Clutching the ring, he slept in the sunlight. It was darkness and cold which woke him this time. Strange how quickly his body readjusted.

He made his way to the portal that night.

No-one there. No obvious alarms waiting to alert her. He passed his real arm over the scanner. No alarms flashing. No voice informing him he was not authorized to travel.

He finally faced the next hurdle. The android arm. He could not travel with that much metal and living electrics without alerting every portal he travelled through.

There were guns in the cupboards, all vintages, all styles. He selected a laser and charged it up. Held it in his right and placed his left on a counter. Hesitated. Put the gun down. Found a clean cloth and put his left down on that. Tried again.

Found himself leaning on the counter, eyes closed, and crying again. He'd been twenty-five when they had forced it on him, but he'd now carried it and used it for twenty seven years. Over half his life.

But the alternative?

He wasn't going back to prison! It didn't matter which side controlled the portal now. His own people would put him in prison just as fast as hers. Taking a deep breath, he gritted his teeth, and sliced.

Retained consciousness long enough to finish the job, but then he fainted.

Woke up to find he had dragged the cloth down with him and what little blood there'd been had bled into it, before the cauterized wound had fully sealed.

He admired the clean neat wound. It was raw and hurt like hell, especially when he tried to wiggle his non-existent fingers, but it was all human, and it was all him.

Now, finally, he was free!

After thirty five years, he dared dream again. He touched the ring and dared think of *her* again. Wondered if she was even alive. Would she be happy to see him? He didn't care. Even if she were married, with a string of grandkids, as was the way of her people, he just wanted to see her again. He'd never even been given a chance to say good-bye.

He set about preparations for leaving.

No credit rating had displayed when he had presented his arm earlier. That meant he had to pay in advance. One of the cupboards held the money of various planets, including inter-planetary standards. There was enough for where he was going. And some in the local currency of his target destination as well. He swapped both with all the money in his pockets.

Ate a ration bar and packed several more. Raided the cupboards for anything else which might be useful. Rescued his few meager possessions from where they were hidden beyond the portal and composed himself.

Did he have everything? He surveyed his collection. Change of clothes, toiletries, money, books, fake ID—he couldn't use it, it was too traceable, but so he could show people when they asked. Credit cards in the fake ID, a dozen ration bars, two eggs, water bottle. He went out to fill the bottle at the pool and eat the remaining eggs. No sign of movement down the hill.

Time to go. Seventeen years he'd been forced to live in this backwater. Seventeen years since his last attempt to escape.

Well, there was no escape more final than death. Smiling grimly, he placed the money on the tray and called up his first destination. He was on his way.

AT the station they directed him to the fields. She was still working the same farm her family had always owned. A fifty something year-old woman, in a country which was not kind to the aging process. He watched from the embankment as she pulled herbs for the evening meal.

She looked up at the stranger watching her, narrowed her eyes, and then drew herself up and berated him, "What you call this? Is thirty-five year. You say you come back one hour with ring for marriage man. Thirty-five year is not one hour."

"I know," he apologized, suddenly giddy with relief.

She was still the same beloved. Old and wrinkled, but still undaunted; still full of the vigor and courage which had attracted him so long ago.

He took the ring from his neck and held it out with his one hand. "I am free now. Are you still free?"

SHE came towards him. Noticed the gaunt hollows in the cheeks, the dark shadows under his eyes. And the eyes. The gentle, loving, humorous eyes, of the young military conscript she had fallen in love with as a girl. She smiled and accepted the ring. "Not still free. Again free."

She slipped the ring on its chain over her neck, and taking his arm, pulled him back towards the house. "Come. Meet you son."

Ruamo's Price
Sarah Celiann

THE PATH THROUGH THE FOREST had not been walked in decades, and Lanai was barely able to follow it, even when accessing all of her ancestral magic. Her mother had not walked this path, but her grandmother had, and if Lanai concentrated very hard she could see the path she had taken through the trees. Behind her, Maile and Malo, her twin guardians, followed, their every senses alert and ready to defend her from enemies she couldn't be on guard for.

They reached a clearing, little more than a small circle of grass in the otherwise unbroken foliage, and Lanai stopped to rest. Maile set her spear aside and handed Lanai a water skin before sitting down next to her. They drank in silence. It was nice to be able to trust someone to simply sit next to her and be still, Lanai thought. Maile's brother, however, was restless, stalking around the clearing, bow half drawn, ready to fire at the slightest movement.

"Are you cold?" Maile asked.

Lanai shook her head. "Are you?"

"No. The Captain was right to make us wear so many layers."

Lanai smiled. Captain Akamu may not have been particularly thrilled to provide supplies to the temple, but once he'd realized they were determined to go, he wouldn't allow them to leave unless properly equipped. He'd provided Maile and Malo with the same uniforms his guard wore, undecorated black leather armor with thick cloth underneath to keep them warm. Lanai wore the same cloth under her ceremonial leather armor, which only she as High Priestess could wear. It was light brown and had been stitched with thread that was the color of the blue waters that surrounded Honua'aina. Around the hem Lanai herself had embroidered the sacred runes that when spoken aloud made up the morning prayer to Ruamo.

The day had started out almost warm, but it had grown cold, and Lanai was certain they would begin to see snowflakes before they reached Ruamo's High Temple.

Malo walked up beside them, his breath fogging the air. "Are we almost there?"

Lanai offered him the water skin. "Halfway."

Malo frowned. "We may have to make camp."

Maile shrugged and pulled a strand of her long, black hair out of her eyes. "Then we make camp. We have the supplies."

"I have never slept without the barrier between myself and those creatures, and I do not ever want to," Malo said.

"Then you should have stayed home," replied Maile.

"Maybe we should have."

"If we had, then the barrier would be no more in a matter of days, and you would still be sleeping outside of its protection," Lanai pointed out. "We are halfway to the temple, and the closer we get, the easier it becomes for me to sense my grandmother's spirit. We will be able to make camp in the safety of the shrine."

"Is there a barrier around the shrine?" Malo asked.

"The High Temple houses Ruamo's spirit. Surely she will protect us within its walls."

Malo shouldered his bow and crossed his arms. "If the city's barrier is failing, why wouldn't Ruamo's power around her High Temple be weakened, too?"

Maile took a drink of water. "Peace, Malo. We will find out when we reach the High Temple. Until then, there is nothing we can do but remain vigilant."

Malo scowled, but said nothing. Maile handed him the water skin, and he drank a little. A single flake of snow floated down from the sky and landed on his nose. He brushed it away, but others followed.

Lanai smiled. "When my grandmother walked this path, snow was a rare, once in a lifetime event. It was hot the day she made her pilgrimage. She wore no armor, only a plain dress and sandals. Her sister had braided a flower into her hair before she left that morning. It was bright red and its perfume swirled around her as she traveled." Lanai closed her eyes. When she tracked her grandmother's spirit like this, it seemed so easy to step back into the past, when the world was warmer and safer, and the morning prayer was sung on every street in the city each day.

Maile shook her gently. "Lanai, please don't get lost in the past. We need you in the present."

Lanai shook her head and the image of her grandmother, so vivid and real, faded away. "I am sorry. I have never had to follow a spirit path that is so old and faded." Lanai stood. "Let's move on. We must make the High Temple by nightfall."

There was a soft crunch from the east, and a Wraith stepped into the clearing. It was short, perhaps five feet tall, and looked like a dying man, with thin, grey skin and no hair. Lanai had been taught that the Wraiths were men once, but that was long ago, and they had been killed so many times that she was sure there was more clay and dirt to the creature than actual skinflesh.

Malo hit it in the chest with an arrow, and then shot another into the socket where its right eye would have been. It fell to the ground and crumbled away into it. Lanai knew it would rise again somewhere else on Honua'aina, perhaps closer to the city or perhaps farther. The Wraiths never stayed dead.

The forest was silent. "Was there only one?" Maile asked, spear in hand.

"They have always attacked in packs," Malo said, readying an arrow.

There was a crash behind them. Lanai whirled around, in time to see Maile stab one of the Wraiths with her spear. It collapsed to the ground in a crumbling pile, and then a second one slammed into Lanai, knocking her to the ground and clawing at her chest with hands made more of rock than bone.

Lanai had worn her armor every day for years when out surveying the barrier. Every single day since she'd come of age, and that was more than two decades of days. The moments where she actually needed it, however, were few and far between, and in those moments she was glad to have it. It may have been uncomfortable, but now it prevented the Wraith from tearing at her skin.

Lanai drew her dagger. It was a short, with a well-worn handle, and one of the few metal objects left on the island. It was her honor as High Priestess to carry it. She stabbed the creature in the neck with it. It drew back, giving her a clear shot at the chest. With a single stroke, the magic animating it snuffed out like a candle, and the Wraith crumbled into a pile of dirt and bone on top of her.

Lanai stood and brushed the remains of the creature off of her. They disappeared into the earth. That, too, was part of Ruamo's blessing. Tumata raised the creatures and Ruamo took their remains back into herself. The cycle would continued until the day when one of them vanquished the other and took their place among the pantheon as the true God or Goddess of the Earth. Lanai prayed that when that day came it would be Ruamo who would ascend. She shuddered to think of a world populated only by the Wraiths.

Maile pulled her spear out of the last Wraith in the pack. All told, there had been five of them. Malo walked across the clearing, picking up arrows, examining their stone tips for damage and putting those that passed muster back into his quiver.

"Is anyone injured?" Lanai asked. Malo and Maile shook their heads. "Then we had best move on before more of them come."

They walked away from the clearing. It took several minutes for Lanai to find the path again, but once she did she found that it was becoming more and more clear as they got closer to the temple. "Ruamo guides us well," Maile remarked.

"Lanai guides us well," replied Malo.

Maile scowled at him. "Can't you keep such thoughts to yourself when we're out beyond the protection of the barrier?"

"What protection is the barrier? Two of the city guard were badly injured by Wraiths just yesterday. And besides that, look at what falls from the sky, Maile. Ruamo's power is fading."

"Ruamo does not control the weather," Maile protested.

"It's a sign," Malo insisted. "Ruamo abandons us. That is why the shrine of worship is nearly empty at the midweek gathering."

"Ruamo is alive and well," Lanai said, placing her hand on Malo's shoulder. "I know that it's hard for you to believe when your eyes see only the things that are going wrong, such as the weather and the barrier. But know this. If you could see through my eyes, you would see Ruamo's touch all around us. She is in the roots of the trees, making them strong to provide us with wood and shade. She nourishes our crops and sustains our livestock. She will provide a way to restore the barrier. I know this in my heart."

Malo bit his lip. "Lanai, I have trusted you since I was a child, but you can't fix everything."

"What would you have us do instead, Malo?" Maile asked.

"We build boats and cross the waters."

Maile scoffed. "If you try to cross the waters you'll only find more water."

"Why did our ancestors build boats, then?" Malo asked.

"To fish," said Lanai, gently stepping around a clump of pohu, a plant that would cause a painful rash if it touched exposed skin.

"There are plenty of fish along the coast. We don't need boats."

"There are plenty of fish now," Lanai said. "Long ago, before the barrier was in place, fish didn't come near the shores. Our ancestors had to use boats to fish."

"And to travel," Malo insisted. "There are other islands besides ours. We used to travel between them. Wahine says-"—"

"Wahine has gone mad in her old age," Maile said. "I love her a much as you, Malo, but she can't even remember where she lives, let alone where our ancestors used to sail."

"Well, I believe her," Malo said.

They were quiet after that. The snow stopped, but the temperature continued to fall as the sun slowly set, until they were all cold even in their many layers. The path, however, became easier to follow, until Lanai no longer needed her magic to follow it. Even Maile and Malo could see a break in the trees that indicated where they should walk.

The last of the sunlight faded away, and they traveled the last half mile or so by torchlight. Lanai was exhausted by the time they reached the temple, but the sight of its sturdy blue stone overgrown with moss and vines lifted her spirits quite a bit. She paused to trace the ornate symbol carved into the three pillars that stood arranged in a triangle outside of the entrance, set back from the line of pillars that formed a perimeter around the High Temple. This was Ruamo's name, written in the old language, which even she could not read. She had only seen it once before, in the waking dream she had entered to inherit her mother's title as High Priestess, but it was exactly as she'd remembered it.

There was a sound in the distance, a rumbling, like something was crawling its way out of the Earth. Maile and Malo reached for their weapons, but Lanai shook her head. "We are safe here."

The Wraiths approached. There were a dozen of them, more than Lanai had ever seen in one place before. They walked slowly toward the temple. Malo notched an arrow, ready to fire. Maile held her spear ready. Lanai simply stood and watched.

When the Wraiths approached the pillars, they simply stopped. Lanai could feel a gentle, comforting power emanating from the runes carved on them. Maile put her spear away and walked up to the creatures, stopping just a foot away.

"I've never seen them this close before," she said. "It's strange, as though I can see the magic animating them."

"Leave them be," Malo said.

"I wasn't planning on trying to touch them, Malo."

They made camp just outside the doorway. Maile and Malo started a fire and cooked stew. Lanai ate it gladly. As soon as she was done eating, exhaustion caught up with her and she fell asleep as Maile and Malo argued over who would keep watch first.

Every night Lanai dreamed of her grandmother, whom she'd never met in the waking world. Sometimes they talked, though Lanai never could remember what was said upon waking. Other times they simply sat and watched the people pass in the court-yard of the City Temple. If they were in her grandmother's time, there were many priests and priestesses, along with students and worshippers. If they dreamt of Lanai's time, the courtyard was quiet and empty, save for the occasional elderly priestess medi-tating under the trees.

That night outside of the temple, Lanai didn't dream at all. She opened her eyes after hours of black unconsciousness to see the sun streaming down through the trees and for the first time in a long time she felt the slow itch of fear crawl down her back.

She stood up and tried to shake some of the cold from her limbs. Malo was preparing a breakfast of porridge and dried fruit.

"Good morning," he said, stirring the pot.

"Good morning. How late did I sleep?"

Malo shrugged. "Maile and I have been up for a few hours."

"You should have woken me."

"We thought we'd let you sleep. We aren't in much of a hurry." Malo gestured behind her.

Lanai turned toward the pillars where the Wraiths had been lined up the night before and gasped. There were now dozens of them, clustered in a giant mass by the pillars, and Lanai could feel the power of the barrier struggling to push them back. They stood still, not moving. Maile sat nearby, leaning against a pillar, spear by her side, watching them.

"How long have they been here?"

"They've been trickling in slowly all night. I haven't seen any new ones for an hour or so, though." Malo handed Lanai a bowl and spoon. "What worries me is Maile. She's been staring at them all morning."

Lanai took a second bowl of porridge and some fruit and brought it over to Maile, who took the food but otherwise barely seemed to notice that Lanai was there.

"Do they frighten you?" Lanai asked.

"No. They fascinate me." She ate a spoonful of porridge. "I've never seen them like this before. Usually I'm up on the wall, and they're far away with the barrier between us. Even theThe handful of times we hunted them as practice there wasn't much time for study. And now, they're just standing there. They don't move. Not even a little. They don't re-adjust their arms or shift their weight from foot to foot. I never realized how much living things move until now."

Lanai looked at the Wraiths. Had she not known what they were, it would have been easy to think they were statues.

"What do you think they're waiting for?"

Lanai looked at Maile, recognizing the fear in her eyes. "For Ruamo's power to fail, or for Tumata's orders to come."

"No," came Malo's voice from behind them, "They're waiting for us to try and leave so they can tear our throats out."

Maile flicked some porridge at him. "Thanks, Malo. That makes me feel much better."

Malo laughed. "You don't want to start a food fight with me. I've got a whole pot of the stuff back there."

Maile stuck her tongue out at him and Lanai couldn't help but laugh. "Come on," she said, gently nudging Maile away from the Wraiths, "Let's find a way to get the temple door open."

The door to the High Temple hadn't been opened in decades, and it proved to be stuck firmly shut. Working together, the three of them pulled on the door and it began to open slowly, bit by bit. When it was about a foot open, Malo gave one last pull and suddenly the door flew open, knocking him over.

There was a rumbling, and Lanai felt the power that had been emanating from the pillars flare so strongly that she felt she couldn't breathe, and then it was gone. The Wraiths let out a howling cry and began to charge at them.

"In the temple!" Maile yelled, dragging Malo to his feet.

They stumbled through the door and as the earth began to shake and debris started to crash down from above, Lanai fell, scraping her knee on the hard blue stone floor. She heard screams, but she wasn't sure if it was her, the twins, or the Wraiths. Belatedly, she remembered her dagger, and just as her hand grasped the hilt, the ground stilled and quiet filled the room.

Lanai sat up. The room was lit by a soft blue glow that came from the walls and ceiling. Lanai wondered if the light was blue or the stone was blue, or perhaps both. The doorway they'd entered through was blocked by a pile of stone and other debris. There were a few cracks between the rubble where sunlight streamed through. Lanai could hear the Wraiths scratching clawing at the stone on the other side.

"We're trapped," Malo said.

"At least we're alive," Maile said. "My spear's on the other side of that rubble, though."

"Along with my bow and our food."

"I have my dagger," Lanai said. "Ruamo saved us from the Wraiths. She will get us home safe."

"Let's hope," Malo said.

It was warmer inside the temple. The room they were in was empty and undecorated except for a flight of stone stairs that led down. Lanai led the way. With each step down she felt less shaken and more calm, more sure of herself. The power she'd felt coming from the pillars above was a mere shadow of the amazing warmth and energy she could feel coming from below. This was Ruamo's High Temple, where the Goddess herself dwelt, but even knowing that, Lanai couldn't shake the apprehension she'd felt since she'd woken that morning.

The room at the bottom of the stairs was small, but felt open, with a worn floor that looked to be a single, giant slab of the blue stone that made up the rest of the temple.

The walls were covered in mosaics made of sand and colored bits of glass. Some of them were the same as the ones that adorned the City Temple. One showed the Goddess deep in prayer as an island rose out of the water in front of her:. _Ruamo Creates Honua'aina_. Another showed Ruamo leading an army of warriors wearing armor with the same blue stitching as Lanai's against an army of Wraiths led by a man dressed in dark robes:. _Tumata's Assault_.

On the wall to her right was a mosaic at least twice the size of the others that Lanai had never seen before, at least twice the size of the others. In it, a woman was bowed in prayer before the entrance to the temple. There were more intact pillars, and the doors were grander, and more open. In fact, the whole temple seemed larger.

The woman in the mosaic was dressed in the same armor as Lanai, the same dagger on her hip. Her long hair obscured her face, but Lanai was sure that if she could have seen it, it would have matched her own.

"Who is she?" Malo asked. "She looks like you."

"That is the first High Priestess of Ruamo," Lanai said.

"Your great-great-great-great grandmother?"

"You'll need a lot more greats than that," Maile said. "That was more than a thousand years ago."

A noise echoed down the stairs, like a crash, followed by scraping sounds.

Malo looked uneasy. "Another earthquake?"

Lanai shook her head. "No. We would have felt it down here."

"Maybe the Wraiths have found a way through the rubble," Maile suggested.

"That's ridiculous," Malo scoffed, "They're not smart enough to clear rock away, and that doorway was blocked solid."

The noises continued. "The inner sanctum is through those doors," Lanai said. She walked over to the doors across from the stairs and stilled herself, letting the warmth of Ruamo's magic fill her soul. When she was ready, she opened her eyes. "I am Lanai, High Priestess of Ruamo. I beg entrance to her temple so that I might protect her people as I have sworn to do."

The door to the inner sanctum swung open silently. Lanai looked at the stairs, then at Maile and Malo. "You may accompany me into the sanctum, but you must remain silent at all times."

Maile and Malo followed her. The sanctum was a small room with an altar made of polished grey rock in the center. There were runes carved on the walls and ceiling here, and they glowed with a soft, pulsing light. Lanai approached the altar and began to sing the morning prayer, but just slightly differently, with a stronger emphasis on a syllable here or a changed word there. Malo paced restlessly, and kept looking back over his shoulder, as if he expected a Wraith to come down the stairs at any moment.

And then, suddenly, without warning or fanfare, there was another woman standing on the other side of the altar across from Lanai. She wore the same leather armor, with the same delicate blue stitching around the edges, though hers seemed softer, as if more decorative than protective. Her eyes were kind, and a string of shells had been braided into her long, black hair.

Lanai bowed to her. "I greet you in peace, Ruamo, Goddess of the Earth and protector of Honua'aina."

Ruamo frowned at her, blue light glowing softly around her. "You're late."

Lanai blinked. "I don't understand."

"You were supposed to be here on your thirtieth birthday, Lanai. That was nearly a decade ago."

"I'm sorry, Goddess. I didn't know."

"Your mother didn't tell you?"

"My mother told me that should the barrier around the city begin to fail I should follow my grandmother's spirit to you, but that was all." Lanai paused. "She was not very devout."

"She told you to wait until the barrier began to fail?" The Goddess shook her head. "I knew she was stubborn, but I didn't think her foolish."

"Ruamo, the barrier around the city is failing. Some have died already. Tell me what I must do to restore it."

"A thousand years ago I gained the upper hand against Tumata and found a way to seal a large part of his power, but I was badly wounded. The barrier is an extension of myself, and I require energy to survive. I must ask you to lend me your spirit, Lanai."

"Lend you my spirit? How?"

"Sacrifice yourself to me. Allow me to absorb your energy."

"No!" Malo cried. "I won't let you hurt Lanai."

"Malo!" Maile hissed, but he pushed her away when she tried to grab his arm.

"Malo," Lanai said, placing her hand on his shoulder. "The barrier is failing. Even the wards protecting this temple are crumbling, and the Wraiths will find their way down those stairs eventually."

"There must be another way. I'm here to protect you, Lanai. I've been trained since birth to do only that."

"And I have been trained since birth to be High Priestess. To serve Ruamo and ensure that the barrier continues to protect the city."

The same unearthly cry they'd heard earlier echoed through the sanctum, and all four of them turned to see Wraiths beginning to stumble down the stairs. Ruamo hissed a word under her breath and the runes in the antechamber flared. Two of the Wraiths crumbled into a pile of dirt and bone on the temple floor. Then the runes went out, leaving them unable to see what lay beyond the sanctum.

"I'm sorry," Ruamo said, leaning against the altar.

Lanai looked at her. "We haven't failed yet."

"Lanai, I won't let you do this——" Malo began.

"You don't command Lanai, she commands us. You have no right to speak against her," Maile snapped.

"If I don't do this, the entire island will perish," Lanai said.

"We can fight the Wraiths ourselves. The City Guard is armed and ready to defend us."

"This is my decision, Malo. I ask that you respect it, even if you cannot agree with it." Lanai drew her dagger from its sheath and looked at it for a moment, feeling its weight one last time. "Both of you, give me your hands."

Maile and Malo each extended their left hand. Lanai placed the dagger in both of their hands. "In the name of Ruamo, Goddess of the Earth, and protector of Honua'aina, I proclaim you High Priest and High Priestess of Ruamo. Our future is in your hands." Lanai let go of the dagger and smiled at them. "There is no one else I would trust with it." Maile's eyes met hers and Lanai thought she saw tears obscuring her dark brown eyes. Lanai squeezed her hand. She hadn't seen Maile cry since she was a little girl.

A Wraith stepped into the sanctum, howled, and charged at them, a handful of others following it. Malo grabbed the dagger by the hilt and stabbed the nearest one in the neck. Maile, unarmed, kicked the nearest Wraith in the chest. It stumbled back and seemed stunned for a moment, but then ran back at her, knocking her to the ground.

Ignoring the Wraiths, Lanai turned to Ruamo. She could feel the memory of all the others who had stood at this same altar over the years, comforting her, giving her strength. The fear that had been crawling along her back since that morning was gone, replaced by that sense of safety that only those in the hands of fate can feel. She let go.

Maile screamed and kicked at the Wraith on top of her, trying to ignore the pain in her leg where its claws had sunk in. Blue light flooded her vision and all she could see were the runes traced on the temple walls. For a brief moment she knew exactly what each and every one of them meant, but that knowledge faded along with the light.

Maile found herself kicking at air. She sat up. The Wraiths were gone, not even a single clump of dirt left behind to indicate that they'd ever been there. There was nobody standing at the altar, and Maile felt a different kind of pain flood through her, far worse than the pain in her leg.

Malo sat down next to her, taking a bit of cloth and using it to bind her wound. "She's gone," he said softly, and Maile realized he was trying not to cry.

"I know," she said, getting to her feet. "Let's go."

Malo stared at her. "We should rest a little."

Maile took the dagger from him before limping towards the stairs. Malo watched the runes in the walls glow ever so slightly as she walked past them.

Red Vapor
Micha Fire

*L*EFT TURN. RIGHT LONG CURVE. *Fast tilt to the right to fit between the two tree trunks. Then quickly tilt back to horizontal while pulling steeply up. Go over the tree tops and in a long left curve fly out over the river.*

Then a sharp turn and back into the red vapor. I can see my house. It's as if it has walls of glass. My family sitting at the table in the dining room. I want to get closer. I want a clearer view of what they are doing. The red vapor is blurring out so many details.

Closer. I'm nearly there. Suddenly I take a steep path up.

Tom woke up, breathing hard. "Not that dream again," he thought. The more often he dreamed it the more details he had at the end, the more his emotions mixed.

Left turn. Right long curve. Fast tilt to the right to fit between the two tree trunks. Then quickly tilt back to horizontal while pulling steeply up. Go over the tree tops and in a long left curve fly out over the river.

This part had been there from the beginning. He remembered the exciting—sensational—feeling of being able to fly like a bird. So full of ease and grace, moving between the trees, then the upward movement and flying over them, and over the town and river. What a magnificent view from up there. Even though everything was hazed by the billowing red vapor. The part with his family had come later. when the dream repeated.

Maybe he should not have tried to have the dream again. Being able to fly had been so exciting. Such a grand feeling that had lasted all day. It made him want to be able to repeat this and have this feeling over and over again. If he had known that the dream would change, and add some feelings of anxiety he greatly disliked, he might not have tried to have the dream again. But only having experienced the grand feeling of flying free like a bird during the first time of the dream, he searched the internet for more information about dreams.

He had found that by thinking about what you wanted to dream before you fell asleep, sometimes you could influence the contents of your dreams. And that was what he had done right the next night. But the red vapor, he could do without that. It blurred out so many details.

So, he had tried to find out what the red shrouding in the dream was. All he could figure out so far was that when he had woken up from the dream the first time, he had been looking right into the red lava lamp blowing bubbles next to his bed. Because of that he had removed the lamp, even turned it off. The red light had always felt so comforting. Not so after that night. Now it was a disturbance.

For some days he had consciously tried to repeat the dream. No success. Maybe the red vapor was a necessary element. Now, for a few nights, he stared into the lava lamp blowing the red bubbles before falling to asleep. It made no difference. The dream did not repeat. Two weeks of experimenting and no success. He was a failure.

He had told his best friends at school about his dream experiments. At first they were interested and even tried it themselves. But none of them had any success either, if they could remember a dream at all. They eventually pushed it aside as a fancy they tried out, like tasting cheese ice cream. As time passed, he forgot all about the dream.

There were more interesting things to do. Like the new game on his computer: Master Invasion Strategy. To invade a foreign country with an army you had to set up and train from scratch. Now this was something even his friends could stay excited about. They could play for hours, instant messaging about the best strategies to win a battle and advance to the next level.

At first Tom had been a lousy player. He was not able to see the big picture. But with tips from his friends and earnest experimenting, he was learning how to solve the battlefield tasks in the fastest and best way possible. It took time. He had to restart the whole game more than once. His friends did, too. The final battle was something none of them had achieved yet.

It was during this stage that his father had gotten angry at him. "This computer game is wasting too much of your time, Tom. If you don't change your behavior and spend more time with your family again, I'll have to take measures."

Tom sighed. He could imagine what type of measure that would be: ban him from his computer. His father had never liked the idea of him having his own. But Dad understood that it was a necessity forced on the children by the school.

Not from the very start though. Those years back it was enough that Tom had known what a computer was and the basic usage of it; always supervised by the parents. They had a family computer, as Tom's father sometimes had some deadlines and worked from home after the office hours to meet them.

But as the amount of homework supposed to be done at the computer rose, like writing essays or doing some research for projects, the time Tom's father had for his work shrank. There had been days the two of them had argued about which work was more important, Tom's, or that of his father, which earned the money. In the end, his parents had decided to buy him his own computer.

That had been an exciting day for him. He got better than his father at using, repairing, and upgrading a computer. Tom still remembered the day when he had gotten rid of that virus on his father's computer. Dad had been so proud, and that made Tom feel good. He had hugged his father—to their mutual astonishment. This had been the first hug since his sister, Jenny, had been born the year before he had gotten the computer.

Tom had felt lowered in family rank since that day. Sure, he had helped his mother with everything that needed to be done around the house and in taking care of a baby: laundry, dishes, even changing her nappies. But he was annoyed that he was forced to give up the status of being their only child. One thing he did not have to give up was his own room. However on some days, having to share the attention of his parents with this baby was worse than before when he had to use Dad's computer with him watching.

Jenny, in Tom's way of thinking, was a family addition that had not been necessary. He couldn't help but blame his father for not having been more careful so that his mother had gotten pregnant again. Tom and Jenny did have good days and lots of fun together; but nothing which felt as good as the praise the day that Tom had saved his father's computer.

And now, because of the game, it was all back to how it had been before that day.

After school, he talked with his friends about his troubles. And to his surprise they had agreed with his father. He really should be with his family more. The game was not so important. Even instant messaging with them after school was not that important.

"You only have that one family, Tom. And you have a good family. They care about you. You are lucky to have them. There is nothing worse than losing a person that cares about you." This was what his friends had told him.

And more along that line. It made him think. Yes, maybe he should spend more time with his family. When he had come home that day, he announced: "From this day on I wish we all could at least eat dinner together every day; not only on the weekends."

Both his parents and even Jenny had stared at him with big eyes for a moment. Then his father hugged him. "Tom, that is a marvelous idea. We can start right this evening." His mother smiled broadly. Jenny ran off to get four plates to put on the table.

That night he had the dream again. Left turn. Right long curve. Fast tilt to the right to fit between the two tree trunks. Then quickly tilt back to horizontal while pulling steeply up. Go over the tree tops and in a long left curve fly out over the river. And that feeling was there too. Free as a bird. And the red vapor. Just as he woke there had been the glimpse of his family at the table, blurred by the red vapor, for the very first time. This was a new part of the dream. The dream that by now he had nearly forgotten as it had been such a long time since he had first dreamed it.

"Ah, that's just me defragging the things my mind has accumulated over the last few days," he said to himself. It was something he remembered from his search about dreams and how to consciously work with them, and about the deeper meaning of dream symbols. Nothing to worry about. He again basked in the flying feeling which he had almost forgotten

This time though, he did not try to consciously repeat the dream. He simply recalled the feeling of flying free as a bird. The dream, however, repeated again the next night, all on its own. And the night after that.

Sure, the main feeling was the excitement of flying like a bird. But there was also this subconscious nagging feeling of not being able to see his family better before he was taken out of the dream by the upward motion.

He could not find any meaning to that. He was as close to his family as he had been for years. And to his surprise, he even cared about the neighborhood now. Mostly elderly people. Sometimes he helped them carry in their groceries or mow their lawn after he was done with the one in front of his own home. Some even gave him a bit of money for those easy tasks. He saved up this money to buy a new, faster computer.

Just a few days ago, a young couple moved into the house on the right. They had a baby. He had seen the baby buggy outside a few times, and had heard the baby crying. But he and his family had not visited them yet. There was a garden party planned for next week at their house. Sure, he could have gone over alone to see the baby or offer to babysit. But to be honest, he was not so keen on babysitting. He knew what that could be like from baby sitting Jenny. And his time was already filled enough with school, family, and yes, this computer game.

And he was so close to beating all his friends in the game. They all had been at it for months now, and no one had yet won the final battle.

Tom was the only one still seriously wanting to win this game. His friends had more or less given up. But they still could provide him with a few strategy options. His best friend had just given him a great hint today. So the first thing he did after his homework was try out the hint: he re-grouped the troops. It seemed to work. He was eager to win this battle and game today, if possible. No matter how long it took.

To finally beat the game would be nearly as good as flying free like a bird. It took up all his attention.

"Tom! Dinner is ready. Get down here at once."

This was the third call from his mother. And this time she sounded dead serious about the "at once" part.

He sighed. It had been a long day at school, lots of homework as well. All he had wanted was to relax from all that stress. He must have lost all sense of time, so captivated by the invasion he was planning.

OK—just this one click here to train some more troops, send the ready ones out to the battlefield, check the status of the troops already at the line of attack. Yes, that should do it.

He turned off the monitor; not the computer. The game would keep on running and, by the time he was done with dinner, the troops should be at the battlefield, ready to fight. Just one more win and this level was through. One step closer to the final battle—and the final win, of course. He had planned this invasion thoroughly. The computer opponent had no chance against his strategy. Not this time. He was an expert by now. He felt proud of his achievement.

Reaching the dining room, the stern look on his father's face quickly brought him back to the real world.

"This was the last warning, Tom. One more time that you can't get away from the computer right away when we call you, and I will confiscate it and keep it from you for a month. If you need it for homework, I'll stand right behind you and watch what you are doing."

"Dad, you can't do that!" Tom knew his father was not joking. The sheer thought of his father watching him doing his homework made him shudder. Maybe he should play through the whole night so that the game should be finished and the threat avoided. Then he would be free to be with his family. Oh, he realized that he had done it again. Put his own priorities ahead of his family's. He had tried so hard to balance the two. Again he had miserably failed.

"Argh, my food is cold. I'm going to nuke it." Tom got up again, taking his plate.

"Nuke it?" Jenny was curious, always wanting to learn all the new words her brother used.

"Yes, nuke it—put it in the microwave oven to re-heat it."

Tom turned and walked into the kitchen. "I want to nuke my food too," Jenny called after him.

"NO!" His father was serious, but Tom, contrary to his usual behavior, just closed the kitchen door. He was not going to eat a cold meal. A bit of microwave radiation wouldn't harm him or the food. He placed the plate in the oven, closed the door, and set it to two minutes.

Just before turning it on he remembered that his mother had told him to never use the microwave without a cover over the food. If he did he would have to clean it all up. He sighed, searching for the food lid. Usually, it was right on top of the oven—not so today. Maybe in the dishwasher? Not there. In the cupboard with the other plastic things? Not there either.

Better hurry or his father might show up and stop him. He wondered why it was so quiet in the dinning room. Whatever, he needed his food hot. So eventually, not finding the proper plastic lid, he took a small ceramic bowl and placed it over the food, completely covering it, shut the door and turned on the oven. "That should do." Tom smiled, knowing he wouldn't have to clean the oven this time around.

Still no sound from the dining room. Not even scratching of forks or knifes on the plates. He went to the door and peeked into the room. No one was there; the plates empty. Had they finished the meal without him? Odd. Maybe a new tactic to get him to be on time for dinner? To think more of them and not just himself?

Bing! The microwave was done. He headed back, opened the door, pulled out the plate, and placed it on the kitchen counter. Using an oven glove, he carefully lifted the hot bowl. No need to have his hands steamed.

And that precaution was good, as the steam that came out was red, blood red. Quickly, he dropped the bowl back on the plate. Something was wrong, very wrong.

Not caring about his meal now, he went back to the dining room. The plates on the table were clean, as if not used at all just moments before. Jenny's chair was standing crooked to the table edge, his parents chairs looked as if they had not been used. Neatly placed in their correct positions, as his father liked it: all the way in with the backs lined up to the table edge, without touching it.. Strange. Where did they go so quickly? It had been mere five minutes since he had left the room to reheat his food.

The house was too silent. He checked the other rooms. All empty. And tidy, like when they would go on vacation. Or if the house was ready for a photo shoot for. Everything looked so clean—nearly sterile. Showroom perfect, except for the three plates on the table.

His room and the kitchen were as he had left them; giving them a familiar, lived-in look. Worried as to where his family might have vanished, Tom ran outside to the garage. The door was shut as always, the car still inside, everything untouched. Did they go for an evening walk without taking him along, or even telling him? Had he again neglected them so much that they saw this as the only measure to make him feel what it was to have no family?

Another oddity he noticed was the silence outside. Just as in the house. No birds, no chirping of insects, no dog barking in the distance. Not even the sound of cars that was always in the background. This was not normal; something strange was going on.

Alarmed, he ran back inside, slamming the door shut. He turned on the TV, switching to the 24-hour news channel. No news. No reporter, no images, not even a pause signal. Nothing. As if the channel had never existed. He switched from channel to channel. The regular shows were running. All that was missing was the news. No news anywhere. Now he felt even more alarmed.

He ran upstairs to his computer, turned on the monitor. The game was waiting for his next input.

"Argh, forget the game," he mumbled and minimized it, opening up the internet and online radio. He searched for news, any news. New news especially. About the silence and missing people. All he found was news older than 30 minutes. Nothing about any strange happenings, nothing about missing people. He sighed. Maybe this was too recent for the news to have updated.

He opened his instant message tab. No one online. OK, at this time it was possible his friends were busy with other things. Checking his favorite social networks, he found that there were no posts newer than from about an hour ago. And nothing about vanished people. And here too, no one seemed to be online. He sighed again. It was all so strange. He tried calling some of his friends, but none answered the phone.

Needing to calm down, he re-sized the game. Might as well finish the level now. He made a few clicks and waited for the game to calculate his score. Yes, he had won this battle and the level. "Ready for the next task?" he was prompted by the game.

No, he was not ready. He wanted to know what had happened to his family. He saved the game status and turned it off. Once more he checked the different news channels. Still nothing.

Disappointed and worried, he turned off the computer. Downstairs, the TV was still running. Slowly, he walked back down, slumped into the seat in front of the TV, and again switched from channel to channel for news. Nothing had changed. All news, and the news channels, were nonexistent.

Uncertain about what to do now, he returned to the kitchen. Yes, he was a bit hungry after all. The kitchen and his room seemed the only normal things in this sterile-looking house. That "messy look", as his mother would have called it, gave him some comfort. So often he had wished his family gone so he could do his thing undisturbed. But not like this. Subconsciously, he had mixed feelings, like he did at the end of his flying dreams. Was there a connection?

Seeing the bowl still covering his plate, and remembering the red steam, he decided to check on his food. The bowl was now cold. Carefully, he lifted the bowl. No steam. He took the bowl off completely.

The red steam had settled back down on the food, covering the meat. It looked slimy. And bloody. The peas, carrots, and potatoes, though, looked normal. With a fork, he poked into the meat. A tiny puff of red vapor came out, not very high. And it settled right back on the meat, making it look even bloodier.

Disgusted, he threw the entire thing into the rubbish. No matter how hungry, he was not going to eat that.

There were still some peas and potatoes left in the cooking pots. He served himself some of that on a fresh plate and heated it in the microwave, with a fresh bowl over it. He still had not found the plastic lid. While waiting for the food to get hot, he threw the previously used bowl into the rubbish as well instead of washing it. As it touched the meat, a tiny puff of red vapor rose up and settled back down. The meat now not only looked bloody but also seemed to disintegrate. Yuck. He checked if there was any other meat left over from cooking, but as usual his mother had only made the four pieces needed. Meat was expensive.

When his food was ready he lifted the bowl very carefully with the oven glove over his hand. Steam came out, as expected. White steam. He smiled, took the bowl off completely, and without bothering to take a seat, ate all of it. He was puzzled as to why only the meat was affected by the red vapor, and not the vegetables and potatoes. But he was not ready to explore that yet. Still a bit hungry, he took the rest of the vegetables, and heated them and ate them. He placed his dishes and the pots in the dishwasher, and poured himself a glass of mineral water from a fresh bottle. Ah, that was good. Finally, his stomach felt full.

Once more, he checked the TV for news.. But again, nothing. He felt very alone. Not that he minded being alone. He could do a lot of things when alone; like playing on his computer all day long and not getting in trouble for it. But not knowing where his family had vanished to or what else was going on made him feel uneasy. He was not in a mood to enjoy this state of lonesomeness. What to do now? Maybe he should check the neighborhood for other people like him. Yes, someone even might need his help.

With new determination, he put on his jacket and hiking boots. He checked that he had his house keys with him, took a deep breath, and stepped outside. He closed the front door behind him, pleased that he had remembered to turn off all the electric appliances and close all the windows. You never know, burglars might find this situation inviting. He wouldn't be home for hours. Outside nothing had changed, all was silent.

With strong steps, he walked over to the house to the right, the one with the young couple and baby. Earlier, when he had come home, the buggy had been outside. Now it was gone. Perhaps the neighbors were out for an evening. He approached the door and listened, but didn't hear a sound. So he knocked, rang the bell, and listened again. No sound. He walked around the house, peeking into each window. No one to be seen.

Just as he was about to move onto the next house, he heard a soft cry. He rushed to the nearest window. Yes, there was the baby in the bed, just waking up. He watched for a few moments, but since no one came into the room and the baby started crying more, he went back to the door. Luckily, it was not locked and, with a last look over his shoulder to see if anybody was around that might see him "breaking" into a stranger's house, he slipped inside. Following the sound, he quickly found the baby's room.

What he saw shocked him. Next to the baby lay a drinking bottle, filled with rose-colored liquid. The baby grabbed the bottle, drank a little, tossed it aside, and cried again. The baby repeated this a few times. Tom picked up the bottle. It was cold. He was about to take it to the kitchen to warm it, when he noticed the red vapor coming out of the teat hole. Holding his breath, he moved the bottle far away from him and the baby.

The baby was still crying, so he picked it up. Immediately, the baby stopped crying and gazed at him with big eyes. But not for very long. Tom was reminded of the times his sister had been a baby. This one was hungry. Now! The pants were full too. With a big sigh he changed the nappies as he had done those years ago, under his mother's supervision. Now Tom could see that it was a boy. He didn't cry anymore; just sobbed a little, looking at him with big, sad eyes. He took the baby to the kitchen and searched for something he could give him to eat. He found an unopened glass of carrot mush. Better than nothing. But even after gently heating this in the microwave oven, the baby refused to eat it, still sobbing softly from time to time.

For a short moment when the baby opened his mouth for a louder sob, Tom could see why it had refused to eat. The whole inside of the mouth was blood red, raw. It was disintegrating like the meat he had thrown into the rubbish at home. Shocked, he nearly dropped the baby. There was nothing he could do for him, or was there?

He put the baby back into the bed, quickly left the house and ran far away down the street, tears welling up.

This red vapor was seemingly destroying everything meat and milk. No wonder there were no other humans around. Maybe even no other animals. There had been no dog barking or bird singing since he had noticed the silence. All of them ate meat in some way and thus got that vapor inside them. He shuddered. Only he had not eaten any meat this evening. Had his family disintegrated like the baby was doing? No wonder there was no one around now. But who then had tidied up all the rooms? What was in the vapor? Where had it come from? Was this the preparation for an alien invasion? His thoughts raced.

He slowed to a walk, out of breath. Was there any vapor around here waiting for him? He hadn't noticed any. He had to go back home, he needed something to protect himself with. He couldn't let himself be disintegrated like his family. Somewhere deep inside him he still had hope that all this was just a bad dream, and he would wake up and his family was still there. Then he could undo all the neglect he had done to them; be a true family member. Now that he seemed to have lost them, he understood how much he loved them, missed them, and how badly he had treated them over the years.

He walked home fast—but not too fast. He didn't want to have to breathe in too deeply. He kept listening for any human or animal sound, and kept looking for any red vapor.

With a sigh of relief, he made it home. He opened the door to his house only as much as he needed, slipped inside, and quickly closed it again. He ran to the bathroom for a wet rag. After tying it over his mouth and nose, he checked the rubbish in the kitchen. The meat in the rubbish was completely gone. So was the red vapor. He poked around in the rubbish a bit to see if it had fallen in deeper, but found nothing. OK, so this stuff didn't last. As long as he didn't touch anything meatish he should be safe for now.

Suddenly, he felt very tired. Yawning, he checked the TV once more only to find no changes. He switched it off and went to his room. Not bothering to check the Internet, he lay on his bed and instantly fell asleep, the wet rag still over his mouth and nose.

He heard a voice call him. It sounded serious, but not as dead serious as when his mother had called him down for dinner. There was an urgent note to it, but it was so soft he hardly could understand more than his name. He jumped up, checked that the rag was still in place, and opened the door of his room.

The voice was now stronger. "Hurry, get in the ship. You have to stop the invasion. The vaccine is already loaded. There is no time to lose, Tom. Hurry!"

Ship? What ship? He ran downstairs, taking two steps at a time, put on his jacket and boots, and opened the front door. He was so glad he had left that rag on. The air was filled with red vapor. In some places, thick. In others, barely visible.

Then he saw it. The ship. Right in front of him, parked at the walkway like his father's car. Amazed by the sight, fearful, yet curious, he walked towards the ship. When he reached the ship, the door opened by itself. He pushed all fears aside and quickly climbed inside.

Here the air was free of red. With one smooth movement he slid into the captain's chair. It formed itself perfectly to his body, the steering mechanism readily touched his hands. At first Tom was a bit timid, but then it seemed he remembered long-forgotten abilities. He started the ship and swiftly maneuvered it down the street.

Once he reached the crossing, he lifted the ship up high over the houses, flying in curves over them. There was no need to activate the vaccine mechanism—the ship was set to automatic for that. All he had to do was fly it, and he did with growing speed and enthusiasm. He truly enjoyed this task, forgetting completely why he was doing it. Only important that he was flying the ship.

Left turn. Right long curve. Fast tilt to the right to fit between the two tree trunks. Then quickly tilt back to horizontal while pulling steeply up. Go over the tree tops and in a long left curve fly out over the river.

Pure fun.

And bit by bit the vapor vanished, and clear air came back. He felt great satisfaction, being only a boy and yet saving the world. He leaned back.

"Tom!" Someone was shaking him. "Get up, Tom. You will be late for school." He opened his eyes and look into the face of his mother, who was a little upset. But weren't they gone, all of them? He must be dreaming. He sat up and looked around.

He was in his room. He couldn't remember how he had gotten here. The last thing he could remember was flying with the ship, eliminating the vapor. Puzzled, he got up to get dressed. His mother went back downstairs. On impulse, he switched on the computer. Yes, perhaps there was news now on what had happened yesterday.

But it still was yesterday.

And somehow, Tom knew the whole thing would still happen. The invasion. His family vanishing. And him coming to their rescue. Or...

Oddly enough, his game still prompted him: "Ready for the next task?" So, he had finished the last battle as he remembered. A time jump back for him alone? Or had he forgotten that he had finished the game already? What had been dream, what real?

He checked his emails.

One line read: "Be ready for tonight." Although it didn't show who had sent it, he disregarded all warnings about safe usage from his father and opened the email. After what he had gone through, he felt he could tackle anything. A computer virus would be nothing compared to last evening. The time stamp on it showed that it had been sent this evening. Been sent ahead of the time he was in now? Odd.

There was nothing much more in the email. Just these words: "No fear. No delay. You know what to do. The world depends on you. Be faster than the red vapor invasion."

It made him smile.

Beauty is Long Thin Legs
Chris Capps

"FRANK, THEY'RE WASPS." As soon as she said it I knew we were in some kind of trouble. I stood there with my phone, watching morning shadows retreat across the porch, listening to my messages. And I heard those words again. She sounded distracted.

"Frank. Frank, they're wasps."

The list of things she could mean by that was pretty long. Clarissa had a habit of providing the most relevant information first. It was something I'd always liked about her, one of a hundred little talents that had earned her a raise last season. Clarissa liked efficiency, and clockwork schedules. And that made me like Clarissa. But this business with the wasps must have meant more to her than it did to me, because she didn't explain much more than that. She started talking to someone else, likely the hotel's night manager, David.

The next message was time stamped 9:41 PM. This would have been about six minutes after I took my pills and laid in bed with the phone downstairs and on silent. I wouldn't have heard it over the bedroom's window unit anyway. It was Clarissa again.

"Frank, David says he'll open up room 102, but he won't do it without your approval. He doesn't believe me. The couple next door to them had to be moved to a different room. They said the television static was too loud, but 102 is the honeymoon suite. It doesn't have a television. Call me."

Nights like this made me wish I made a habit of charging the phone by my bed. Whatever was happening—whatever had happened—I was helpless to intervene. I thought about the visitors I'd sent to room 102. The big hats. Strange, quiet, possibly in town for some kind of a convention. People like to show off their eccentric personalities to hotel night staff. You know, "Look how strange I am. Isn't that something?" It had been different with the big hats. They seemed nervous, awkward. Uncomfortable in their own skins. And then there was the one that spoke—the one wearing the sunglasses.

Four more unheard messages. Next message. 11:31 PM.

"David went home. He said he quits. The static went quiet about fifteen minutes ago and I—look, I listened at the door to see if I could figure out what he saw. They were talking, but I couldn't understand them because one was laughing, that exhausted breathless kind of laughing like someone was tickling them. And when one stopped, another picked up right away. And there was another sound, like a balloon with a hundred tiny squeaking holes in it that had formed without popping it. I don't know what that was. It was a constant rush, just air forced through a perforated surface, but with so many different tones. I know how all of this must sound, but please come down right away."

Next message. 11:52 PM.

It sounded like she might have accidentally dialed my phone. Two people were casually talking in the background. An unlikely sound was growing, thousands of buzzing wings, millions, and the needle click of something tapping across the phone's receiver. The message ended at the two minute mark. I could have sworn one of the voices talking belonged to Clarissa. But she sounded calm, talkative, like she was at some kind of party.

Next message. 4:02 AM.

"This is Ben Davis. Sorry to call you so late, but I just walked in and no one's at the front desk. I've got one of the maintenance guys behind the counter. He says he's been holding the fort since midnight. I don't know where Clarissa or David have gone. Give me a call as soon as you get this, and sorry again about calling so late."

Next message. 8:09 AM.

"Frank, this is detective Ed Palmer. Please call your hotel the moment you get this. Thank you."

"Fucking Christ. Twelve years from now I'll be able to forget. For me life starts again at 43".

"They say you never forget the rough stuff," I said, impotently dispensing the wisdom of a middle aged hotel manager. I don't know what I was trying to say. I wasn't exactly comforting him, but he looked like he'd seen a thing or two in his life. He shook his head, surprised at what I had just said.

"Oh no, you can. Just need time. Lots and lots of time. Enough time and you can forget anything."

He reached over to where the lotus pod was in the potpourri arrangement and he closed his hand around it as hard as he could, his fist shaking as he crushed it into a fine dust, methodically sprinkling it over the rest of the dried flowers. Afterward, he looked at his hand and rubbed it on his pant leg,

"Smells nice," he said, "Those holes ran pretty deep in them. I don't know how they weren't dead when they showed up. Bodies were ice cold, except in the holes. Those were hot. Was the guy with sunglasses there when they checked in?"

"Yeah," I said, "He's the one I talked to."

"Holes went to his eyes," Palmer said. His tone had changed, like he was talking about an exhibit in a museum, "Had hundreds of em running out of the sockets. I think something tunneled in, or tunneled out."

"Tunneled out?" I said.

"I had this idea," he said, "It was weird. They had the wrong thoughts. That's how my brain explained it to me. Like it was a rule pulled from a dream or a bad... you know a bad trip. They thought the wrong thing and it made a body for itself in their heads. Abstract made concrete. A little wasp that grew and tunneled and bred until it didn't need them anymore. Don't know why they came here. Guess they wanted to talk. I kept thinking, 'we've all got little wasps in our heads.' Sure."

There was a strange honesty in Palmer's voice. I may not be a detective, but I've met a lot of people. Something in his voice grabbed me—something I trusted.

"Sex cult," the action figure said from behind us. He must have been watching the other detective for a while now, listening in on our conversation. I was surprised to see him so candid with the sensitive details of an ongoing investigation—but I don't think for a second that he was doing it to satisfy my curiosity. It was more useful for me to believe what he was saying. Sex cult was what the newspapers were going to say, if they said anything at all. I was sure of it.

"What about their heads?" Palmer said.

"CDC says sex cult. What about the heads? They had big hats with wasps in 'em and they glued those to their heads and died because—well, that's what happens."

"There were tunnels," Palmer said, "Networks running down through to the one guy's eyes. He knew it looked weird. That's why the sunglasses."

"What do you want from me, Palmer?" the action figure said, "You just quit. Now button up or you're walking home."

I stood up and walked over to the counter, leaving the two men to argue. We weren't going to see much business today. And sex cult suicide was a good headline, so maybe we'd never see normal business again.

"Dear God," I said to myself as the phone rang for the first time that morning, "Don't be a reporter."

I picked up the phone, but before I could introduce myself or the hotel, I could hear a tired familiar breath speaking in sultry tones,

"Beauty is long thin legs. Long thin legs tapping against glass like a whole family in a single body. Its eyes are lavender, seeing everything."

"Clarissa," I said, lowering my voice and ducking my head down. It was conspicuous, more-so than I could have afforded in a room full of cops, "What happened?"

"Frank," she said, "You're not going to believe this. Listen carefully, hold it in your imagination as I describe it."

"There are a bunch of dead people in room 102," I said, "And there's cops all over."

"Listen carefully, Frank," I heard Clarissa say, "They're not people. They're wasps. Long thin legs. Long thin legs tapping against glass like a whole family in a single body. Its eyes are lavender, seeing—"

I could feel it. Something about what she was saying, the notes of her voice, the breath of it—it was more seductive than any Clarissa I had ever met. There was life to those words. Like she was pouring something secret into my brain with every syllable. Every inch of me recognized it the way you'd recognize danger from the bright yellow and black coloring of a wasp. You're born with that kind of knowledge.

"Clarissa," I said, "I'm going to stop you right there. Did they tell you something?"

"They explained it all to me. The whole thing. They gave me the words that brought something up in my head. You don't know how life feels to the universe until you feel yourself growing something right in your brain."

"Are you trying to tell me everything?" I asked, "Is what you're about to say going to grow something in my brain?"

"Yes," she said, inhaling excitedly to get the next words out quickly. That fraction of a second was frantic. She wanted to share this with me. I stopped her.

"Buzz off."

And I hung up.

There's a sign next to the phone these days instructing employees to hang up the instant someone says the words 'Beauty is Long Thin Legs' on the line. Clarissa doesn't waste time, and she doesn't bother with introductions. She calls once a day at precisely 9:55 PM when the night shift staff is most likely to be by the phone. She's never visited, never called more than once per day. But wherever she goes, she's always by a phone at 9:55, calling us. Trying to tell us what beauty is. Trying to tell us what those wasps told her.

Odd the newspapers never picked up on the story. A brief local spot ran of a single man committing suicide in room 102 of our hotel, but no one was really interested in who did it, where they came from, or why. It just faded from memory almost as quickly as it appeared.

The CDC—or whoever they were—cleaned up really well, taking the carpet and everything else. Never heard from them again. Never talked to them at all, come to think of it.

Detective Palmer and I are still in touch. He still calls from Ohio. Says he has dreams sometimes about baby wasps trickling out of meaty hats. Years later he would tell me he had heard words crying from those split open hats—a chorus deep in the hive, all shrieking the same thing. I never asked him what they said.

I imagine it started with,

"Beauty is..."

Salvage
MJ Kobernus

Near Orbit, Palsenz
Year 2387

THE SHUTTLE APPROACHED THE LARGER SHIP'S DOCKING PORT slowly, performing an intricate ballet of trajectories and vectors, matching speed, angle and rotation until it mirrored the other vessel precisely.

"*Argoss III*, this is the shuttle *Heimdal*. Requesting permission to dock." The radio remained silent. First Officer, Stephanie Chu looked to the pilot and shrugged. "Still no response, Pål."

Captain Pål Knutsen acknowledged this with a nod. But he had his orders. Dock with the *Argoss*, and enable ingress for the salvage team. He triggered a burst from the central reaction control system, giving the shuttle a push sufficient to allow it to move slowly towards its vastly bigger host. With a clang that reverberated throughout the smaller vessel, the shuttle mated with the *Argoss*, its inexorable progress countered by the torsional and compression systems that absorbed most of the collision's impact. With a glance at the control panel, he saw that the Orbital Docking System indicated the seal was tight. All green. He flipped the comm channel open.

"OK, boys. You're clear to disembark."

Stephanie pulled her headset off. It floated away gently. Raising an eyebrow, she said, "Boys?"

Her partner shrugged. "Just a figure of speech. You be careful, Steph. Make sure that seal is tight. I don't care what the panel shows." He gestured to the ODS which continued to give its electronic assurance that the docking ports were cleanly mated.

"I always am, Pål. Don't worry about me."

She quickly moved to the small hatch in the bulkhead behind them. Making good use of the handholds, she swung around and pivoted through the narrow opening, flying through with the speed of long familiarity. This put her in the central fuselage where the tech-engs from the *Bitter Sea* were waiting, already suited. The six men and three women were checking each other's EV suits, before tapping their partners' shoulders to indicate final approval. At zero gee, they could move easily in the heavy, articulated bodies, but they were bulky and cumbersome under normal grav conditions.

Stephanie punched the code for the airlock and a door slid open revealing a small chamber just big enough to hold four of the suited figures at a time. The first group entered, some of them carrying silver cases containing the instruments and tools needed to assess the condition of the third colony ship, which steadfastly refused to acknowledge their presence. She activated the close routine and the hatch slid shut silently. Watching through the tiny sight glass, she could see the expedition leader manually operate the docking port. The shuttle vibrated for a moment as the port dilated open, and the tech-engs passed into the airlock on the other side.

One of them turned before entering the *Argoss*, giving her a thumbs up gesture, then sealed the hatch behind him. The panel displayed a flashing green light. They were in. She repeated the process for the three remaining crew and watched as they too disappeared into what some people were already referring to as the ghost ship. She shook her head ruefully. Stupid to let rumour affect her like that. So the ship had suffered some kind of environmental disaster and most likely killed everyone aboard. That was no reason to start getting superstitious. And yet, she could not shake the feeling that something was wrong.

INSIDE the *Argoss III*, Officer First Class Jensen examined the external pressure and air sensor unit mounted on the sleeve of his suit. With a nod to the others, he started to unclamp his helmet. Quickly, they helped each other, hanging their suits in racks that lined the wall of the small chamber. In just a few minutes, nine heavy EVO suits slumped against the airlock wall.

Jensen sniffed cautiously. He was the first of his family in almost three hundred years to breathe air not filtered through the *Bitter Sea*'s scrubbers. It was disappointingly familiar. The same aroma of rubber and steel. But there was a hint of something else too. Something he did not recognise.

The airlock opened into a narrow corridor, its once white walls now grey, several of its lighting panels dimmed or broken. Noting the condition, Jensen felt his fears for the people aboard the *Argoss III* mounting. No one had been doing any maintenance for a very long time, it seemed.

"Alright folkens, let's get to work." He gestured to the Drive Techs who carried a crate between them. "Finn and Cho. You two get moving. Find out what state the main drive is in. The rest of us are heading for the control centre."

The two drive techs nodded, lifting their heavy crate easily in the zero gee, and headed down the corridor. Even though their names denoted a familial heritage that could not have been more different, they looked surprisingly similar. Both men were tall, with high cheekbones and dark hair. Finn's blue eyes spoke of his Norsk roots, while Cho's brown were rooted firmly in Shanxi province. They moved at a steady pace, their boots providing solid traction on the floor. Theirs was the longest journey, as they had to go through the gen-pop section in the third sphere in order to get to the engines, but there was a control station in section two that could provide some answers first. They turned left at the junction in the corridor without hesitation. They did not need to think about where they were going. They were as familiar with the layout of the *Argoss* as they were with the *Bitter Sea*. The colony ships were all built identically, down to the last nut and bolt, even if each did its own unique 'flavour.'

The great vessels had left Earth in the wake of the Final Fall. They had maintained close communications during the first generation, but after forty years, the *Argoss* had gone quiet. It also maintained a longer and harder acceleration program than the other three ships, so after many decades it had pulled too far ahead to be tracked easily. And though it was clear that it had not exploded, as had the luckless Truman seventy years into their journey, it was equally certain that something had gone catastrophically wrong.

After eight generations, only half the expected colonists had arrived safely at their new home, a G star system with a Kepler-classified Super-Earth planetoid. But this would be enough as each ship was fully capable of establishing a colony on its own. However, the success potential of any fledgling outpost increased with greater numbers. When *Endurance* and *Bitter Sea* entered the Palsenz star system, there was much celebration when the *Argoss III* was discovered to be waiting for them in a geo-stationary orbit.

Each of the giant ships had been sponsored by a consortium of privately held companies with cooperation from national groups on Earth. The *Bitter Sea* was a joint Sino-Norsk enterprise, with lesser representation from several other countries. As a result, most of the colonists on the *Bitter Sea* had Eurasian features, with a prevalence for high cheekbones and almond shaped eyes, even those with blonde hair. In contrast, the *Endurance* was largely of North American manufacture, with a large percentage of Southern American and a small minority of central Europeans. The colonists aboard *Endurance* were much darker in complexion, with a prevalence of brown eyes and darker hair. The vision of a melting pot for humanity had become reality only after its almost utter extinction.

Officer Jensen began to lead the group of engineers, technicians and computer operators on the long march to the control centre, located in the third and most forward section. The *Heimdal* had docked in the middle section, which contained the engineering, hydroponics and various other support industries. This was the heart of the great ark and it should have been a hive of industry.

The modular design always reminded Jensen of pictures he had seen as a kid; a bulbous bug, with a large abdomen, smaller thorax and tiny head. Each section was bigger than the previous, and all were connected by multiple limbs and tubes.

Only the third section had gravity. The General Population pod was based upon a design from the twentieth century; a Bernal sphere. The entire core of the sphere was hollow and housed the majority of the ship's crew and personnel. There were no passengers. If your ancestors were not specialists or would not work, they did not go. A constant three quarter gee was maintained by spinning it along a central axis ensuring that the population could maintain sufficient muscle and bone mass throughout the long journey to their new home.

The salvage team led by Jensen continued through various corridors, some of them entirely dark, requiring them to use their light beams on scatter setting, creating odd, looming shadows out of nothing. It was in one dark passage that they found the first *Argoss* crewman; or what was left of him. The synthetic material of his uniform was perfectly intact, in contrast to the skeletal remains within. It looked to Jensen as if the man had died leaning against the bulkhead, then simply fallen over.

The Med Tech drew a handheld scanner and went to work. She looked up, face grave. She said just one word, but it chilled them all.

"Radiation."

At that moment Jensen's ear comm chirped, announcing an incoming signal. He keyed it to relay, so the others could hear the drive tech through their own comms.

"Chief, there's something not right here. We're at the engine control centre. There's no sign of any activity, but the nav system shows that a containment coil was aligned recently."

Jensen understood enough about the singularity drive to know what a containment coil was, but he did not understand why this was important.

So?"

"So, the procedure is not automated. It has to be done manually."

Jensen let the significance of the words filter through. Someone must have been performing the alignment. "Well, that's good news. There must still be some crew alive, right?"

"Well, that's the thing chief. I can access the main Control Comp System from here. There's a secondary interface in engineering as a backup. I requested a head count."

Each person aboard a colony ship had a tiny sub dermal implant, which allowed the CCS to track their location as well as the individuals' bio readings. It would also constantly monitor how many people were aboard.

"I may regret asking this. How many are there?"

"Zero chief. There are no crewmen currently registered."

"But you said that the alignment was done manually."

"Yes, sir."

"Hmm. Okay, thanks Finn."

The implants were inserted into the gluteus maximus of all newborns. This was protocol; everyone had one. If there were people aboard that did not have the bio tracker, then that could only mean one thing. He turned to his team. "There may be a break in the social structure. It could be they had a mutiny. Keep on your toes."

The group nodded in response. They continued along the corridor, coming upon more of the hapless crew that had died suddenly, killed by a flash radiation burst, most likely from the ship's own reactor.

When they reached the junction to the Control Centre Pod, the most forward part of the ship, Jensen felt a sense of relief. He opened the connecting portal. It was an airlock, since the control pod was effectively a separate system to the rest of the ship. Although cramped, the *Bitter Sea* personnel squeezed into the small chamber. They cycled through and as the adjoining portal opened, they got their first glimpse of the ship's control centre, the bridge.

A dozen of the *Argoss* crew were arrayed around the room, some still at their workstations, others haphazardly fallen, or sitting slumped against a bulkhead. The blast of radiation that had killed them had been over in a second. They probably hadn't even felt a thing.

But the gen-pop sphere would have better shielding. Sure, it was closer to the reaction core, but its hull was meters thick. Still, if there had been any survivors, the engineers would have reported it by now.

Jensen went to the nearest computer terminal and punched a few keys at random. Nothing.

"Let's get to work. We need these systems up and running."

His team spread out, carefully moving the bags of bones that had once been people. They stacked them in a corner of the control room, then began to pull apart the panelling to get at the computer's inner systems, looking for the fault that had put the control centre offline.

Engineer first class Markus Han was first to get his terminal running. He turned to his partner. "Li, look at this." He pointed to a digital readout that displayed a set of numbers. Li narrowed his eyes.

"It looks like the containment field was taken offline."

"Yeah, that's what I thought."

"But . . . that would kill everyone. Why would they do that?"

"No idea. But it looks like someone wanted to pull the plug on the whole crew."

"Sir! Over here, please."

Jensen hurried over to the techs, who were still staring in shock at the data on the screen.

"It was sabotage, Sir. The drive failure. Someone did it deliberately."

Jensen swore, shaking his head. "What in hell would possess someone to do that?"

Markus Han peered closer at the data, and he visibly paled. "Sir . . . it was here. They did it from here." He pointed to a section of the screen displaying an array of numbers. "They overrode the safety protocols. That's the captain's own authorisation code."

"What?" Jensen stared in puzzlement at the data on the screen. Drive tech was not his field, and he could not comprehend the lines of scrolling data. "The command crew caused a deliberate drive containment field failure? Why the hell would they do that? It would kill everyone on the whole ship!"

Markus nodded. "Yeah. Everyone. And everything."

Jensen activated his comm unit. "Finn, report in please."

There was no answer.

"Lieutenant Cho, please respond."

The technicians in the control room looked to their leader, whose hand had automatically gone to the holstered weapon on his right hip.

LIEUTENANT Cho levered the panel away from the wall, exposing an intricate array of wires and tubes. He reached in and pulled a breaker from its panel, examining it carefully before reinserting it. Then he keyed the reset and pulled his arm out. Immediately there was a hum, and lights on instrument panels around the room illuminated.

"Nice," said Finn. "Just a tripped breaker. Good call."

"Not my first rodeo," Cho replied.

"Your first what?"

"I dunno. I saw it in one of the movie archives," Cho said. "Seemed appropriate."

They both laughed. Movies were a major source of entertainment for the crew of the *Bitter Sea* and *Endurance*, however no new films had been made in the hundreds of years since leaving Earth, so they were stuck with re-watching films from a time and place that hardly made sense.

With the computer systems running, they began preliminary checks. It was not long before they discovered the recent maintenance performed on the drive, which they related to Jensen, along with the fact that there were no registered crew remaining.

"Somebody must have done the alignment though," said Cho thoughtfully. "Or maybe they died after completing it? Can we run a filter and find out when the last crew died?"

Finn typed rapidly, feeding instructions into the computer. The answer was quick in coming.

"Says here that the last crew registered was 2192. That was when the ship went silent."

"So everyone was killed two hundred and eighty years ago?"

"Looks like."

"Okay. Then who realigned the coil?"

Both their comm units chirped and Jensen's voice sounded as the door to the control room hissed open. Cho and Finn whirled around. It was not one of the other salvage team members. What came through the door may have been distantly related to humanity, but it wasn't human.

They had barely enough time to scream.

WITH no answer from the drive technicians, Jensen was clearly worried. "Get the systems online. We need to find out what the hell we're dealing with."

Markus looked up from the computer terminal he was working on. "No response from Cho or Finn?"

"No."

"Want me to check on their vitals?"

"You can get their bio data?"

"I think so. Shouldn't be a problem to use the system to check on our chips. Just need to change the scanning frequency."

He typed several commands into his terminal, then input the frequency range of their own bio sensor implants. Each ship used a different frequency, and it was easily updated with the new data. He keyed a final command. The number on the screen showing current crew headcount made him visibly pale.

Jensen looked over his shoulder and swore. There were five signals, all in the CC. "Okay, that's it. We're leaving. Get your gear. Something is clearly wrong and we are not equipped to deal with it. We're going back to the shuttle."

He tapped his comm device. "Shuttle *Heimdal*, this is First Officer Jensen. Do you copy?"

"This is Chu. We hear you. Everything okay?"

"No. We're coming back. Something killed two of my team, and we are not prepared for this contingency. Recommend immediate evac."

"Roger that, we're ready to go. Just get back here safe."

Jensen pulled the gun from his holster. Only one other member of his team carried a sidearm, and she quickly pulled her weapon. Jensen looked at her. "Heat it up, Leoni."

Leoni Hansen thumbed the safety off, and the power quickly starting to build with an audible hum. Within seconds it was ready to fire a charge powerful enough to kill a man.

"I'll take point, you take the rear. Everyone else in the middle and move quick. Whatever killed Finn and Cho may well be coming for us."

Markus had been typing into the data console and finished the input with a final decisive tap. He shook his head in wonder. Jensen moved over to stare at the screen.

"What is that?"

"I reconfigured the internal sensors to pick up any bio readings, regardless if they were chipped."

"I didn't know it could do that."

"Yeah. Well, we had to figure out how to reduce the rat population a few years back, so we worked out a method to use the sensors to track heat signatures."

Jensen nodded. There was a number on the screen. His eyes widened slightly, then narrowed. "So, there are currently over a dozen bio organisms on the ship."

Markus swallowed. "No. Those are the ones in the passages between us and the central pod." He tapped a few keys, and entered a new command. The screen showed a different value now. "This is for the entire ship."

Nine hundred and eighty-five bio signatures.

"Are they human?" Jensen asked, as he thumbed the safety off his pistol.

"No. Their core temperature is too hot. If they were human, they'd be dead."

"Then what the hell are they?"

"I don't know," Markus replied. "But we're gonna find out."

The screen clearly indicated that several of the bio signatures were converging on the command centre.

CAPTAIN Pål Knutsen flipped a series of switches, engaging the drive initiation sequence. Stephanie Chu floated horizontally behind him. He punched a series of commands on the terminal to his side. Internal cameras and sensors were now recording everything.

"I have to go in, Pål," she said.

"I know."

"I'll be careful."

"Fuck careful. Be lethal."

She nodded, then pulled herself towards him. She wrapped arms around him in a brief hug before jack-knifing and pushing off his chair towards the hatch. She went through, barely touching the sides, and at the last second she grabbed a handle and pulled herself into a vertical standing position, relative to the floor. She opened a locker, and removed a heavy multigun. Designed to be used in any situation, the multigun could be configured for lethal and non-lethal bursts. She flicked off the safety and set the weapon to rapid fire, heavy charge. It whined as the power started to climb.

Turning to the airlock, she punched in the code. The door opened and she stepped through.

First Officer Jensen tensed as the airlock doors opened. He moved cautiously into the corridor, expecting …. he did not know what. The six members of his team followed close behind him.

"Okay, let's go."

He moved briskly, each foot carefully placed. It was still a zero G environment, which meant that an attack could come from literally any direction. He eyed the ceiling and was reassured by the fact that there appeared to be no ducts, or other access points. At least here.

They had been making quick progress for almost ten minutes when they entered a dark section, and even though they all used their light beams, there were too many dancing shadows.

They didn't see the attack.

A muffled yell broke the silence, which quickly changed to a gurgle, and the salvage team instinctively clumped together. Eyes wide with fear, their light beams randomly illumined each other's faces, trying to see who was missing. Li, the Chinese kid. Markus let out a groan.

"Goddamn and to hell," he said, his voice a trembling whisper.

"Keep moving," Jensen commanded, and the group moved forward again, this time noticeably closer to each other. Not that that would matter - Li had been in the middle of the pack.

They passed a junction, where tubes led out to service points on the central pod. That was when they lost Leoni.

She had time enough to scream and fire her weapon. A blue flash lit up the service duct, but if she hit whatever had attacked her it made no difference. Their light beams revealed no sign of her.

"We're moving too slowly," said Jensen. "Run!"

STEPHANIE stood waiting for whatever was coming. She tried to will herself into a calm mental state. She had never been in combat before; none of them had. And yet they had trained. Simulations of all kinds, in case the planet they arrived at had hostile fauna, or intelligent and unfriendly natives. No one had believed in the latter possibility, but here she was, standing outside the airlock on the *Argoss*, waiting to engage an unknown enemy with unknown capabilities.

She took a deep breath, then dropped into combat stance, going to one knee, steadying the heavy weapon, using her arm as a support, braced against her thigh. She aimed down the corridor, her finger lightly touching the firing stud.

Markus Han appeared first, running with the clumsy, almost comical look that people had in zero G. He was followed by a man she did not recognise, then came Jensen, firing behind him as he ran.

The three made their way towards her, and then she saw it, a glimpse of something fast, dark. Her breath came in a gasp, but her hands moved of their own accord, tracking the thing, aiming, firing. Her first blast missed. The tech-engs lumbered past, and she took aim again, her eyes going wide as black claws reached for her. She fired, hitting the creature in the torso. It flew back, a tumbled mass of red ruin with stick like arms and legs.

More followed and Stephanie tracked them quickly, firing in rapid succession, laying down an enfilade that came dangerously close to overloading the multigun.

The creatures were oddly angular. Neither bipedal nor quadruped. Their limbs seemed to work in any direction, allowing them to move with erratic, quick turns. They had short bodies, with small heads. They got close enough that Stephanie could see the colour of their eyes as she fired blast after blast. They were human, intelligent and filled with hate.

Markus Han reached the airlock and started to open the chamber. The others piled in and she followed, after laying down an intense barrage to discourage any of the creatures from getting too close.

Stephanie initiated the airlock cycle. No one spoke, only their harsh breathing disturbed the silence. Jensen holstered his pistol, his hand visibly shaking.

Stephanie examined the survivors. They seemed dazed, as if they did not understand what had happened. Then something thudded against the airlock door. She span around, hitting the control on the view panel. The outer camera mounted above the door relayed the carnage in the corridor. Blood, bodies and twisted limbs filled her vision. Stephanie looked away, almost retching. Just then the cycle finished, and the door to the shuttle's cargo bay slid open. They stumbled as one from the airlock.

Stephanie put the multigun back into its cabinet and slammed shut the door before she returned to the cockpit.

"Welcome back," said Pål. "Things got hot, I see."

She almost laughed with the release of tension as she thrust herself into her co-pilot's seat.

"What the hell were those things?" Pål continued.

"They were us, I think. If we lived in an unshielded environment for centuries."

"Human? You've got to be kidding!"

"I wish I was."

Pål eyed the control panel. A red light blinked. "Everyone is back then. No one left behind?"

"Everyone that is coming back is here," said a voice behind them. Stephanie swivelled around as Jensen floated slowly through the hatch.

"Then who the hell just cycled through the airlock?" said Knutsen.

Screams from the two men in the cargo hold ended abruptly. Pål cursed and punched the main drive at the same time as the attitude jets. The *Heimdal* surged forward, attempting to rip itself away from the great bulk of the *Argoss*. The sound of rending metal reverberated through the ship as it wrenched free.

Jensen pulled his gun, aiming along the length of his own body. Then his disappeared, pulled into the hold. Stephanie launched herself out of her chair, and went through the hatch, slower than usual, but faster than she wanted. There was a blue flash as Jensen's gun fired, then again and again. Another scream, this one inhuman.

Inside the cargo hold, she bumped up against Markus. His throat had been torn open and blood bubbled out, floating in a long red stream towards a suction vent as the automatic maintenance systems kicked in. The other engineer was also clearly dead, one side of his head stoved in. Stephanie felt a momentary shame that she did not even know his name. Jensen was alive, holding his hand over a cut on his upper left arm. The thing had slashed at him with razor-like claws.

She got a good look at it this time. It was floating, with impossibly long and stick-like limbs moving in odd directions. If this thing had once been human, it had been a very long time ago. It was hairless and smooth and dark skinned, but it wore clothing made from the same material as used by the crew on all the ships. But this only covered its groin, like a loincloth. There were no tools, or weapons. Its head was small, its mouth wide with a bank of needle like teeth.

"Is it dead?" she asked hesitantly.

"Yeah. I put enough of a charge into it to kill a dozen men. It's dead, alright."

"We need to get it back to the *Bitter Sea*. They need to know what happened."

Jensen nodded. One look at their 'cargo' and no explanations would be necessary.

"Did you radio them?" he asked. "Let them know what the hell happened?"

Stephanie shook her head. "No. The ship's on the other side of the planet, and the *Endurance* is still exploring the gas giant. We don't have line of sight for another thirty minutes or so."

The thrust of the engines kicking in pushed the creature up against a bulkhead. Stephanie secured it with webbing, then started forward to the cockpit. "Get yourself strapped in, Jensen. We're not gonna hang around."

He nodded, then secured himself in much the same way that Stephanie had tied down the creature.

She propelled herself through the hatch and pivoted, swinging down into her seat. She strapped in as Pål banked the *Heimdal* sharply to avoid a support strut on the *Argoss*.

They had to warn the other arks. She started to relay what she knew of the situation into the databanks, updating the ship's log.

Jensen put the shuttle in a close orbit, using the planet's gravitational pull to slingshot it to greater speeds than would be possible with engines alone. Stephanie's hands started to shake. She gripped the console firmly to steady them.

"Shit, what the hell is that?" she said, pointing to a flashing red light. Collision. Warning. Missile. Had the damned mutants fired on them?

"They must have launched some of the *Argoss'* mines. Goddamn."

The mines had been designed to explode in close proximity to a moving target. Intended for clearing asteroids, they would be just as deadly to the shuttle.

The explosion that blossomed on the port bow rocked the ship, knocking out the fusion drive and painfully slamming the occupants in their restraints. Pål cursed as the ship streaked towards the surface of Palsenz, vapour from a blown seal turning to a trail of ice as they plummeted.

Stephanie Chu had been well trained. She followed protocol, sealing the hull breach, but nothing she could do would restart the engines. The planet loomed huge through the narrow viewports. Then they were rocked as they hit the outer atmosphere, causing the shuttle to buck and twist as it fell. The temperature inside the cabin rose noticeably, but they would not burn up; the vessel was too well built for that.

"Brace for impact," Pål screamed, his hand reaching for Stephanie's.

They went down, ploughing into the rock and sand of the Badlands. Then the shuttle hit a large dune and seemed to skip, becoming airborne again before landing nose first and slewing around, sliding backwards. One of the stubby wings tore off against an outcropping of rock. Stephanie cried out as she gripped Pål's hand.

Finally, the shuttle came to a shuddering rest. Lying on its side, partially buried in red sand, the *Heimdal* had left a ragged scar on the face of the planet that almost mirrored the one on Stephanie Chu's scalp. Blood began to trickle down into her eyes as she passed out.

SOMEONE was moaning. The sound registered slowly as First Officer Stephanie Chu regained consciousness. It took a moment more before she realized she was making the noise herself. She tried to move but gave up, gasping, the pain in her head timed perfectly with her heartbeat, each pulse a needle in her brain.

Her eyes were sealed shut by something sticky. Raising a hand, she wiped at the substance until she could finally open them, but the cabin lights were out. What was this stuff? She probed her head gently, grimacing in pain when she found a ragged gash.

The crackling blue arc of an electrical short punctuated the dark. Other senses awoke, the acrid stench of burning plastic assaulted her nose. Panicked, she tried to sit up, pushing against the straps that held her. Hopefully the automatic systems had managed to take care of the fire. But what the hell had happened? She fell back into her chair.

Then the memories came flooding back. The mission to assess the *Argoss*, the attack on the salvage crew, their escape and the proximity mine that had taken out the drive.

The salvage team had gone aboard the abandoned *Argoss* and then ... Pål! Her hand reached out for the control panel, desperately feeling for the correct switch. She triggered the cockpit lights and they illuminated, sending shockwaves of pain through her cranium. Blinking rapidly, she turned to examine her partner. Captain Pål Knutsen was strapped into his chair beside her. His chest rose and fell in a regular rhythm and she breathed a sigh of relief to see him alive. They had been together since training;

WHEN I got to the hotel, the trench coat pointed at me. He was more the action figure of a detective than a person, complete with the styrofoam cup accessory kit and a badge hanging around his neck.

"Detective Palmer?" I said.

"Wrong," the action figure in a tan coat said, "Palmer quit. I'm just watching the place 'til the CDC gets here. You sit over there."

He motioned for me to sit in the lobby's waiting area. It was typically empty in the early hours, but there was a man in a white business shirt looking at a newspaper. The classifieds section.

Right when I sat down he nodded to himself, and said,

"I've got an uncle in Ohio that runs a construction company. Do construction guys get health insurance?"

"No," I said, "Are you Palmer?"

"Yeah," he said, eyes still on the paper.

"What happened?" I asked.

He looked at me, his mouth open, making a visible effort to make eye contact. He was trying to share something, but he couldn't get it out. There was a wall somewhere in him. Finally,

"You checked them in?"

"Big hats?" I said, "Sure I did."

"Big hats," he said folding the newspaper and putting it beside him, "Yeah. Those weren't hats, friend. We took one off, pulled it hard and it came apart—sang like a pumpkin ripping open."

"And?" I said.

"And. Yeah and. And the sound lasted just a little bit too long. There were tunnels in those big hats. A whole city of tunnels. Like a hive. Just big holes in the meat of 'em, honeycombing all through like a—"

The detective turned to look over at the table near us. On it was an arrangement of potpourri, with a large black lotus seed pod resting at the top. Inside the pod were holes and little seeds peeking out from its black recessed pits. The detective didn't compare the two out loud, but he then looked away from the seed pod, and said, the shuttle *Heimdal,* and its captain, were her world. Hitting the release on her chair straps, she climbed to her feet on uncertain, weak legs.

The planet's gravity was higher than the spin in the gen-pop sphere of the *Endurance.* Used to spending much of her time in zero-gee, now she felt heavy, clumsy.

With one hand always touching a bulkhead or handhold, she moved to Pål, feeling for a pulse at his neck. It was there, strong, steady. Good, he would be fine. She bent and laid her head next to his, giving him the briefest of hugs, then turned and made her way through the narrow hatch into the central fuselage, crawling slowly where usually she would fly. It was pitch-black but she palmed a switch and the fuselage lights flickered into brightness, illuminating the large hold.

Strapped to the starboard bulkhead were three bodies. Two tech-engs from the *Endurance* and one of *them;* one of the dark-skinned things that had attacked the salvage team. Its head was small, its mouth wide with a bank of needle-like teeth. The creature's stick thin arms and legs articulated in odd ways. It was barely recognizable as human. But she had seen its eyes. There was no mistaking what it was, what it had been.

A mumbled cursing caused her to spin around. The only survivor from the salvage team was struggling with the strapping that had kept him safe during their forced landing. One arm had been gashed open by the mutant before it was killed, but that did not appear to be bleeding anymore. Even so, Jensen looked pale.

"It's okay," she said. "You're safe."

"Where are we? What happened?" He coughed and blood flecked his lip.

"We're on Palsenz. Somewhere in the Badlands, I think."

He snorted in dry amusement. "You and I have different understandings of the word *safe.*"

She nodded at the sentiment. It perfectly mirrored her own thoughts. Although Palsenz supported a meager biodiversity, the Badlands were different. Even from orbit, the *Endurance's* sensors detected strange readings from the region.

"We're lucky to be alive," she said. Jensen nodded but looked unconvinced. Unspoken was the thought that although they had avoided the frying pan, they might well be in the fire, as the Badlands comprised a large area of blasted rock and desert with no life and bizarre topography.

But Stephanie Chu counted her blessings. If they had crashed on any other planet in the system, they would be dead. The gas giant was a raging storm of hydrochloric acid and the rest ranged from impossibly high gravity to tiny, airless rocks. Not the best place for a forced landing. At least Palsenz had air.

"Here," she said. "Let me help you."

She pulled the strapping free, and Jensen collapsed into her arms, grimacing.

"What is it?"

"I don't know," he gasped. "My ribs . . ."

He stood straighter as he got used to the gravity. "I'm okay, really."

"Good. There's a medkit on the bulkhead there," she pointed to a box fixed to the wall. "I need to check on the captain."

As Jensen opened the medkit, Stephanie crawled into the cockpit. Pål was still out, but unbelievably he was snoring. Typical! She gently shook his shoulder. Then harder. "Pål."

"What?" His eyes blinked opened, after a moment focusing on her. "Damn, you look a mess."

Stephanie chuckled. Her hand went to her long black hair, matted with blood. Usually it needed careful control to stop it from floating all over the place, but now it hung lank and sticky against her scalp. No doubt she looked bad, but that was the least of their problems.

"I should take a look at that cut on your head."

"No, it's okay. Check the comms, please Pål. We need an evac off this rock."

"You sure? It looks nasty."

"It's not bleeding anymore." She gently touched her scalp, then winced. It was not life-threatening. It could wait.

Knutsen hit the strap release on his chair and sat up straight. He did not look any the worse for having survived the forced landing. Stephanie felt a momentary irritation at that. His blonde Nordic locks were not even mussed.

"Assuming that the *Endurance* is in range now," he said, hands reaching out to flick switches, "it will take a couple of hours at least before another shuttle can reach us."

He donned his headset. "This is the shuttle *Heimdal*. *Endurance*, do you read?"

No signal. He tried again, then threw off his headset. His sigh told Stephanie everything she needed to know. Instantly she turned and hit a switch marked EPIRB. It was old tech but it would broadcast their position for as long as the ship had power. The *Endurance* might not be in range for some hours yet, but they could just sit tight and wait for pickup. She thanked her ancestors that the *Heimdal* had held together, coming down in one piece. It might even be salvageable. Whether it was testimony to Pål's skill as a pilot or divine intervention was moot. She would light a joss stick once they were out of this mess.

"How's Jensen?" Knutsen asked, with a nod towards the hold.

"Broken rib, looks like," Stephanie replied. "Might have pierced a lung. Not good."

Knutsen levered himself out of his chair with a grunt and flexed his shoulders. "The gravity is higher than I expected."

"It's only a little more than Earth normal. We've been running on three quarters gee for too long."

Knutsen shrugged noncommittally and crawled through the hatch into the fuselage. Stephanie followed and clambered down into the hold. Knutsen stopped in shock at the sight of the mutant and the two dead crewmen hanging limp from the wall.

"What the hell is that?"

Jensen had used some of the strapping to wrap around his chest. He was pulling it tight, wincing with the pain. Stephanie stepped forward, helping him tie it off. He had evidently come to the same conclusion as she had; broken ribs. Knutsen glanced in his direction, giving him a quick once over, before returning his gaze to the mutant.

"You going to be okay, Jensen?"

"I'm fine. Don't worry about me."

"These things attacked you?" he asked, nodding towards the alien. "Unprovoked?"

"We didn't even know they were there until they started killing us."

Knutsen shook his head in wonder. The *Argoss* was known to have had a major tech failure, but to find out that it had been caused deliberately made sense only if the mutants had posed a serious threat to the mission. The captain may have reasoned that it was better to preserve the arc for the other colonists, than let it fall prey to the mutated crew. If every living thing on board was killed, then the ship would arrive at its final destination and wait there, hale and whole until the other arcs arrived. And this was just what had happened. Except the mutants had evidently survived.

From the cockpit, a shrill siren sounded. With a nod, Knutsen ordered Chu to check it out. Stephanie crawled back into the cockpit. Almost immediately she was back, her face drained of its natural color.

"Pål! You'd better get in here, now."

Knutsen crawled back into the cockpit. Stephanie pointed to a series of readouts on the port side of his station where the lights had changed from green to yellow. The drive was not dead. It was going critical.

His eyes widened at the sight, but he wasted no time trying to reverse the problem. There was no fix for this. He leaned in towards Stephanie, speaking loudly in order to be heard over the incessant siren.

"Get everything out that we can carry. We need to make it to the minimum safe zone. I don't know how much time we've got, but I'm not taking any chances."

Stephanie nodded, pulling a medkit from a bulkhead. She made her way into the hold where she punched in the code to open the weapons locker. Knutsen followed, pushing two emergency kits with him. The kits contained basic field rations for three days, a small amount of water and foil blankets.

Stephanie slung the heavy multigun—the same she had used to defend the airlock against the mutants—over her shoulder. It was designed to be used in any situation and could be configured for a variety of lethal and non-lethal payloads. She checked to ensure that it was set to *High-Charge*, a killing level.

Through either luck, or judgment on Knutsen's part, the shuttle had come to rest on its belly. The airlock should be the easiest exit but a quick glance through the porthole showed only the fine red sand of Palsenz covering the tempered glass. The hatch was clearly buried.

That left only one way out, the payload doors. Stephanie hit the release mechanism, then punched in her authorization code. With a groan, the ceiling began to split, widening as the overhead hatches opened outwards like the ribs of a great beast, splayed to reveal the tender organs within.

Instantly a fierce wind carried sand into the bay, whipping around in a frenzied gyre. Stephanie turned to Jensen who was helping himself to a multigun.

"We need to get as far away from the shuttle as we can. The drive is overloading. Take this medkit and start climbing."

She passed him the medical supplies and pointed to the far end of the bay where handholds set into the bulkheads formed a ladder. Jensen nodded, slinging the rifle over one shoulder and medkit over the other. He made his way past his dead crew and the mutant, giving the latter a slightly wider berth, then began to climb, head turned to the side to avoid the stinging sand.

Stephanie watched Jensen climb, noting how he struggled to raise his right arm. Not good. Knutsen appeared at her shoulder and she jumped.

"Hell, you gave me a start."

His answering look held no apology. He just pushed her towards the ladder. She understood. No time to waste on pleasantries. She scaled the ladder quickly, climbing out, turning her head from the caustic wind and the tiny sand grains needling her face.

She slid down the fuselage, onto the stubby wing of the shuttle, then jumped, landing next to Jensen. The jolt when she hit the ground almost knocked the wind out of her. Nevertheless, she slapped Jensen on the shoulder and tried her best to give him a smile.

"Congratulations, Officer Jensen. You're the first man to set foot on Palsenz."

He nodded, but did not look like he appreciated the distinction as he was trying to shield his eyes from the sand. Equally, Stephanie did not feel anything special for being the first woman on the planet. If they survived, maybe then.

A moment later and Knutsen joined them. They set off, making their way through twisted rocks that coiled and spired at odd angles, many of the fingers of stone ending in points, like granite daggers. Care was needed. A fall here could be deadly.

The wind howled, almost drowning out her voice. Nevertheless, Stephanie attempted to shout above it. "How far to be safe?"

Knutsen strained to hear. He grimaced as he worked out the meaning of the almost jumbled words that came to him.

"At least three kilometers," he shouted in reply, holding up three fingers.

Stephanie nodded and leaned into the wind, pushing hard to make progress. It would have been smarter to go the opposite direction where the wind would help propel them, but the almost sheer wall of stone that lay there contradicted that instinct. Had the shuttle changed its angle of descent by just a tiny margin, they would have impacted the cliff face, and that would have been that.

They began their trek away from the shuttle. After some time, Stephanie found she could walk naturally, no longer needing to lean into the wind. She checked her wrist display, measuring their progress. Barely two klicks. That was not far enough!

They pushed on. Finally, a break in the wind allowed them to observe their surroundings in more detail. With the sand no longer menacing her eyes, Stephanie raised her head. There was a rocky outcrop nearby and she quickly clambered up before turning to survey the horizon, marveling at the vista of an alien planet. Home.

What she saw was a bleak, forbidding landscape of rolling red sand dunes and oddly striated rocks that rose from the ground like bony fingers. It was like a garden of stone, she thought.

She turned to look back the way they had come. Already their footprints had been erased and the shuttle was no longer in sight. She felt a pang of regret for its loss. She and Pål Knutsen had been assigned to the *Heimdal* as cadets and it had practically been home to them. Like many co-workers, they had taken their relationship to another level, becoming lovers. It was common for those who worked in close proximity to marry and have children. Any stigma that had once existed had long since disappeared within their insular culture where perpetuating the species was more important than outmoded social mores. Of course, this did not mean that there was not a chain of command. Stephanie was First Officer on the *Heimdal*, but it was Pål who had made Captain. That meant his word was law, even here, on the planet's surface.

"Orders, Captain?"

"Our first priority is to get out of the blast zone, which I believe we have done. Next is shelter. I think these sand storms might get rough."

Jensen smiled grimly at that. "Not much shelter here, by the looks of things."

"No," Knutsen conceded. "We'll just have to keep moving and hope we get lucky."

From her vantage point, Stephanie could see further than the others. Her brows furrowed. "I can see something." She pointed to the east. The others turned to look. "Something glinted. Like a reflection off glass."

"Must be wreckage from the *Heimdal*," Knutsen asserted.

"No," she replied. "Not that far east. It doesn't match our approach vector. There's no way there could be anything from the wreck there."

Stephanie continued to peer into the distance, but there was nothing except endless sand. Then suddenly she saw it again. A glint, and it was gone. Could it be a reflection from binoculars? She hopped down from the mound, landing in a crouch, and opened her mouth to speak.

They felt the explosion before they heard it. The ground heaved, throwing them down, Jensen's face contorting in pain. The horizon behind them flared into white. Then it darkened as a huge cloud of sand rose into the sky, consuming it, clouding out the sun. Then came the wind, howling, tearing at them, ripping their clothes with wave after wave of jagged sand.

Stephanie covered her head with her hands and screwed her eyes tightly closed. Then as suddenly as it had begun, it was over.

They climbed to their feet, dusting themselves off, shaking sand from hair and clothes. Jensen spat, saliva and blood instantly absorbed by the desert. For a moment, no one spoke.

"I'm sorry," said Knutsen. It was not clear if he was addressing the shuttle, his crew or their passenger. Stephanie laid a hand on his arm.

"Pål, before the explosion . . ." she paused to formulate the right words in her head. "I saw something. It looked to me like someone was using binoculars out there."

Captain Knutsen twisted his mouth in a wry grimace and shook his head. "Couldn't be. There's no way a rescue party would be here so soon."

Stephanie held his gaze, her brown eyes holding his blue. "I know. That's what worries me."

He turned to look in the direction where she had seen the flash of light. "You don't think . . ."

"I don't know what to think. But something is coming this way."

Jensen looked at them, his gaze alternating from one to the other. He seemed to be having problems breathing but he managed to spit out a single word.

"What?"

Stephanie bit her bottom lip. "If it's not a rescue, then either they're indigenous, or it's *them*. From the *Argoss*. The mutants."

Jensen laughed nervously, until he realized she wasn't joking. "You can't be serious!"

Knutsen nodded. "Makes sense. There were shuttles missing from the hull of the *Argoss*. We just assumed they were destroyed or lost during the journey. Maybe those things *used* them to make landfall."

Stephanie unslung her multigun, holding it in combat ready position. "If that's true, then we need to get as far away from them as possible. I don't plan to die on this rock."

Knutsen spat sand and wiped his mouth. "Agreed. Let's move out."

They set off, walking as quickly as they could in the shifting sand. Changing direction to the west, they used whatever rocks they could find for cover, trying to make it as hard as possible to be seen by whatever was coming. Thankfully, it appeared that there would be little chance of anyone following their footprints, as the wind started to pick up again and they were soon erased.

Jensen stumbled and Knutsen moved to help, wrapping one of the man's arms over his shoulder. Supporting half his weight, Knutsen urged him on.

The day ended abruptly as the sun sank below the horizon. Darkness was not absolute, as the evening sky was awash with stars. Palsenz' own tiny moon appeared as a bright dot, moving over the surface of the night.

Exhaustion brought the group to a halt soon enough, and they huddled in the lee of an overhanging rock that was not quite a cave, though it did provide some protection from the wind.

Stephanie rolled a head-sized rock into the half circle of their shelter. Then she fired her multigun with a low power setting at it. She held a continuous beam on the stone until it began to glow white-hot.

That done, they shared some rations and sat back, the heat radiating from the rock suffusing them with more than just its warmth. It comforted them, made them feel somehow less vulnerable.

Jensen carefully maneuvered himself into a supine position. His breathing was ragged, and he had a waxy complexion to this skin. Stephanie put two fingers on his neck.

"Relax. I just want to check your pulse."

Jensen gave the barest of nods. His pulse was fast. She did not need to time it to know he was experiencing problems. Plus, he felt hot. There was a thermometer in the medkit and she fished it out, pressing it against his neck. A moment later it beeped. 103 degrees. He was burning up.

She poked about in the medkit bag and found a strip of pills marked 'General Antibiotic.' She examined the instructions, then popped two out. She passed Jensen a bottle of water and the pills.

"We'll need to keep a watch during the night," said Knutsen.

Jensen struggled to raise himself, but Stephanie pushed him back down. "No. Not you. You're on meds, have a damaged lung and a fever. We'll manage."

Knutsen nodded approvingly. "Steph, I'm pretty wiped. Can you take the first two hours, then wake me?"

"Absolutely. Don't worry. I'll keep the rock hot."

STEPHANIE didn't wake Knutsen at the appointed time. Instead, she took a walk, making her way to a high point of jutting stone a short distance from the camp. She climbed it, then settled in, wedged between two twisting spires. From her position she could see the sleeping men, the heat rock still glowing a faint red. But she could also see the wider plain, and even though it was night, there was sufficient light to make out the nearby rocks and dunes.

She snapped open the sight-port on the multigun and lifted it to her eye. Scanning the horizon, focusing on the east, she searched for any sign of movement. Nothing. Switching to infrared, she tried again.

The desert was an even tone of yellow with patches here and there of darker umber, indicating warmer sand. But there was nothing 'hot' out there. Stephanie let out her breath, unaware she had been holding it. Whatever had been trying to track them was gone.

She grinned and was about to jump down when some instinct made her look again. This time she scanned the area much closer to their camp, less than a klick distant. And there it was, something moving, registering as a brilliant red blob in her gun sights. Then another and another. Three high heat sources slowly converging on the location of the overhang under which Knutsen and Jensen lay sleeping.

Her stomach clenched, and without thought she thumbed the safety off the multigun, aiming at the nearest of the heat sources. Whatever it was, it was only 300 meters away. She fired.

The shot missed, impacting a dune, creating a spectacular heat rose in the infrared spectrum. She switched to night vision, and what she saw almost made her freeze rigid with shock. A mutant, much like the ones she had seen on the *Argoss* and *Heimdal*, with the strangely articulating limbs and smaller head. But this one was still recognizably human. It crouched low, turning to look towards the other creatures it travelled with. They scuttled away, as if aware they were suddenly visible and in danger. In a moment they were all gone, hidden behind rocks or dunes.

But now they would be more careful. She mentally berated herself for missing her target. With a snarl of rage, she hopped down and hurried back to the camp. She kicked hard at Knutsen's foot, then Jensen's. Knutsen was on his feet in a second, but Jensen merely moaned.

"What is it? What happened?" Knutsen checked his wrist display. "Why didn't you wake me?"

"Never mind. They found us," Stephanie replied. She had her back to them, the multigun raised high, scanning the area in case the enemy returned. "I saw three mutants coming directly towards the camp. I don't know how, but they can track us. We need to keep moving."

Knutsen nodded curtly, then knelt beside the comatose Jensen, checking his vitals.

"He's not looking good." He gently peeled back an eyelid, using a light from his wrist display to check Jensen's pupil response. "He's unconscious, not sleeping."

"Then you'll have to carry him," Stephanie replied. "I'll take point." She grabbed up the second multigun, slinging it across her back, then a medkit. Knutsen donned the remaining emergency kits, then with a grunt, bent and lifted Jensen across his shoulders. He staggered to his feet.

Stephanie gave him a sympathetic look. "We need to circle back to the crash site. That's the first place any rescue team would look to find us."

Knutsen gave the merest of grunts. He took a step, then another. His face was locked into a determined grimace. Stephanie led the way, switching between infrared and night vision while sweeping the area ahead and behind. Now they knew for sure what they were facing, their only hope of survival was to hide. Superior firepower would only work for so long, and the Ancestors alone knew how many of the damned creatures were on the surface.

As they made their way, Knutsen occasionally stumbled so Stephanie had to catch him. It was obvious that he was growing tired. Attempting to distract him, she described what she had seen.

"It's as though there were two species," she said. "The one I saw appeared almost human. It had a larger head and I'm sure it had normal feet. It was definitely different to the ones on the *Argoss*."

Knutsen did not answer. It was all he could do to move in the heavier gravity with Jensen's weight and his own. Stephanie continued.

"Also, they reacted immediately to the fact that I could hit them with a charge. The mutants on the arc did not seem to care. They attacked with a ferocity that seemed . . . well, I think it bordered on madness. But these others, they displayed caution. Which makes me think they're smarter. Or simply not insane. Either way, it makes them more dangerous."

Knutsen grunted. Each step he took was a deliberate action, requiring focus and concentration. After only a short while, he was sweating. Slowly he lowered Jensen to the sand.

"Need to rest," he gasped out.

Stephanie kept up her scanning, switching between modes on the sights. There had been no other sign of the creatures since she had fired on them, but they were still out there. She could feel it in her gut.

"We're not more than 3 klicks from the wreckage of the shuttle. We can take 10 minute breaks in every 30. Think you can manage that, Pål?"

He looked up at her and she was shocked at the exhaustion written into every line on his face. She put a hand on his shoulder, giving him a squeeze.

SUNRISE on Palsenz came slower than they were used to. On the *Endurance*, a day was split into divisions of fourteen hours of daylight and ten of night. Daylight was simulated by a plasma ball suspended in the middle of the sphere. As a result, the sun was always overhead no matter where you were. At night, however, it was shielded, creating the illusion of a regular day. It had long since been set to emulate the approximate timings that they would find on Palsenz itself, in order to acclimate the colonists.

Stephanie watched the orb of the sun rising over the horizon with her mouth hanging open. It was unlike anything she had imagined. Her whole life had been a preparation for the moment they arrived and claimed their new home, but now she realized that their existence on the *Endurance* had been a mere reflection of reality. And a poor one at that.

They were now less than a klick to the crater left by the *Heimdal*. Fragments of the shuttle littered the ground around them. Pieces impossible to identify, twisted and burned. She felt regret and loss. It had almost been their home, they had spent so much time in it. On the plus side, the debris would make it easier for a rescue team to find them.

Stephanie took a good look around, doing a 360 degree turn. Nothing. But from the corner of her eye, she thought that maybe she *could* see something. Snapping her head back, she focused on a nearby dune, only a hundred meters distant. She put the gun sight to her eye, but there was no movement there now, and no indication that there had been anything. She was jumpy, that was it. Just her nerves getting frayed.

As she was turning back she saw it again. This time there was no mistaking it. The small head, the thin limbs; mutant. One, then another and another. The three that had been tracking them. They raised themselves, standing as tall as they were able, clearly wanting to be seen. Stephanie swallowed dryly, wishing she had not already finished the last of her water ration.

Why did they just stand there?

"Pål. They're here."

She indicated the dune with the mutants. Knutsen looked up from his burden, seeing them. His eyes widened with shock, then closed in dismay.

"We'll have to fight." He stared about himself, obviously hoping for a defensible position. The shuttle explosion had left a crater and they were on its edge. Either they moved towards the mutants, or they moved further into the crater.

To Stephanie, the footing looked treacherous, with jagged shards of metal protruding from the sand. But mercifully, there seemed to be a narrow path free of any major obstacles, and it led directly to a large piece of the *Heimdal's* hull.

"We go down," she said.

That piece of the hull would give them cover, acting as a shield. Knutsen glanced to the crater, assessing, then nodded. As he made his painful way to the crater's epicenter, Stephanie held back, her eyes never leaving the dune and its three very visible occupants.

But why were they just standing there? What were they doing? It was almost as if they wanted her to look at them. To distract her!

She whirled around but it was too late. Pål was already too far away. She saw the sand erupting before him, two mutants emerging from a hidden trapdoor. They grabbed at his legs, pulling him down. Before she could even call out they were gone.

She shrieked as despair and anger filled her. Turning back to the mutants on the dune, she raised the multigun, but they too were gone. With nothing to vent her rage on, she ran down to where she had seen Pål and Jensen disappear. Yet no matter how hard she searched, she could find no sign of the trapdoor. The sand seemed undisturbed. She fell to her knees, a strangled scream escaping her raw throat.

When she looked up again, the three mutants were almost on her. One of them had blue-grey eyes, almost like Pål's. But the stunted faces and smaller heads with wide mouths sent a surge of adrenalin through her as well as a sense of certainty. With Pål gone there was nothing left. Raising her gun, she pointed it at her own head, then reached for the firing stud.

The closest mutant reacted. Its eyes opened wide and it raised a hand as if to order her to stop, to desist. Then she heard it. The distinctive roar of a class III shuttle making an atmospheric landing. The whining of the drive as the attitude jets kicked in was unmistakable.

She was rescued. They were here! Unable to believe her senses, Stephanie Chu looked up just as the shuttle began a near-vertical descent. The pilot was skilled, no doubt. One of her colleagues from *Endurance*, most likely Chang. She felt the briefest sense of justification. She had made it. Even if she died now, it did not matter. The rescue had come.

She looked to the mutants, but they did not appear concerned. One was covering his face from the onslaught of wind and sand, but the others kept their eyes locked on hers. None made any attempt to flee.

Incredulous she stared at them. Slowly she turned her gun around, once again assuming a combat stance. The shuttle landed behind her. She could hear the airlock opening. She smiled, grimly triumphant.

"You should run."

The mutants did not react, merely observing her with calm equanimity. Stephanie waved the gun. "GET AWAY!"

Someone behind her spoke. The voice was accented, but understandable. It was not anyone from the *Endurance*. Could it be a shuttle from the *Bitter Sea*?

"I am the Speaker. We will not hurt you."

Small, oddly jointed hands reached out. Stephanie turned and stared in wide-eyed horror. Mutants were emerging from the shuttle. One stood directly beside her. In an instant she was disarmed. One of the three unclipped the gun-strap, relieving her of her heavy multigun. Another took the one slung across her back.

A strangled noise emerged from her throat as she tried to speak. Unable to comprehend what was happening, she sank to her knees. Finally, she found her voice.

"Why? Why did you attack us? On the *Argoss*?"

The mutant named Speaker looked at her and for a moment Stephanie thought that she could see sadness within its eyes.

"We are not like those poor wretches on the arc. They are our great shame. We have abandoned them. The *Argoss* is their home and this planet is ours."

Stephanie struggled to get to her feet, but found her legs too weak. Clawed hands reached out to help. Speaker looked up at her as she stood, taller than him by a full head. Up close she found the mutants not quite so repellent. But they had a strange smell, like dried leather. Speaker addressed her again.

"Your kind are our ancestors. Those on the *Argoss* are our close cousins. But they are not like us. We cannot live with them, so we gave them the *Argoss*. But this planet is ours. If your people are to live here, then an agreement must be reached."

Stephanie looked over to the shuttle. It looked exactly the same as the *Heimdal,* and for a moment she believed it *was* her ship, that this was all a bad dream. But the strange creature before her belied that.

"We set out from Earth to colonize this planet," she said. "This is our home."

"No. It is *ours*. We got here first. But your kind will be allowed to settle. There will be an agreement about boundaries, possibly trade. We will keep your crew members as surety until we have concluded negotiations with your leaders. Your people are quite safe. The injured one is being treated by our physicians. He will recover."

At this news, Stephanie felt her strength abandon her and she almost collapsed. Pål was alive! She took a deep breath, composing herself.

"What makes you think we can reach an agreement on sharing the planet?"

A curious coughing sound emerged from the mutant. It took a moment for Stephanie to realize that it was laughing.

"You have no choice. We have mastered the secrets of the Predecessors, the species whose planet this once was. We have had a long time to understand their heritage. Your kind will be allowed to settle on this planet but knowledge of the Predecessors will be denied. Come."

Speaker led her to the shuttle. Once aboard, it quickly launched. Inside there were two crew members, plus Speaker and his retinue. Stephanie watched with professional interest as the crew operated the vessel within the atmosphere. That was a skill more art than science. The pilots knew what they were doing.

"We will deliver you back to the *Endurance*." He passed her a communicator. "With this we shall forge our agreement."

Stephanie felt her head swimming. It was too much, too fast. But a thought occurred, nagging. They were so certain, so assured!

"What if we cannot come to terms?" Once again she thought she saw sadness in the creature's eyes as Speaker looked up at her.

"Then you will have to leave this system." He turned his back to her, watching on a vid screen as the great bulbous shape of the *Endurance* appeared. "Either that, or we will be forced to destroy you utterly. Palsenz is ours."

CONTRIBUTORS

Credits

MJ Kobernus - Executive Editor, Nordland Publishing

Micha Fire - Executive Officer, Antares

David R. Grigg - Associate Editor, Antares

Cover artwork: Ashraf E. Shalaby

Authors

Oliver Ashford

Oliver Ashford is a developer and author from London writing post apocalyptic fiction, hard sci-fi and singularity fiction.

Website: http://www.oliverashford.com

Twitter: http://www.twitter.com/oliverashford

Adam Baxter

Adam happily lives in Western Canada with his wife, two children, his annoying dog and several of his regrets, which include, but are not limited to, eating that deep fried pickle stuffed with a hot dog at the Calgary Stampede.

Adam works as an educator, and his current position has allowed for a focus on integrating technologies into learning, and developing computer science literacy in classrooms. In his spare time Adam can be found reading, contemplating spaceships, changing diapers, hunting down dragons in the Rocky Mountains, appeasing his spouse and occasionally, when time allows, rearranging words into pleasurable patterns.

Sales: www.amazon.com/Adam-Baxter/e/B00920B2TS

Chris Capps

"Blood weeping from the walls. Type O. Six lives saved." is the shortest story Chris Capps has written.

The twitter handle where he occasionally writes microfiction is @cappswriting.

If you'd like to hear more of his work, you could start with Season 02, Episode 09 of the horror podcast Manor House for his piece "Faller and Bucker."

There's also "Our War with Molly Nayfack" on Amazon, and a post-apocalyptic adventure series that starts with the title "Beware the Well Fed Man."

Chris Capps lives in Illinois and has a birth mark in the cornea of his left eye.

Twitter: @cappswriting

Sarah Celiann

Sarah Celiann is an author and playwright from Chicago, where she stages her own productions.

She is part of The Ed Greenwood Group's Sessorium of Creatives and will have work coming out through them soon.

She loves fantasy, though science fiction also calls to her.

Website: www.sarahceliann.com

Twitter: @sarahceliann

Calvin Demmer

Calvin Demmer is a crime, mystery, and speculative fiction author.

His stories have been published or are forthcoming in/at Bards and Sages, Ravenwood Quarterly, Shotgun Honey, Mad Scientist Journal, and others.

When not writing, he is intrigued by that which goes bump in the night and the sciences of our universe.

Website: www.calvindemmer.com

Micha Fire

As a teenager Micha Fire, artist and writer, moved with her family for five years away from Germany and lived in Papua New Guinea, Australia and one year in Japan, thus English has become a second mother tongue to her and the favourite one to express her thoughts in writing. Having lived overseas has influenced her stories as they can occur any place in the world.

She collaborates in anthology projects: NovoPulp, Theme-Theology and Antares Anthology.

Visit her website for more writing, drawings, paintings and handcraft art.

Her photography, another art hobby, can be found on G+.

Website: www.micha-fire.net

Sales: www.amazon.de/-/e/B00HM6ZAQ4

D. C. Golightly

D. C. Golightly is a proposal writer who dabbles in fiction, so any escapism he wishes to pursue to free himself from the shackles of corporate America tend to spill into his stories.

He has three fantastic children and a wonderful wife that puts up with his love of comics and cookies.

David R. Grigg

David Grigg is a retired software developer who lives in Melbourne, Australia.

David had several short stories published professionally during the 1970s and 1980s and in 1976 he had two short fantasy novels for pre-teens published by Cassell Australia.

During this period, David was deeply involved in the Australian science fiction community, eventually becoming Chairman of the 43rd World SF Convention held in Melbourne in 1985.

Since retiring, he has returned to writing fiction, and a number of his stories have appeared in recent online and ebook anthologies. His stories are available at:

Website: rightword.com.au/books

Jill Hand

Jill Hand has an upcoming novel from Kellan Publishing called The Blue Horse, about time travel and a quest for a fantastic cryptid that actually existed. She writes speculative fiction. Her work has appeared recently in Aphelion; Bewildering Stories; Cease, Cows; Suspense and T. gene Davis's Speculative Fiction.

MJ Kobernus

MJ Kobernus is the founder and editor in Chief of Nordland Publishing. He is the author of the Guardian 'Blood' series and the self-proclaimed creator of Flash Philosophy. He can sometimes be found living under a bridge in southeast Norway.

When not scaring goats or people, he likes to play guitar, ride his vintage motorcycle and dream of sailing into the sunset on a sailboat. You can find him via;

Website: nordlandpublishing.com

Blog: metaphysicalgeometry.blogspot.no

Twitter: twitter.com/MikcKobernus

Facebook: www.facebook.com/mkobernus

Jordan Legg

I'm originally from Oshawa, Ontario, and I hold a degree in English and Creative Writing from the University of Windsor. I've been published in Allegory eZine, MTLS.ca, On The Premises, and several anthologies, among others. When I'm not writing I enjoy drawing, soccer, reading, cycling, and maintaining my beard.

Twitter : @JordanLegg2

LynC

LynC is a 50 something year old widow, thoroughly enjoying semi-retirement, which gives her plenty of time to travel, write, read and enjoy her family. Hah!

She has had four short stories published, with two more on the way. One of her short stories—"Nematalien"—was nominated for an award in 2013. Her first novel - Nil By Mouth (Satalyte Publishing) - published in 2014, was shortlisted for both the Aurealis Awards (SF Category) and the Norma K Hemming Award in 2015.

She resides, with her two adult children, four cats, and one canary, in a hidden area less than ten kilometres from the Melbourne CBD (in Australia) surrounded by creeks and wooded hills.

Website: www.lyncwriter.com.au

Facebook: www.facebook.com/lync.lync

Kyle Owens

Kyle Owens lives in the Appalachian Mountains and his work has appeared in Aberrant Literature, Saturday Night Reader, Bete Nore Magazine along with several anthologies.

Stephen Wilcott

Stephen Willcott is a software architect, living in San Diego. His fiction has appeared in Pseudopod, Arcane Anthologies, Silver Blade Magazine and Static Motion.

Besides pulp fiction he enjoys translating Old English. He's currently working on Beowulf. You can follow his progress here:

Website: ingeld.wordpress.com

Copyright

NORDLAND PUBLISHING
Follow the North Road.

nordlandpublishing.com
facebook.com/nordlandpublishing
nordlandpublishing.tumblr.com

www.nordlandpublishing.com